Praise for *Th*

"At first, you'll think, wow, these three friends are a bit out of control, aren't they? And then you'll think this is really scary, so you'll catch your breath, but then bad gets worse. Still, you can't put the book down. There are mysteries here to be solved. John Hughes handles this page-turning tale of depravity, mayhem, and evil with sensitivity and mettle. He an enchanter, casting his spell with fresh and provocative language, hypnotic sentences, and irresistible characters. So grab yourself a drink, a stiff one, make it a double, settle into your easy chair, open *The Boys*, and begin. You're home for the evening. And I promise you this, Lucas and Lowell will haunt your dreams."

—John Dufresne, author of *I Don't Like Where This Is Going*

"It is what remains undefined that speaks most definitively in this startling journey about friendship. As three outsiders wander one into the other in a conservative college classroom, relationships, secrets, and desires rearrange across a landscape that becomes devoid of borders or mirrors. It's a place where accountability exists only in mutual dark stirrings and a teethed and restless intellect. Inside dorm rooms, honkytonks, and the muddy rivers of rural Arkansas, the dialogue is so bitingly substantive that even peripheral characters and the mundane have measure. Meanwhile, angling head-long at full volume down country roads is the momentum of a dark reckoning. An excellent read that defies labels and expectations."

—Laura Sobbott Ross, author of *To the Patron Saint of Wayward Daughters*

"John Calvin Hughes' *The Boys* is up-to-the-minute Southern grit, with a strong nod to the best of the region's literature and at its heart a profound question: Why do people commit evil acts, and who is really to blame? Hughes has a wonderful eye for the language, habits, and milieu of today's college students, and yet produces a timeless portrait of a strong Arkansas family. This murder-mystery-within-a-mystery may at times shock the reader, including with the very first scene, while also regaling them with a clever plot. The protagonists/antagonists are all smart, savvy, intellectuals, but what lines will they not cross? The reader will enjoy finding out."

—Glenda Bailey-Mershon, author of *Eve's Garden*

"Bright young woman goes to a liberal arts college in the South, meets a couple of glib, handsome, would-be philosophers in class who might be the worst kind of bad influence. In John Calvin Hughes' witty and often lyrical prose, our protagonist reveals her own intelligence, and her awareness of her confusing need for male validation, especially from this pair of adventuring show-offs. In this dark Svengali tale, a question forms that keeps the pages turning: will she follow *The Boys* anywhere? Even if it's straight to hell?"

—Susan Lilley, author of *Venus in Retrograde*

"A freshman girl at a small Arkansas college forms a unique bond with a pair of bright, mesmerizing, inseparable boys. As her feelings deepen, she senses something unsettling about their three-way relationship and the mysterious events on campus. Hughes has crafted a richly Southern thriller with a plot that unfolds so lyrically, so naturally, that you feel like you're riding shotgun on a dark country road. *The Boys* reminded me of one of those classic thrillers like Diabolique or Vertigo, with a set of well-drawn characters and a story that just keeps moving forward, where you know something's wrong but you're not sure why it's getting under your skin until it hits you like ice-cold river water. I read the last hundred pages in one night; I had to know what happens."

—Jude Atwood, author of *Maybe There Are Witches*

"One of the marvels of this strange and off-kilter novel, where at one point 'every light is halo ringed and every line gone non-Euclidian,' is how beauty shines in the midst of darkness and violence. In a freshman university experience like none other, Darling's enmeshment in the perverse escapades of two new male friends deepens in every scene. She becomes so gripped by the need to belong with these particular boys, that boundaries of self and violation blur. In this Blakeian examination of innocence and guilt, Darling may be 'unraveling the braids of starlight and love' but, the novel asks, what does love, anyway, have to do with desire? Readers are left to wonder how Darling will find a place in the world now that she has realized a kinship with darkness."

—Darlin' Neal, author of *Rattlesnakes & The Moon Darling*

"Jean Bramlett, the main character in John Calvin Hughes's *The Boys*, is a first semester freshman at an Arkansas university when she meets 'the boys,' two upperclassmen who will change her life forever. Darling is smart and funny, but the boys are smarter, funnier, and certainly more experienced. Like many young women in her situation, she is smitten with their physical beauty, their intelligence, their fearlessness, and their never-ending analysis of everything which include riffs on philosophy, literature, Madonna, and the power of language. She falls for them both and wants them both. Hughes's command of the language is deft and compelling, his wit clever and genuine, but the beauty of the story is how we are given insights into what it means to be a girl and young woman, to become entranced with the universal desire to love and be loved. Darling learns, like most of us, the ambivalences of life, that one is badly mistaken to believe the world is black and white, when the grey is all around us."

—James Ladd Thomas, author of *Lester Lies Down*

THE BOYS

John Calvin Hughes

Regal House Publishing

Published by
Regal House Publishing, LLC
Raleigh, NC 27605

ISBN -13 (paperback): 9781646033287
ISBN -13 (epub): 9781646033294
Library of Congress Control Number: 2022942689

Regal House Publishing, LLC
https://regalhousepublishing.com

Printed in the United States of America

For Janie, again.

Was it really murder
were you just pretending
lately I have heard…

In the dark dorm-room closet, Lucas reeks, a sour, dirty-laundry funk. He presses against me, listening to Lowell persuade the girl out of her clothes. Lowell is naked, beautiful, a werewolf in a carnival forest, god into swan. Lucas's elbow bumps the side of my breast and I wonder if he is going to feel me up, and if so, it's about time. We're peeking through the crack in the closet doors. The girl is on her knees before Lowell and he is pulling her shirt over her head. Her breasts are tremulous, tremendous, wholly improbable. Lowell pushes her onto her back and tugs her pants off. That's when Lucas steps out of the closet with his phone. The girl—what's her name?—gasps, but Lowell lies down on top of her and covers her mouth with his. He's irresistible. Her eyes flick at Lucas, panicked for a second, then she buries her face in Lowell's shoulder.

Lucas is videoing. He nudges me and says, "Phone, Darling."

I don't want to see this through my phone. Not that I haven't seen Lowell naked before, but now, in this shadowy room, atop this girl, he is perfect, airbrushed, photoshopped perfection, every flaw smudged in chiaroscuro and shade. Lucas drops to the floor with them to get some kind of porn angle, I suppose, but I need to see her face. The moment he penetrates her. And there it is: her eyes widen, a little insuck of breath, head thrown back. Lowell raises up onto his elbows, eye to eye, nose to nose, sharing his breath with her as he begins to fuck her.

Do I wish I was her? I suppose I have to admit that I do.

"Darling. Phone."

I watch the rest on the screen.

❧

Lucas and Lowell sit shoulder to shoulder on the bed staring at Lucas's iPhone. The room smells like Cupid's jockstrap. They grin, comment, bump shoulders, ignore the girl—Carla, that's her name—as she rises and dresses and moves toward the door. She watches Lowell the whole time, slowly pulling up her slacks, carefully buttoning her blue silk blouse that I imagine she so lovingly chose for her evening with him; she watches him, yes, even now over her shoulder as she fumbles with the door handle, her face impassive, as she tries not to show whatever it is she's feeling. What does she need? What does she want to take away with her, besides his seed, which will be running down her leg before she gets out of the dorm? Will she hesitate at the end of the hall, relive the act as she pushes through the door and out into the night? She's not having trouble with the handle. She wants Lowell to look at her before she goes, I'm guessing. She doesn't want to be *that* girl, again I'm guessing, girl as fuck buddy, girl as sperm receptacle. Even now, even as the boys make the crudest comments imaginable about her body, she wants Lowell to look at her, a glance, just a peek, to intimate, however imprecisely, that she's more than just another piece of ass. When she gives up and opens the door and the light from the hall pours in, she finally looks at me, and even though we have two classes together and even though she knows my name, Darling, I imagine she wonders, *Who is this girl*?

I wonder that too. I also wonder, why Carla? The answer—it seems obvious now—her breasts. Her breasts are iconic, legendary, something out of a men's magazine, out of a teenage boy's most salacious fantasies. Almost but not quite absurd. And yet, Lucas and Lowell are never obvious, never just clichés. They long ago chucked cliché out the car window and it is now a dusty smudge in the rearview mirror. Everything they think, everything they do or say, seems wonderful and new, crushing, outrageous, radical, beyond any defensible paradigm. And somewhere out there before them (before us?) is even more, an etherical and ethical void toward which they constantly hammer, like prophets blinded by the fiery breath of God. So, if not the breasts, why Carla?

What am I really asking? I'm asking, *Why not me*?

❧

"Let me see your phone," Lucas says.

I hesitate.

"What do you think will be on mine that isn't on yours?"

"Problem?" Lowell says.

Lucas sneers. "I don't think she appreciates our handiwork."

"Are you not entertained?" Lowell stands up, arms outstretched, turning round and round, doing the *Gladiator* thing, but naked.

This would be the time, I think, for one of them to snarkily suggest that what I am is jealous, that what I want is to be the one on the floor, under Lowell, under Lucas, under somebody, getting fucked and filmed. But no. They don't go there.

"Darling. Phone."

I drop it into his outstretched hand and walk over to the window.

They scroll through my phone, first reading my messages and emails, checking my grades, and finally looking at the video of Carla.

"Look at this crap. What is this, Darling, an art film?" Lucas says.

"I am not up for a Siskel and Ebert," I say.

"Did you see her tits, Darling?"

"So?"

"So? They were epic, they were monumental. They were—! Where's the tit shot? This is mostly her face."

"Your storyboards weren't specific, Spielberg."

"Ah," Lowell says. "Attitude from Darlin'. Well done."

"And here. Look at this. What is this? A video essay in praise of the anatomy of Lowell Horatio Whitebread the Third? Let Us Now Praise Famous Asses?"

"Let me see," Lowell says and takes the phone. "Nice. You have a good eye, Darlin'. And, of course, the camera loves me." They both laugh. "Send that to your phone." Lucas forwards the video and tosses my phone back to me. "But Lucas is right. It's an art film. You should change your major to cinematography."

I say there is no cinematography program at Chandler College and I have no major as yet, but they ignore me. They're busy humming soundtracks for the video. I take one more long look at Lowell and leave.

It's September, so technically autumn, but Arkansas autumn, so it's warm, still eighty-five degrees at ten o'clock tonight. White globes on arching poles light the campus sidewalks. I stop equidistant between two of them and take out my phone and watch Lowell on top of the girl. His body, even digitized, even shrunk to grainy video on a tiny screen, scores me like whipping sand, scourges me like a nine-tailed sacrament. It's one thing to sing the beloved (*do* I belove him? them?), but the guilty, scorching, river god of the blood is another altogether. I'm in some penumbra. I'm caught between worlds. I'm the ladybug without the lady, flying away from my burning home and children into—what? I don't know what I want or what anyone wants from me. What godhead could ever rise out of me, sticky with desire, fragrant with sweat and cum and unrecognizable stuff? Where are the limits of my desire? What did I ever want in my entire life as badly as a cock wants to burst from its denim prison and push into a damp, tight hole, hurling every night, every heart into unending chaos? Why am I comparing myself to a penis?

I don't want to go to my dormitory. My empty room. I want to turn around and go back to theirs. Why did I leave in the first place? Jealous of Carla? Really? Jealous of Carla in a video on a phone? Am I that narcissistic? *Pay attention to me? Look at me?* Is this what I want to say to them? *Take my clothes off? Lay me on the floor, on the bed?* What? What?

I walk past the dorm and out into the dark beyond the buildings, up the Hill toward the abandoned observatory, the high point of the college. Of the county. It's a make-out place, a pot-smoking place, and everybody just calls it the Hill. When I reach the top, I turn around like Lot's wife and look at the campus spread out before me: the clock tower in the Christian Center, the Kubla Khan domed top of Murrah Hall, the brick facades and serpentine paths. The school is a dream of what a college should look like, colleges in movies, on brochures in guidance counselors' offices. The library is the newest building, a wide-open space, with emphasis on information technology, stacks shrunk and shrinking in the post-print twenty-first century. The exception is law books, undigitized, shelf after shelf stretching out into the recesses of library, gold and red like the towers of Byzantium.

The night is hothouse humid, the air thick, the stars watery and wasted looking. I feel heavy with it, like my clothes are pulling me down, heavy as if soaked and soaking with wet air. I wish a wind full of interstellar space would gnaw at me, scoop me, hollow me out, fill me with relentless waves of need. The planet isn't big enough for my emptiness. I'm a cliché, a socket, a sheath, an absence waiting to be filled.

But with what? With whom? The boys? More?

They first noticed me the second week of the fall semester in Dr. Whitman's history of Western Philosophy class, a sophomore-level class I had somehow been allowed to register for. Actually, they let me register for English Lit, too, another sophomore class. *Why?* Lucas, who had obviously read Nietzsche and Cioran and some others, was arguing the problem of evil with Whitman. Lucas was saying that there were no objective standards of evil, that what was evil in one culture, say cannibalism, was acceptable in another, that ethical variations were merely cultural, different cultures enacting different practical moralities. "The killing," Lucas said, "of human beings, for instance, is not an absolute evil. Some people"—and here he smirked his famous, scarred smirk—"just straight up need killing." The students tittered. Professor Whitman granted that there are bad people, not that they necessarily needed killing, but that sanctioned killings—wars, capital punishment, for example—might exist as temporary responses to popular needs in some societies. Even so, he said, unsanctioned killing, killing outside legal permission, might still be demonstrably, objectively evil. Whitman wanted to offer us at least one human action that is undeniably evil across every cultural and historical boundary. But before he could get there, Lowell spoke up and said that moral decisions and consequences have to be looked at on a case-by-case basis, and that such a procedure is incompatible with the broad view and theoretical paradigmatic approach required by the practice of philosophy, and that while ethics or meta-ethics might reasonably remain part of the philosophy curriculum, morality should probably be relegated to anthropology.

I tend to be overly empathetic and believe I know what everybody is thinking and, especially, what they're feeling, and I got the uncomfortable and squirmy impression that Whitman was on the defensive at this point. These two young men had him on the ropes. And I liked them, liked how they seemed to have skipped flowering altogether and had instead pushed their essences into early fruit, how they saw themselves as Whitman's equal and not just students in his class. I'm so very Rilke, don't you know.

Whitman clearly wanted to—shoot, *needed* to—demonstrate an objective standard of right and wrong. And even though he is a Christian, he is also a philosopher and a professor of philosophy and was not willing to appeal simply to the received wisdom of his religion to win an argument with a student. Whitman, unwisely, I think, decided to go with an emotional approach: "Imagine a father who, finding that his three-year-old son had wet the bed again, chooses to beat the child's legs with an electrical cord and push his head down into a filthy toilet. Surely you gentlemen don't want to suggest that the actions of this father might be dismissed as 'merely' cultural.

Surely you want to be on the side that declares such actions to be unequivocally wrong?"

The class murmured their assent to the professor's reasoning, and the boys were quiet. They seemed done, maybe defeated, or maybe just bored with the argument. So, I spoke up. What did I think I was doing?

Let me stop right here and say this would not be the last time I would wonder, *What did I think I was doing?*

I said, "Dr. Whitman, sir, your example is heartbreaking, certainly, and very much so to the softhearted, of which I am one." He smiled at me and started to say something, but I continued: "I feel obliged to point out, though, that the underlying argument in this example is based on another—let's say invisible—thesis, and that is that human life is somehow special, unique, worth preserving at any cost."

"And I believe that is true—" he began.

"But," I interrupted him, "think of the many examples in which we might find that other concerns are more important than human life."

"For instance?"

"Off the top of my head, the sacrifice of lives in war."

"*Dulce et decorum est.*"

"Good one, sir, but that seems to sidestep, however poetically, a phenomenon we safe and protected children of the middle class today may have forgotten called 'the draft.' A great many of those young men, and I'm thinking here of the war in Viet Nam especially, maybe even the vast majority of those young men, were not volunteers, ready to die 'sweetly' for their country, but, arguably, victims, helpless victims murdered by the State for reasons that were not always entirely limited to the safety and security of the homeland. Maybe something to do with oil company interests and other big-money concerns?"

(I had binged Ken Burns over the summer.)

He had an answer to this, I could see, so I pushed on before he could speak.

"And what about the example of people who murder abortion doctors?"

"I don't think," Whitman began, "that any reasonable person can justify that."

"A famous utilitarian once suggested that the needs of the many fetuses outweigh the needs of the few abortion providers."

Somebody in the back of the room shouted, "Spock!"

"I don't mean to hog the discussion here," I continued, "but let's put the value of human life into a reality-based scenario." I stood up and looked around at the room: "Classmates. Fellow budding intellectuals. Let me ask you this. You're in a burning building. It's just you, a ninety-year-old man who happens to be in the process of dying a painful death from prostate cancer, *and* the last original copy of the Constitution of the United States. You can save only one. Which do you carry out? Which one do you save?"

I was flushed, breathing hard. Shoot, I was burning like a house afire. But it wasn't fear. Or stage fright. Or embarrassment. I wasn't ashamed of the simplicity of my reasoning or the dishonesty of my examples. I knew that what I was saying was a smoke screen, a red herring. No, what I was feeling—the heat, the tightness in my stomach, the breathlessness, my face burning like a burning mask—all came from their eyes on me, the two boys lounging at their desks, looking at me now, the boys I had stood up to support.

No, I won't do that. I won't equivocate. I won't dissemble. I won't lie. I didn't stand up to support them. I could care less about such philosophical niceties. I stood up to get their attention. If my eternal question is *What did I think I was doing?* then I'm going to have to admit that this is what I thought I was doing: getting their attention. Back when I imagined I had an intelligent thought in my head, I had stood up to impress them, to astonish them, to burn in their eyes like a mad photon, to fall into their orbit like a dark orphan planet.

From that point, the class degenerated into a reductio black hole of Lifeboat Scenarios, and poor Whitman found his students, young people that he had hoped to turn into good citizens and good neighbors and good parents, carrying the *Mona Lisa* and the *Starry Night* and their childhood teddy bears out of hypothetical burning buildings ahead of actual people. He tried to keep a straight face but kept looking at me askance. On the other hand, Lucas and Lowell were grinning at me like the proverbial possum eating briars. They looked ravenous. I thought, *Oh golden child the world will kill and eat.*

Near the top of the Hill is an abandoned observatory. It is a cliché out of a picture book for kids, exactly what you'd think an observatory should look like. Silhouetted against the wetly starred sky, it is a blind eye still turned toward the heavens. In daylight, you can see the facade is scarred, the paint on the western side scorched black by fire. Supposedly fire. At least that is the rumor, the campus legend. Once upon a time, so I'm told, the observatory was the site of the greatest and most infamous Chandler tragedy, a grand Romantic tragedy out of some old gothic novel. The story goes that the last astronomy professor died there, along with his beautiful young student-mistress, and in killing themselves, they destroyed the workings of the observatory, simultaneously eradicating the astronomy program altogether. Pardon my poetry, but to hear it told around campus, the two lovers, scorned and derided, humiliated and shunned, thought to bathe their love in celestial light, in the blinding white light of Truth and Beauty and all that Keatsian rigmarole, in order to become one, and not just in a spiritual way, but in a quantumly physical way, and to that end, the professor focused the gigantic lens of the telescope toward the sun at high noon, thereby compacting and compressing the hurtling photons, both particle and wave, into the tiny room until neutron and proton and electron fractured and professor and lover were returned as broken atoms and ash to the chaos of the early and unformed universe.

That's what I heard anyway.

I scrape my fingernail against the burnt wall and wonder

at the composition of the residue. How much professor, how much lover, how much compressed sunshine? I put my finger in my mouth but cannot taste the mystery. Maybe time has undone the done or maybe my tongue is not the proper tool for unraveling the braids of starlight and love.

From up here I can see not only the whole campus, but the entire town of Barnesville. This is the highest point in the county, assuming the credibility of college brochures in the age of Fake News, maybe highest in the state. I worked hard to get here, to the top of Arkansas, put a lot on the line, in my father's manner of speaking. My parents wanted me to go to the junior college in my hometown, just six miles from our house. And of course, that made perfect sense. Barnett Junior College was cheaper; I could live at home, under the watchful eyes of my parents and neighbors and friends. But you know, so many problems. The junior college looks for all the world like a prison. A strip-mall prison, and that was just not for me. No, I wanted to come to Chandler. It was everything I dreamed of when I imagined myself matriculated, the girl-poet, the lost daughter of Plath and Rich and Akhmatova, in my long sweater and black leggings, my books pressed against my breasts, my gaze downward, mysterious, desirable. The high ceilings, the clerestory windows, the brick walls with actual ivy fingering its way up toward the very cloths of heaven.

My father had looked at the brochures and at the financial materials and shook his head. "What do you think they can teach you there that you can't get at the college right here?"

I looked at my mother for support. She was torn. It wasn't hard to empathize with her: she wanted so much for me, everything really. Still, she hated to lose me, hated for me to move away. But it wasn't just that. There was something else. I didn't know what then. Also, my father was putting nothing on his hands, so I didn't know how much of this she was following.

Once my father told me that he had grown up wanting to be a disc jockey. I asked him, *What's a disc jockey*? He looked at me like I had started spouting the Russian language or something and then told me that down in Little Rock there is a radio station, KAAY, and that back in the day, way back in the day apparently, it had been a Top 40 station, until eleven o'clock at night when an old boy named Clyde started playing what was then called "underground" music. And to hear my daddy tell it, old Clyde did as much talking as he did record playing, long rambling monologues that touched on ideas and notions and philosophies such as what matched up with the hippie mentality of the music he played. Daddy said that the station's nighttime signal was so powerful it reached all over the Mississippi Valley and up into the Great Plains and whatnot. And that's what he dreamed of being: a voice in the night, sounding out across the piney woods of Arkansas and beyond, playing whole sides of albums, spouting Eastern koans and obscure philosophical doctrine and ringing wind chimes. But all that was lost, he said, when he fell in love with a deaf woman.

A man with a dream that didn't come true.

"Daddy, Barnett is only one step above a technical school." I was signing while I talked. "And a baby step at that. I want to go to a *college*. You know, a real college. One with beautiful old buildings, ivory towers, real PhD-style professors in the classroom." I didn't know the signs for a lot of what I said, but Mama was watching my mouth intently.

"No, I guess I don't know. I just can't see how all that equals the difference in cost. And what do the buildings have to do with any of it. A classroom is a classroom. An education is an education, isn't it?"

"Yes and no."

"So, what if you did your first two years at Barnett and then transferred to Chandler?"

"Shoot, I don't want to do that."

"That's not much of an argument."

He was right. It was a child's argument: *I want to do what I want to do.*

Finally. Finally, my mother.

new friends—she wants—freedom—independence She said this

with her hands. American Sign Language. My mother is that deaf woman, the one my father gave up his dream of music and his voice in the night for.

"So, you're tired of your parents, is that it?" He managed to sound hurt and reasonable at the same time, no mean feat.

"I'm not tired of you." I may have put too much emphasis on the word *tired.*

My mother sat down with us then and signed to my father: *something new—she wants—different—remember—before—your father wanted you work with him—his job*

My father looked down at the paperwork, but Mama lifted his chin and looked into his eyes: *your father like you felt same—wanted you work with him, lumberyard—why? —you leave him—he not want—not the job—you— lose you he not want*

My father said, "I know," and he signed it too.

lose you he not—your own way you found—you success—for you and for me and for Darling

Mama was good in that moment. But something wasn't right. She was saying that she wanted me to go to Chandler, but there was something else. Something she saw in the papers spread around on the table. Something that gave her pause. Even so, she was on my side. Daddy shuffled the paperwork around some more, looking at my grants and loans, and finally saying, "It's gonna be tight, Darling."

"You're right. I think it's going to be worth it, though."

Ultimately, he relented. He gave me what I wanted. He said he would set up a direct deposit of seventy-five dollars a month from his checking account to mine to help me with day-to-day expenses. "Don't spend it all on beer," he said, smiling.

Can I put some of the blame for all that went wrong on them? I guess Lucas would say so. The smear of influence, he'd call it.

As the students shuffled out of the classroom that day, that "First Day," as I came to think of it, in my sad, silly, adolescent mythologizing way, I hung back by the door, though I had another class to get to. Lucas and Lowell stood at the front of the room talking to the professor. They were all smiling, sharing in something, something beyond what went on with the other students. They were beautiful. All three tall, handsome, confident, articulate. Professor and students, ethics and logic, aesthetics and theory, moonlight, poetry, blood. And what did they encompass? *Was this, were they, everything I ever wanted? I realized just then they were everything I ever wanted.* And why didn't I suspect that before, before I came here, before I saw them, before they manifested themselves out there in front of me like a fire in the rain on a lonely path, like the carvings at Carnac, the burning bush? Then Lowell turned and saw me and the look on his face was so familiar, so welcoming, a look you might expect to see in the countenance of someone who loves you and sees you every day but who still takes pleasure in you. I think I smiled back. I tried to, anyway.

When the professor turned away from them to gather his notes and books and load up his briefcase, I ducked out into the hall and headed toward the exit. In a quick second, the boys were walking on either side of me, already in the middle of a conversation. As we stepped outside, they stopped on the portico and Lucas said, "Let's get some lunch, Richie Rich."

Lowell laughed and looked down at me and said, "He means 'dinner,' Darlin'."

Lucas said, "Since it'll be you fingering the profound, and deep, money bags of your daddy's lucre, you can call it 'sloppin' the hogs' or 'feedin' the chickens' or whatever Faulkner-fried metaphor 'strikes yo fancy.'" Mocking our southern accents.

"I have another class now," I said.

They looked at each other over my head.

"What class?" Lucas asked.

"Music Appreciation."

Again, they looked at each other and this time laughed. "C'mon," Lowell said, taking my arm with a gentleness that bespoke a legacy of cotillions and mimosas and fancy dancing. "I got the Big Joe Williams yonder in the car. He eats Grieg for breakfast. What's your name, sweetheart?"

"Darling."

"Seriously?" Lucas said.

"That a nickname?" Lowell said.

"No. That's my name. Darling Jean Bramlett."

"Your parents ought to have their asses kicked," Lucas said. "Where are you from, Darlin'?"

"I'm from right here in Arkansas. Helena."

"Then you'll appreciate some 'Piney Woods Blues.'"

"I just might at that."

I sat in between them on the front seat, feeling like nothing so much as the little sister. Lowell has a really nice car, an SUV of Cadillac origin. He drove past all the restaurants and fast-food joints on the main drag and out beyond the city limits. Down Highway 62 and he finally turned off onto a side road headed out into the country. It occurred to me that they might be taking me out somewhere into the deep, deep woods to fuck me. *Little fuck sister.* I was right up against being scared. I had deliberately drawn their attention. And gotten it. Was I now the lost lamb, bleating for help and inadvertently calling down the wolf? I looked out the windows at the flashing green scenery. I had no idea where we were. Lost as a goose. And I didn't know these boys from Adam's off ox. Two weeks into my dream of college and now what? Love? Sex? Death? The reach of Big Ideas? And come so soon?

Who are you kidding, Darling? Even now you have to admit you'd have dropped your panties for them in a New York heartbeat and never looked back.

Lowell pulled over in front of a small building, a shack really, with a faded hand-painted sign that read Mister Willie's Lonesome B-B-Q. A smoker the size of a Volkswagen radiated waves of heat and sweet, tart smoke. Lucas jumped out of the car and met an old man coming out the front door of the place. They shook hands. The older man said something about the music. Lowell ejected the CD and got out of the car too, shook the man's hand, and handed him the disc. The old man turned it over and over and nodded and slipped it into the front pocket of his overhauls.. Lucas crooked a finger at me. We went onto a small screened-in porch and sat in kitchen chairs around a wobbly little table. It was hot as tarnation and we ate finger-scalding ribs and corn on the cob like we were starving runaways, washing it all down with watery sweet tea. We were sweating and sauce was running down our arms and our knees were knocking together under the table and it was so crazy and we were all laughing and eating and making faces—it was hell-hot paradise. The old gentleman brought us slabs of pecan pie on paper plates for dessert, which the boys ate with their hands.

Afterward, they led me around back of the place and down a worn dirt path to a spring. There they peeled out of their clothes without a glance back at me and plunged into the water, whooping and splashing, their white bodies sparkling in the shadowy green water. I walked down to where I could wet my feet and splash my arms and face and waited. For what? For them to say, *Strip. Come on in. Show us what you got*? They raced and dunked each other like kids, and when they got tired of that, swam slowly around each other face-to-face, whispering like lovers. They sank out of sight, and I could see them swimming underwater toward me. I backed up onto the bank and sat down in a sunny spot. They walked out of the water, stood shoulder to shoulder facing me for a long second, as if inviting my gaze. I didn't turn away. I didn't look up at their faces. Eye-level with their cocks, I tried to keep my face impassive, as if such business for me were common enough. They sat down on either side of me and leaned back onto their elbows, drying themselves in the white light. Their cocks nestled in sparkling curly black hair. I waited to be pulled back onto the ground. Surely this was the moment.

It was not the moment. They talked over me about some story they had read for their American Lit seminar. Something by Flannery O'Connor. I hadn't read her. I knew the name, but she wasn't in the curriculum at my high school. We read Welty and "The Bear" and *Cat on a Hot Tin Roof*.

"You cannot drag that last-century Romanticism into a discussion of the Misfit," Lucas said.

"I don't think that's what I'm doing."

"I'm sorry. Are you or are you not suggesting that a spirit, God, or whatever it is in your phantasmagoric and incorporeal universe, is actually entering the story? And affecting its outcome?"

"Are we pretending that she's *not* Catholic?"

"And that Grandma's epiphany is, in fact, *revelation*? From on high?"

"'Revelation' may be too strong a word. What's wrong with 'epiphany'?" Lowell said.

"Well, for one thing, it doesn't come from God."

"I don't know about that. You are familiar with the etymology of the word, aren't you? What do you think, Darlin'?"

"I haven't read this story or book or whatever y'all are talking about."

"Haven't read O'Connor? *A Good Man is Hard to Find*?"

"I recognize the truth of that, but nope."

Lowell said, "She recognizes the truth of it."

Lucas said, "Yeah. Funny."

"I can't believe that you, a southern girl, haven't read O'Connor."

Lucas said, "That's what she's in college for, Beauregard. To learn. To be exposed to stuff."

"Plenty of exposure here today," I said and looked pointedly back and forth at their respective penises.

"Darlin'," Lowell said, ignoring that, "while we may abandon traditional religious explanations and propositions, even to the point of abandoning God," and here he nodded at Lucas, "don't you think that there is surely a vast unseen world all around us, possibly one inaccessible to our poor five senses? One that an additional, say, ten senses, the properties of which we cannot even imagine, might reveal to us? Isn't it possible that the limits of science and of language are blinding us to other coexistent realities?"

"I believe in luck," I said.

"Well, that's something," Lowell said.

"Don't get me started on luck," Lucas said.

"Or we'd be here all day."

They laughed, and Lucas got up and shook out his clothes and put them on. He climbed back up the path. I followed him. Near the top he turned and called to Lowell, who was standing in a circle of light falling through the trees, still naked, arms outstretched. Posing? For whom?

"Come on, Narcissus. Don't fall in," Lucas said.

Lowell turned and looked up at us, smiling.

"Show off," Lucas muttered.

"Hit him," Lucas said.

We were taking what I assumed was the long way back to campus, down potholed two-lane farm roads, dusty dirt roads, sometimes overlaced with tree canopies that dappled the sunlight onto the ground like Impressionist paintings.

Lucas was pointing at a boy on a rickety bicycle.

"In my Escalade? No, Erskine, that bike would surely scratch the paint. Not gonna happen," Lowell said.

"Where's your spirit of adventure?"

"Nice target, though. Can't you just see him flying off into those cotton bushes?"

"Like an arrow to my heart."

I hear them before I see them. Lucas hectoring, Lowell's soft-voweled replies, and finally their silhouettes separate themselves from the surrounding dark, Lucas's manic-dancing, Lowell's slow shuffle.

"Told you she'd be on the Hill," Lucas says.

"Darlin'," Lowell says. "Why aren't you home in your soft and safe dormitory bed, surrounded on all sides by the sweet sighs and breaths of the thousand-and-one virgins asleep around you rising up to Paradise like so many unanswered prayers?"

They sit on either side of me, then lie back and open their faces to the sky, at home in the denatured world. I catch a whiff of something dead nearby. I lie back too. *And if one of them took me to his breast, would I shrivel in the power of his magnificence? For what is Beauty if it cannot be bothered to destroy us?*

"Is the observatory story true?" Lucas and Lowell are juniors; I, an uninitiated freshman.

"So many kinds of truth, Darlin'. Would you be satisfied if I said it was figuratively true?" Lowell says.

Lucas says, "It's bullshit. A, I don't think the physics works, and two, I heard the astronomy program just ran out of money. My understanding is that the Arkansas legislature, satisfied as they seem to be with a Biblical guesstimate of the cosmos, just stopped funding the thing."

"What is it that appeals to you about the story, Darlin'?" Lowell's voice is soft, softening toward his southern accent, which he usually dampens, but allows out, even exaggerates when it suits him. "Sex and death? Well, that's common enough, isn't it? But you're not common at tall, are you, sweetheart?"

"God loves the common folk, I've heard," I say.

"Hm. Lincoln? And maybe that's true, though one might suggest the common folk take fairly regular ass-kickings from the World Historical Spirit, as Hegel might say, whereas the exceptional among humans do much better."

"Or much worse," Lucas says. "Hello? Lincoln? Duh."

"Yes," Lowell says. "To exercise the Will to, well, the Will to anything, is a risk. Greatness comes at a closely milled risk."

"Milled?" Lucas asks.

"For every successful Napoleon, there are a billion failed ones, gone to dust, lost to history. That French boy took some big chances. And they paid off. But they didn't have to. It wasn't Fate."

"Milled?" Lucas says again.

"If it wasn't Fate, what was it?" I say.

"An infinitely variegated set of threads leading out of multiple causes toward one remarkable outcome," Lowell says.

Lucas snorts. "He's talking about your 'luck,' Darling."

"I don't think that's what I'm talking about."

"Yes, it is. Good luck for Napoleon, bad luck for the wannabes."

"I'm not completely sold on the idea of luck, no offense, Darlin'. It's like unto Fate, only—"

"How did you get the scar, Lucas?" I interrupt.

They are quiet now. The wind soughs ever so softly in the oaks below us like a long, satisfied sigh. Lucas's scar runs from the corner of his left eye in a graceful, if ragged, curve to his chin. "An accident," Lucas says.

Lowell coughs.

"Something to add?" Lucas says.

"It's your tale," Lowell says. "Told by—"

"There was a misunderstanding, then a fight, and the one guy had a knife, and then there was no money for plastic surgery."

"Redaction at its finest, Darlin'," Lowell says.

"Sure," I say. "Details have been left out, based on a true story, the names changed to protect, etc."

"The scar has served me."

"He embraced it a long time ago," Lowell says.

"*My* tale?"

"Right. Sorry. Are you telling the tale?"

"It was a case of mistaken identity."

"That's what Nietzsche said all along," Lowell says.

"I was coming out of Refugees—"

"That's a gay bar in San Jose," Lowell says.

"Will you please, please, please, please, please, please, please stop talking?"

"Ah. Nice. Suggesting, then, that the scar came from an abortion. A little air let in, don't you know."

"A lot of my friends were gay. Coming out of the bar, we ran into these homophobic fucks. I just wasn't in the mood to back down right then, and well, as I say, a misunderstanding," Lucas says.

"An abortion?" I ask, confused.

"The death of the self. The birth of the anti-self," Lowell says. "In seven years the human body replaces every single solitary cell and we are made completely anew, but sometimes we must accelerate our evolution."

I'm not going to get the whole and true scar story, at least not tonight. None of that cell stuff's true, either. It's an interesting trope, seven, the holy number, the new-made body and all, but no. On the other hand, even though his metaphor collapses, I get what Lowell's saying. I have accelerated my own evolution. From small-town hick to budding nihilist. From half-assed poet to apprentice anarchist. It's coming on toward dawn. No one has suggested going to our dorms, getting some sleep, going to class. The pale ghost of the moon rising in the morning sky. Two buzzards circling above the trees north of the campus.

It bothered me, the thing about Flannery O'Connor. I hate it when I'm behind the curve, when it feels like everybody knows something except for me. I guess I shouldn't have been bothered. The next three months were going to constitute a litany of things Lucas and Lowell knew or knew about which I didn't.

I am from Helena, a town smaller even than Barnesville, where Chandler College is. Like everyone there, I went to Eliza Miller Primary and then Central High. I was pretty enough to be invited onto the cheer squad, but I wasn't popular. I only got called out for cheerleading because they needed one more reasonably attractive girl. Three girls do not a cheer team make. But apparently you can get by with four. Even at practice the other girls mostly ignored me. The problem was, I didn't cultivate the right friends. You see, I wanted to be a poet. Or so I thought. I loved Anne Sexton. I loved Elizabeth Bishop. Glück, Rich, Plath. Ah, Plath. The book *Ariel* was my totem. I didn't really understand all the poems in it, but I didn't need to, for I loved the sound of the words. And the idea of the poet herself, cold, abandoned, feverish with inspiration, burned in me like a gas stove. It didn't matter that I didn't understand those poems because, of course, Plath was crazy, and so by the time I got to *Ariel* in the tenth grade, after reading *The Bell Jar*, I didn't expect to make complete sense out of her. I was satisfied to let her "flow over" me. But Shakespeare got my goat. As my father says. I had to draw the line there. With Shakespeare. Tenth grade was *Romeo and Juliet*, and I had decided that I was going to get a head start. This would be my first encounter with the Bard.

I checked his sonnets out of the library and took them home and spent a weekend reading them. And not just reading them. Poring over them. Getting more and more frustrated, more and more filled with despair. And I don't think I got the gist of even five out of the whole hundred and fifty something of them. How in the world could the most popular poet in the English language (according to Mrs. Griffith) be completely incomprehensible to me? Me! Darling Jean Bramlett, a straight-A student!

By Sunday night I was so frustrated I was in tears. So I broke down and I googled him. Yes, I did. I googled the very Shakespeare himself.

And I found lots of explanations and interpretations of the sonnets. And I thought, *It means that? That's what it says? Shoot, why didn't I see that?*

I realized that if I were going to maintain my status at school and, indeed, my very self-image, I was probably gonna need to google *Romeo and Juliet* too. I had already bought the requisite paperback copy and now I dug it out of my backpack and opened it to the first page.

SAMPSON
Gregory, o' my word, we'll not carry coals.
GREGORY
No, for then we should be colliers.
SAMPSON
I mean, an we be in choler, we'll draw.
GREGORY

Ay, while you live, draw your neck out o' the collar.
SAMPSON
I strike quickly, being moved.
GREGORY
But thou art not quickly moved to strike.
SAMPSON
A dog of the house of Montague moves me.
GREGORY
To move is to stir; and to be valiant is to stand: therefore, if thou art moved, thou runn'st away.

Nope. Not a word. Not a single word. And so, not for the last time, I felt left out, I felt like I was too provincial, too ignorant to read even the almighty Bard, the finest writer of English. But I decided right then and there that I was not going to be defeated. Not by Shakespeare. Not by anything. If I had to google every single thing I ever needed or wanted to know and didn't, then that's what I'd do. If I had to google the whole world, then so be it.

By the time our class got to Romeo and his Juliet, I was all over it. I had annotated my copy like a mad monk illuminating the *Song of Songs* with pornographic glee.

And from then on I no longer waited for my teachers to assign books or acquaint me with authors or illustrate philosophical principles. I did it. I went ahead and did it: I googled the whole world. I read the life of Byron on the *Encyclopedia Britannica* online. I read the History of Philosophy on Wikipedia. I read the *Duino Elegies* on some Minnesota kid's copyright-exploding website. I became the Google Autodidact of Helena. I became the person I wanted to be.

Or I thought I wanted to be. Or I thought I wanted to be back then.

In high school, I hung out with the English geeks. There weren't many: pimple-faced Roger, sweet Annabella as round as an Oreo, Franklin, dressed in all black year round, hopelessly closeted. And blindfolded. They wowed Mrs. Driscoll with their teen imitations of the Romantics and were exempted from term papers in lieu of poetry manuscripts. I didn't think virgins should write poetry, so I was holding off putting quill to vellum.

The four of us walked in the woods around campus and prayed for inspiration. And fame. Roger reciting Keats, Franklin declaiming Byron. Anabella giggling and peeking at Franklin, oblivious. Roger fell in love with me. Of course.

I mean, it was inevitable, wasn't it? He didn't know any other girls. As the philosopher Hannibal Lecter has said, we begin by coveting that which we see every day. Roger began by sending me poems through the mail—the actual postal mail—handwritten in a "style," I guess you'd call it, that I'm sure he thought was calligraphy, poems he didn't show the others or turn in to Mrs. Driscoll. In due course, which is to say senior year, I let him take me out.

He squired me to the one and only movie theater in Helena and then to the drive-in the next town over and to the Denny's and the Waffle House and other such dining establishments as are available in the reaches of north Arkansas. His father let him use the family station wagon. He was kind and solicitous and deferential, but I just couldn't find it in myself to desire him. Is that even something we can control? Can we choose to desire something, someone? I couldn't. My controlling emotion was pity: I felt sorry for him. Truly sorry. He so wanted to fuck me. I mean, he really, *really* wanted to fuck me. So much, in fact, that he cried. Literally cried. Literal tears. On several occasions. "Just let me open your shirt." I had spent a fair amount of time considering the problem and the logistics of jettisoning my virginity. Some writer in some novel I can't remember now said that the idea of virginity was contrived by old men so they'd have something to defile. Maybe so, but it was definitely the heavy bear I dragged around with me, the cross on my shoulders, one of the many stumbling blocks to my poetic aspirations. And so—as well him as another, like what's-her-name said. Better him, in fact, than some football player trying to fuck his way through the cheerleaders, the pep squad, and the student council.

It's not that I was immune to sexual desire. I had been responsible for and, more importantly, capable of my own orgasm since fourth grade. My best friend, Julie, and I had discovered that her mother's couch cushions were extremely companionable, and we humped them from the time we got to her house after school until her mother got home from work around four. We played "house." Wherein "house" was prepubescent wives and cushiony husbands. When the boys started bragging about jerking off in the sixth grade, we rolled our eyes and nudged each other. We'd already been there. That was the same year my father told me about intercourse. He and I had been doing math homework together and when the last problem was done, he just dropped it on me. In glorious detail. I went straight to Julie's house and told her all about it. She slept over with me that Friday and playing "house" changed irrevocably that night.

She got on top of me. Then I got on top of her. We pushed against each other, like bony couch cushions, I suppose. It was good, it was nice, we both came, but it changed something. I'm not sure what or how, but for some reason we never played "house" again after that night. We never mounted the cushions together anymore either. It was like we just agreed, somehow and without saying anything, never to mention any of it again. Ever. And we never did.

Then with Roger, well, I'm going to have to admit that what I enjoyed most was the perverse thrill of delaying him. He wanted me so bad. Shoot, every button undone was a victory for him, a joy, a revelation, an epiphany. One night in the back of the station wagon out at the Tracks, a make-out place by the abandoned railway station, three buttons in, he kissed the tops of my breasts and tried to pull my bra down to get at my nipples, but I stopped him and he satisfied himself kissing me where I allowed him. Night after night he charged the battlements of my resistance. His joy, his desire, his total want of me was intoxicating. Orgasm was great, who knew that better than I, a tight fist of pleasure that creaked my bones and blew the top of my head off. But I really didn't need him for that. I could give myself orgasms, and I did, at home, in my bed, after he had dropped me off. But his need for me, his hunger, was a sea of roiling black water inexhaustible in its reach. On top of me, fumbling, rubbing, sniffling even, he was ravenous, famished for me. I imagined him fiercely masturbating in his car on lonely roads while I lay in bed fingering myself.

I tortured him. It was wonderful. *What was wrong with me?*

Unsnapping my pants. Unhooking my bra. I let him take off my jeans the eighth time at the drive-in. He pushed his nose against my panties and wept. Was it the slippery texture of the fabric or the smell that drove him to such desperation? Or simply the proximity to that which he wanted more than salvation. I was his Christ, spread out in the back of the station wagon as if on a cross. I went home that night with my underwear soaked in equal parts spit, tears, and me.

Desire is narcotic. Not that I desired anything. I was addicted to being desired.

The summer after senior year, when I was going to leave for Chandler in the fall and Roger would be going to UA in Fayetteville, he called and asked me to go with him to the Tracks. I told him to bring a condom. I imagined I could hear the phone shaking in his hand.

Ninety degrees at ten p.m. We lay on a quilt and sweated all over each other. His sweat was oily. And not in a pleasant way. But I was excited. The grand thing finally here. He kneeled over me and pulled on the rubber. He was trembling.

The act itself was brief and unexceptional. He drooled on my face when he came.

He cried and apologized. Not for drooling on me, which I don't think he even knew he'd done, but for fucking me. For debasing me, he said, spoiling me, degrading me, ruining me, defiling me. I bit back the urge to ask if he needed a thesaurus. He loved me, he said, and I deserved better, so much better, than he had treated me.

In an act that had little enough pleasure in it, he somehow found a way to make things worse. I thought about saying, *Don't dirty or degrade or demean or debase this delightful moment.* But that would have been cruel. So I didn't.

What does that even mean? I'd tortured him and his hormonal systems for months. Did I think mocking him now was worse than lying under him night after night, denying him, watching the pain and confusion on his face? I was a terrible person, I suppose. I suppose I still am.

The day after they took me for barbecue, the boys were waiting for me outside the women's dorm. They were both in short pants. Lucas was wearing a T-shirt that said *Don't Sweat My Swag* and Lowell was in a Polo. They're tall, over six feet. Lowell's hair is Edgar Allan Poe black and long, curls crowding his collar. Lucas wears a buzz cut.

"Long pants, Darlin'?" Lowell asked.

"It's cold in Murrah Hall."

We headed toward the cafeteria. Even at seven in the morning, it was already hot. The sky hazy, the wind mild. Everyone was walking briskly toward their breakfasts or their classes. There was still a "first week of school" air about things, even though it was the second week. People were still smiling and excited to be here. I felt the same way. Like the first week of senior year in high school but to the fifth power or something. I was wondering if that amplification was because I'd actually gotten here, gotten to Chandler despite all the odds, or was it because of the boys walking on either side of me. We rounded the corner at the Christian Center and that's when three girls stepped up and looked me squarely in the eyes. They were smiling, friendly, but there was something else? What?

And there was one more girl. Standing a few feet behind the others. Beautiful, dark hair, slim, and in her beret looking like a French movie star from the fifties. She was staring at me like she knew me. And didn't care much for me. What was that about?

In fact, even though the girls were looking at me, I thought they had stopped to speak to Lucas and Lowell because I didn't know them. I didn't really know anyone here yet. Then I turned and saw that the boys had fallen back and were leaning against the brick wall of the Christian Center. Lucas gave me a wry smile and whispered something to Lowell, who dropped his head and didn't look at me.

One of the girls was from my algebra class, a tall redhead. She was dressed in a yellow blouse and matching shorts. I was put in mind of Big Bird, and a remark was on the tip of my tongue, but I swallowed it. She said, "Hi. You're Darling, right? I'm Clarissa. We have Dr. Simpson together."

"Yes. I recognize you."

"This is Suzanne and Lindsay," and both girls chirped "hi" in unison. "Anyway, Darling, we're from Delta Delta Kappa. Have you seen our house?"

The Delta Delta Kappa house is a colonial style, red brick, white columned, three-story building, the largest Greek house on campus. The 2DKs are known to be the rich girls.

"Yes," I said. "It's pretty. Must be nice to live there."

"Oh," she said, "pledges don't live there." There must have been a look on my face because her smile disappeared and she quickly added, "College regs say that freshmen have to live in the dorms. You know that, right? You can't move off campus or into a Greek house."

"Yeah. Sure, of course."

Her smile came back on like a lamp. "Anyway. We're looking for pledges—"

One of the girls behind her said, "New members."

"Right. New members. Quality girls. Anyway, we think you would be a great addition to the Deltas. Now, our Open House is tomorrow night. We would love to have you come by and meet all the girls. And don't forget that Rush is only two weeks away."

"I hadn't really thought—"

"You'll love it, I swear. This is not last-century toga parties and panty raids. We're totally twenty-first century orientated. We do a lot of good for the community."

One of the girls behind her said, "Charity work."

The other girl said, "We're the primary sponsor of a women's shelter."

Clarissa said, "For battered women. And their children."

"That's very nice," I said.

"Have you thought about joining a sorority, Darling?"

"No. Actually, I haven't."

"Well, I don't mean to brag, and I'm sure all the other houses think the same thing about themselves, but DDK is the best house on campus. You couldn't make a better choice."

"Maybe you do mean to brag," I said, but with a smile.

"You got me," she said and laughed. "Anyway, the advantages are myriad."

Myriad.

"Like what?" I said and looked over my shoulder at Lucas and Lowell who were listening while pretending not to. *Why was I even talking to this girl? I couldn't afford the sorority life even if I wanted. Shoot, I'd already blown the seventy-five from my dad for this month.*

One of the girls behind Clarissa spoke up: "It's about the connections you make, Darling, and not just with us. You'll be hooking into a network of Deltas all over the business world. Delta Delta Kappa is not just a four-year college experience. It's a lifetime immersion."

"Sounds like a marriage," I said.

Clarissa said, "Marriages come and go, Darling. Sisterhood is forever. Anyway, you should also consider that if you join us, you will be able to live in the nicest place on campus. Next year, I mean. And statistics show that Greeks have significantly higher GPAs than independents. In fact, Delta has the highest collective GPA at Chandler. Higher even than the so-called Honor Society."

"Really? That's impressive."

"Yes, it is. Look, Darling. You're not going to find a better house on campus. You should think about it."

I said this very carefully: "Are there any Black girls in your sorority?" I tried to modulate my voice in such a way so that she could not tell whether I thought this would be a plus or a deal breaker.

Two lines appeared between her eyebrows. This had, I thought, caught her off guard. Of course there were Black women in the sorority. It was 2016, for God's sake. Why was she hesitating to answer? Finally, she cocked her head to one side and said, "We try to look past things like race, Darling."

"To what?" I said. "Money?" She blushed at the evocation of the word. "I'm sorry, Clarissa," and here I said her name the way she'd been saying mine, a careful amalgam of intimacy and condescension. "My folks aren't rich. To be embarrassingly honest, we're just poor white trash from Helena. I'm at Chandler on a fragile, liable-to-collapse-at-any-moment edifice of small scholarships and big loans. I cannot afford to buy any friends right now."

The two girls behind her backed up a couple of steps and looked away.

Clarissa's lines deepened. She stepped in close and lowered her voice. "You're clever, Darling. Very smart, very verbal. You live up to your billing one thousand percent. You're just what we're looking for. A first-class bitch and I like that. Now, I don't know if your performance this morning is for me or for those two degenerates over there, but you can consider my invitation withdrawn. Anyway, I'm not going to embarrass you right here, right now, as you have embarrassed me. Take your clever repartee and go on your merry. Sorry to have wasted your time."

And she turned and walked away. She and Suzanne and Lindsay went over to the French movie-star girl and Clarissa said something which prompted that girl to say loud enough for me to hear, "It's a waste of time. She's already pledged." And she nodded toward the boys.

Lucas and Lowell stepped up on either side of me and stared at the French movie-star girl until the lot of them turned and headed toward sorority row.

"Who is that?" I said.

Lowell nudged me and we walked toward the dining hall.

"Who is who?" Lucas said.

I sleep through Intro to Sociology, but I make it to English Lit, though I am in my sleep pants. Dr. Blackwell is savagely critiquing some antique poem called "Trees," scrawling a drawing on the board of the creature that the poem seems to be describing, mouth to the ground, eyes to the sky, arms waving like a drowning man. She clearly hates the poem. I've never heard of it and judging by the faces of the other students, neither have they.

When she finishes with the poor author of "Trees," she recites from memory a poem by Yeats. "The Song of Wandering Aengus." This is one I do know, and it is beautiful. Transported by her own recital, Blackwell commands the room, head high, eyes closed, hands clasped to her very bosom. *The golden apples of the sun.*

"So enough for now of 'talking' about poetry. Who would choose to be the lightning rod when they could be the lightning? And so, we will write our own poems."

The duration of the class is taken up with whining and questions and offensive countermeasures: "This isn't creative writing!" "Does it have to rhyme? What about iambic pyramider or whatever?" "I can't write a poem!"

I shouldn't be worried. A poem, sure, of course. I am the poet-child in vitro. Or something. The problem is, I haven't written a word since I got here. Despite setting aside an hour a day to write, I just can't get going. A radical self-consciousness has fallen on me like the proverbial house. My internal editor works faster than I do. A word is not off the pencil good, and I already hate it. Should never have read that dumbass Prufrock.

It's not like I never wrote anything. All through senior year I wrote lyrics for Tommy Steele who had himself a cover band that played around Sharp and Lawrence and Independence counties, but who wanted to do his own original material, and make his way to New York City, and become the next Bruce Springsteen. So, he would write some music and then burn a CD of himself playing it and give it to me with the title of the song and ask me to write the words. He was all, *the title of this is Atomic Lampshade, or this one is Desecration Row*, and it was easy to fill in the blanks right up to the chorus (which was always just the title over and over) with little rhymes and half rhymes, cold, hard, screamable words that meant nothing. Or less than nothing. Shoot, they weren't meant to mean anything. Evocation was all. The joy of the lyric which need only seem and never be.

The boys catch me coming out of English and convince me to cut Music Appreciation (again). They want to drive up near the Missouri border to check out some state park.

"Are we taking up camping?" I say when we're headed east in the Escalade.

"Really it's about access points to Kings River. From what I've read, the river widens right there at the park into a virtual swamp," Lowell says.

"River into swamp," I say.

"You never know when you'll need a swamp," Lowell says.

"I cannot even imagine what that means," I say.

"You can't spend enough time on rivers," Lucas says. "The river is the core metaphor of life."

"The what?" I say.

"I'm just kidding," Lucas says.

"Well, speaking of metaphors, I have to write a poem for English."

And one of the many things I love about them: they know I want to be a poet, but they don't rag me about never actually writing any. They don't make fun of me, belittle my aspirations, mock me. They want to help.

"I don't have to be, you know, the best poet in the class. I just don't want to be the worst. If there were just some way to write a poem and then not have to be responsible for it, like the parent of some teenage spree killer. You should have seen Blackwell taking apart this poem called 'Trees.'"

Lucas says, "That poem deserves vivisection. Though Kilmer is American. Why is she doing Kilmer in English Lit. It's *English* Lit, right?"

Lowell suggests a found poem.

"How could you go wrong?" he says. "We'll find some grocery list or advert on Facebook and arrange whatever it is into 'lines' of poetry and voilà! Poem. Done. Boom."

I say, "Well, that's not a bad idea—"

Lucas isn't having it. "No, what you want is a Dadaist poem. We print out a bunch of words, cut them up, throw them into the air, then pick them up and put them together in whatever order they happen to fall. Now that's the way to do 'how can you go wrong.' There is no wrong. With Dada, it's not you. It's chance. Say, for instance, we pick some 'found' thing and make it into a poem, and then it comes to pass that your teacher hates it. Well, you have left yourself open for criticism since it was you who chose that found something to make into a poem. People could complain, 'What did you pick that for? It's boring.' But Dada? Really? Who can gripe about the choices that Chance, Fate, the Universe, the Oversoul has made? 'You don't like what the Universe has provided, well, that's not my fault.'"

"I think I have some of those refrigerator poetry magnets."

Each raises an eyebrow.

"They were a gift."

"Yes," Lucas says. "Let us by all means add the God of Magnetism into the mix."

It's about an hour to the Kings River State Park. We drive in, past picnic areas, a visitor center (closed), camping spots with hookups for trailers and farther on, places for tents and such. It's deserted. A sign says "Canoe Rentals" and we follow it to a turnoff toward the river. At the water's edge is an old building with a couple dozen canoes stacked outside. As we're getting out of the car, a guy steps out of the building. He's an old hippie type, tall, with long black and gray hair, cutoff jean shorts, flip-flops. He's surprised to see us. He reeks of pot.

"Hey, y'all," he says. "I'm John. Wanting to rent a canoe, are you?" He's brushing ashes off his shirt. I think it's a woman's blouse.

"Got one big enough for the lot of us?" Lowell says in his finest southern drawl.

"As long as you're not including me, any of these will fit the three of you just fine."

"Well, let's haul one down to the water then," Lowell says.

Old Hippie John and Lucas unchain a yellow canoe and drag it to the river and throw paddles and life jackets into the bottom.

Old John says, "Right through here the current ain't too strong. Here's the thing, though. Whichever direction you go, in about an hour y'all need to turn around and come back. You don't want to be out there after dark. Kindly getting a late start, you know."

"'Preciate it," Lowell says and climbs into the canoe. I sit in the middle with Lowell up front and Lucas in the back. From the rental joint, the river broadens southward and this is the direction we go. Fifteen minutes later we are floating among trees with water stretched out on either side of us out of sight. It's not a river anymore. At least not recognizable as such. I'm put in mind of a Cajun swamp such as I've seen on television.

Lowell lights a joint and the smoke drifts back over me. Lucas says, "Did you get that off Hippie John?"

Lowell turns and silently offers it to me. I shake my head. It's dark under the canopy of trees. The air is full of birdsong and the water mirrors the ripply dark of the leaves, another Impressionist painting.

"This river's got a real Monet thing going on," Lowell says.

"Should have left you back at the Love Shack," Lucas says.

"I was just thinking about Impressionism myself," I say. "Actually, I seem to think about it a lot."

"Freshmen," Lucas says.

The boys aren't paddling. We drift along at the same speed as the fallen leaves and sticks and insects in the water.

"Still," I say, "this is beautiful. It has to make you feel good, huh?"

Lucas says, "There is a negativeness in the universe. We endure the hideous lonely emptiness of existence. Nothingness. The predicament of Man forced to live in a barren, Godless eternity like a tiny flame flickering in an immense void with nothing but waste, horror, and degradation, forming a useless bleak straitjacket in a black absurd cosmos."

Lowell turns around and looks at Lucas, frowning. "You didn't just think that up. That's out of a movie."

"What movie?"

"I can't remember."

"Give me a title, Mr. Know Everyfuckingthing."

"I need a minute. I'm going to find it. Where's my phone? I can look it up, Herr Plagiarism."

"Not out here, Eudora. There's no signal."

"Besides which," Lowell says, leaning back and laying his head on my leg, "You're positing Nothingness as an entity, which is in full violation of your Nietzschean world view."

"I'm not positing shit."

"Really? Up your diction, Stand Up Comedy Boy."

"I'm just expressing a response to the random nature of nature. The lack of reason and purpose. It's a reasonable reaction, I think, to the suggestion that we're floating along here in a Monet."

Lowell says, "The problem with your theory is that nature is not random. There's patterning. Where do you suppose the Teleological Argument comes from?"

"The who?"

"Stop it. Ontogeny recapitulates phylogeny."

"Debunked."

"Maybe."

"In any case," Lucas says, "patterns in the physical universe are just the result of predictable forces. Gravity, magnetism, quantum flux. The strong force, the weak force. All meaningless."

"What about patterns in human affairs?"

"Confirmation bias."

Lowell laughs. "Let me tell you a story."

"Fuck all. You Confederates. I swear to God. Is there anything you don't have a story about? Or the overwhelming, gut-wrenching urge to tell it?"

Lowell sits up and turns around to face us. He's gorgeous. Hair lifted by the soft breeze, face haloed in the diffused light falling through the canopy of green and brown. My thigh is burning where his head lately lay.

"My father grew up poor."

Lucas snorts.

"It's true. He and his brother Paul and his sisters, Evie and Melissa, lived in the deep country with my grandparents, who were a mere step above sharecroppers."

"What does that mean?" I say.

"That they actually owned the poor dirt they farmed."

"What did they grow?" I ask.

"Not the point. Whatever it was, it didn't keep the great ballyhooed wolf from the door. Paul and my father started hiring themselves out to construction jobs here and there around the county and eventually started their own construction business, which is how they pulled themselves up."

"Made themselves rich," Lucas says.

"Yes."

"So, you're outlining a 'pattern' of avarice, greed, and social mobility?"

"No. I haven't gotten to that story yet."

"Jesus! Enough warming up. Enough foreplay. Get to it before the bourbon kicks in, Faulkner boy."

"It was my grandmother what told me this story, don't you know." Lowell is exaggerating his accent now. "Paul and my daddy were little, Daddy five or six and Paul four, I think. Evie comes running into the house and says, 'Paul's in the water.' Granny goes running out the house and down to the road. There was a big ole washed-out place in this dirt road where water had collected, and there she found Paul floating face down in it."

"Lord a mighty," I say.

"So she yanks him up by the feet and shakes him upside down and squeezes the water out of him and somehow—he's not dead."

"Miracle," I add.

"Yeah."

"Nice story," Lucas says, "signifying nothing."

"Not done," Lowell says.

"I'm shocked," Lucas says.

"So it's forty years or so later. Paul is playing golf at this country club he belongs to—"

"Rich folks," Lucas says.

"—and he's on the ninth green up near the clubhouse and he sees this commotion over by the pool. Ambulance, folks gathered round, some hollering and crying and whatnot. So he drops his putter and runs over there. And just as he gets there, the paramedics are stepping back from the laid-out body of this teenage boy and they're saying, 'He's gone,' and people are weeping and hugging up on one another. The boy had drowned in the pool, you see. Well, old Paul says, and I'm quoting my Bible-spouting grandmother here, 'Fuck that,' and he drops down to his knees by the boy and gives him mouth-to-mouth, every once in a while stopping to do some chest compressions. The paramedics tell him they've been working on the boy for ten minutes with no luck and that Paul should just give it up. But he won't. He breathes into the boy and pumps on his chest for thirty minutes, and damn if the boy doesn't start breathing and coughing up water and comes right back to life and Paul is the big hero. Story goes that that young man went on to graduate high school and the University of Mississippi Law School and is a highly successful Capitol Street lawyer right this very minute."

"Wow," I say.

"Wow's ass," Lucas says. "Your point?"

"Not there yet."

"Seriously?"

"Some years later Paul and some of his friends are canoeing the Homochitto River, doing an overnight float. They've camped on a sandbar and are bonfireing and drinking expensive bourbon and smoking fine cigars and generally enjoying the good life. During the night, a flash flood washes away the sandbar and everybody on it. A couple of the guys drowned, a couple more survived, and Paul, or his body, was never found."

"Have mercy," I say.

"Now the point?" Lucas asks.

"Pattern. Water, Paul, life, death. Can't you see it?"

"Are you crazy? That's not pattern. It's—poetry or something."

"Forced to disagree. Water, the source of all life, a pattern of turning points in Paul's life and death."

"Stop. Please. You're embarrassing yourself."

"Maybe. Or maybe it's simply the pattern of tragedy that runs from Oedipus through Achilles down to—"

Lucas sits up straight and says something like *nnh, nnh,* and points at a murky dark place. He drops his paddle into the water and the canoe slides left. Lowell puts his paddle in and they pull hard to port, I guess you'd say.

"Darling. Scull," Lucas says.

"Skull? Where?"

"Paddle, Darling."

"Toward the skull? Is that what you mean? Where's it at?"

"Between the A and the T," Lowell drawls with all his might.

Lucas says, "There's no skull. Just—never mind."

We slip up next to a place that might be called the "bank" if there were any solid ground instead of just shallow water and grass and weeds pushed up three feet high. You couldn't've stepped out here—not earth, but not river proper.

What we've come to see is a formation of bent-over weeds and bushes and skinny trees, twisted in such a way as to form a cave-like opening. Inside is darkness and a smell out of your nightmares, equal parts rot and death and putrefaction.

"I know we ain't even fixin' to go up in there," I say.

"And Darling reverts to Helena-speak. It's a panic-sight thing, isn't it?" Lucas says.

"I will not be defined by my accent nor my inflection at any particular moment." I don't know the term panic-sight, but inferring from context, I think, yeah, that's probably right because I really do not want to go into that hole.

"I am put in mind of a quote heah," Lowell says. He's in full Scarlett O'Hara mode now, accentwise.

I say, "It gaped like a dark open mouth." I read "A Good Man Is Hard to Find" in the interim. *Shouldn't I be reading such things so as to impress my professors instead of these two?*

"Look at little Darlin', trotting out with the O'Connor allusion." Lowell laughs. "Well done, Sissy."

To this day, that's what my father calls his sister. Sissy. Even though she died two years ago. The dead sister.

The boys tie the canoe to a spindly tree right in front of the opening. A snake swims out and a bullfrog croaks from within. "Nest of water moccasins," a phrase from back in my childhood somewhere, worms around in my brain's gearbox. The water, the swamp, these woods seem to be growing darker. Of course, my panic-sight may be getting worse, glaucomatizing even.

"I think this place might be evil," I say.

"Evil?" the boys say in unison.

"Can't you feel it? I feel something here, something dark and cold, even in this heat. A place can be evil, can't it?"

"For example?" Lucas says.

"I don't know. That weird-ass suicide forest in Japan? Teotihuacan?"

"Tay tee a what?" Lowell says.

"There are places that make me feel good. If there are places that make me feel good, then aren't those 'good' places? And if there are good places, why not evil places?" I say.

"Let me guess," Lucas says and waves the paddle around over his head, hurling black drops of water which I instinctively duck. "The library makes you feel good, the soft chairs, the smell of the books. Sitting on the bank of a river watching the swirl of leaves in water, the dance of light in the ripples, the liquid silver voices of birds in the trees—all this makes you feel good, no?"

"Maybe."

He sneers. "No maybe, Darling. You want to live in a poem, a beautiful poem, a nineteenth-century poem, Keats, I'm guessing, but everything you bring to your worldly experience is wish fulfillment. Those things you experience that are like your poem-world are good and those that are not are evil. Or banal."

"So, when I consider this dark and terrible hole you've brought us to and I feel dark and terrible, that's just my psychology. It's all coming from me, is that what you're saying?"

"Yes, Darling," Lucas says. "It's so obvious. It's right there in your grammar. You feel, and the world corresponds to your feeling."

His voice softens here. He sounds like he actually cares about me, wants me to understand, when he says, "There is no evil in the world, but what man has wrought. The universe is morally neutral."

Maybe his voice didn't soften. Maybe that was just me, wanting to be cared about, projecting that need onto him. And I see now that's probably what he would say too.

"Man doesn't make hurricanes or disease," I say. "Those seem to be evils man didn't create. And man didn't make this hole in the river, I don't guess." I'm trembling a little bit.

Lucas doesn't say anything back. He looks off, back upstream. I can't tell if I've caught him in a paradox or if he's just fed up with my recalcitrance.

Or if I've rejected his care for me.

Or if I'm too dense to see his point.

Lowell stands up in the front of the canoe, almost turning us over, nearly blinding my panic-sight, and strips. In this gloaming of greeny black shadows, he is marble smooth, as if rubbed by the loving hands of a Renaissance sculptor, gleaming, radiant in a fall of white light spilling through an aperture in the tree sky.

I grip the sides of the canoe, trying to keep him from tumping us into the water. He turns away from us and looks toward the swamp cave. His behind is a peach. Or an erotic poem.

Lucas pulls out his phone and photographs him.

Lowell says, "Lucas is not entirely correct here, Darlin'."

"Where's your phone, Darling?" Lucas asks.

"I left it in the car."

"Cliché, at this point," Lucas says.

Lowell says, "The universe is not neutral. It is, for lack of a better phrase, what it is."

"You had to get naked to say this?" Lucas asks.

"It moves, like music moves, only in time, cutting its path with no discernible goal. It creates and it destroys. There is no Good or Evil for there is no consciousness, at least as we know it. Consciousness is, above all, about choice. Does the universe choose to expand? To hold stars together in galaxies, or is that all the function of physical law?" He turns to look at us. "Darling, you come up to the front. I want to get some pictures of you."

When I stand up, the canoe tilts again, and Lowell and I have to pass each other awkwardly, holding on to one another and sort of shuffle-stepping by. I'm pressed against his naked body. He's all sweat and musk and some aftershave or cologne I don't recognize. Maybe it's disingenuous to say I am not doing it consciously or on purpose, but in those couple of seconds when we are face to face, I arch my back, just a little, I swear, so that my breasts are sort of "there" against him.

What do I want? The answer is obvious. Because I am a cliché, just as Lucas said. I want what I had with Roger, with the couple of other boys I let take me out in high school. I want him to want me. I want him to be filled. With an ocean of want. A glacier of desire. His desire and want overwhelming him. I want him to want me, to want inside me. Outside me. I can say it. I want him, both of them, really, begging for my body, my heart, my soul. Or. I want them to want what they want of me. What do they desire?

Would I let them kill me, if that's what they wanted?

I have to consider the very real possibility that I'm a perv.

Lucas scoots over and Lowell sits next to him, mashed together on one seat. Naked and dressed, soft hearted and hardheaded, dark and dark. I'm bent over holding the sides of canoe. Lowell motions for me to sit down. He says, "In the scalding interior of the sun, hydrogen is broken, the promise sworn between one neutron and one proton broken again and again, becoming helium, the mayfly helium already dying as soon as it is born, becoming iron and so on until the sun collapses and flames out, flames out like shook foil, some poet says. And who would bemoan 'O poor hydrogen, poor helium, to have lived and died, and for what?' You see, those are the sorts of things that folks will think, for the will to anthropomorphize is strong. But we, too, Darlin', are but hydrogen and helium and iron, no more permanent than the smallest immeasurable unit of time."

"I'm not gladdened by that," I say.

"Darling, can you give me something other than the resting bitch face, please," Lucas says.

Facing them, their phones, firefly flashes trapping photonic versions of my face. And the dark cave behind me.

"That's not her rbf, old son," Lowell says. "That's worried Darlin'."

"Darling. Do you imagine that there is such a thing as a perfect murder?" Lucas asks.

Not gladdened even more, I say, "Like maybe killing me here and stuffing me up in that hellhole?"

They look at each other. And then laugh.

"We love you, Darlin'."

"And we'd get caught," Lucas said.

"Would you?"

"Yeah. And that wouldn't be the perfect murder, would it?"

I think for a minute. "Well, if you're really asking and if this is really not about me, I suppose a perfect murder could be done. But there would be limitations."

"Preach, sweetheart," Lowell says.

"Well, let's start with this well-known fact and investigative given. In 99.9999 percent of murders, the perpetrator is someone the victim knows, mostly husbands and wives, though also children and coworkers. Neighbors. Did you hear me? *Someone the victim knows.* I know you."

Lowell laughs. "She knows us."

"Yeah. funny. Darling, we're not gonna kill you."

"Shoot, I hope not. I'm just joking, Lucas."

He sighs. "So. Ninety-nine percent?"

"Yeah, and since the cops know this, they always look first at the people within the victim's immediate circle. Eventually they find a motive, one-third of the three-legged stool of guilt presumption."

"Yeah. Three-legged, huh? What?" Lucas asks.

"Means, motive, opportunity. Cops look for all three. One isn't enough for a conviction. But once they do find one of them, they start looking for the other two, even if it takes forever. No statue of limitations on murder."

"Darling. Statute."

"What?"

"It's statute."

"What did I say?"

"Statue."

"Bullshit."

"Carry on then."

"So, you couldn't kill some asshole jock that you both hate or, let's say, Dr. Richmond, who never gives As."

"That polecat son of a bitch," Lowell says.

"Wait," Lucas says. "There must be lots of people who want Richmond dead beyond us. People in the department, students he's screwed over or felt up. Surely there would be a long line of suspects ahead of us."

"Us? This us?"

"Figuratively."

"So, figures of us. Okay. Anyway, once the cops are there

on campus, we are in the suspect pool. And they'll never give up. They will eliminate every possibility until they get to us. What does Sherlock say? Eliminate the something something something. Suddenly it's all the walls closing in, concentric circles tightening around us, the center of the labyrinth just ahead."

"Listen to Darlin'! Going all Harold Bloomy on us," Lowell says.

"If you really want to get away with it, the best option is to kill somebody we don't know. What am I saying? *We*?"

"Where's the fun in that?" Lucas asks.

The wind has picked up and turned the canoe around so that I'm facing the hole. *I was gladdened when they said unto me.* But I am not gladdened now.

"Shall we stop a moment and review why we're even talking about this?" I say.

Lucas says, "No. Let's don't. And fuck all this Leopold and Loeb shit. What are we? Scientists? Engineers? Nerds in white lab coats, holding clipboards? Running some experiment? From which, by the way, we have removed all subjectivity? I don't know about you, but I wouldn't even remotely want to do that. Kill somebody I don't know for no reason. Bullshit. I want to feel what I do. I want to wallow in the sty of the subjective. I want to come from a place of will."

"I get so hard when you go all Overman on me," Lowell says.

"Well, better close your eyes then because I'm about to go full-bukkake Nietzsche all over your all-too-human face."

"Spray me, then."

"There is the will to power and then there is everything else. You're going to kill some random stranger? What's your emotion? Neutral? Objective observation? For what? To see somebody die? To see a stranger die? You can see that every night on television, in both fiction and nonfictional accounts. And since they're both on TV, they are, for all practical purposes, the same thing. I don't need any neutral experiences. That's what I have college for. That's what these professors do. They drag the emotion and subjectivity screaming out of every aesthetic or scientific or creative discussion in favor of the cool dispassion of analysis. No, no, no. I want to feel something. If I have enjoyed seeing my enemies punished, and I have done, then how much more will I enjoy watching one pay the ultimate price, as they say on TV?"

"And yet everything you just said places Darlin's three-legged stool between us and that goal."

"Risk is part of crime," Lucas says, but not with much fire.

"That's true, but there is no need to take it on unnecessarily. Kill Dr. Richmond. I know I might like to, but howmanyfold do we increase our risk versus killing someone completely unconnected to us?"

"Well, you could use forensic countermeasures," I say.

They look at me.

"The fuck you say," Lucas says.

"Where did you pick up such nomenclature, sweetheart?"

"*Law and Order.* Everything I know about investigation and the criminal justice system comes right off *Law and Order.*"

"TV girl," Lucas says, with a mean voice.

"Kill the prof, frame the jock," I say.

"Probably doable," Lowell says.

"Lots of planning. Lots of work," I say.

The boys seem to consider the options. Eventually, they unknot the ropes and paddle us back the way we came.

"Paddle, Darling," Lucas says.

Coming back against the current, though it is meandering at best, is still harder than straight up floating downstream, so I pick the paddle up out of the brown water in the bottom of the canoe and row.

Lowell does not put his clothes on. When we get back to the rental place, Old John comes out to help pull the canoe out of the water. He looks at Lowell and then at me, but if he has anything to say, he keeps it to himself.

❧

Friday night I barely make the dining hall before it closes. The boys have decided to wash and wax the Escalade at the Super Self Wash out on 62 and supper at 7-Eleven. I'm the last through the line, which works out for me because almost every table is empty. I pick one in the back near the wall. I have accepted a grilled cheese that smells plasticky like they didn't take the wrappers off the slices, and two red Jell-Os. The sandwich is cold and I'm eating the Jell-O when I spot Carla on the other side of the cafeteria. When she sees me, she says something to the girl she's with and then picks her way through the tables toward me. I am somewhat surprised.

She plops down in the chair opposite me and fixes me with a flat look.

"Are y'all going to put it on Twitter or something?"

She's wearing J'adore, but behind that is the acrid smell of fear.

"Y'all?"

"Them."

"Where are you from, Carla?"

"Little Rock." Pause. "The nice part."

"The white part."

"Yeah."

"Yeah."

"So, are you?"

"I'm not gonna do anything. I deleted it off my phone," I say.

"But them?"

"I don't mean to hurt your feelings, but I think they've forgotten about it."

"But they have it."

"Probably. Maybe. I don't actually know. They delete stuff off their phones all the time."

I look down into my Jell-O. I'm hoping she's done now and will leave. No such.

"Are you one of them?"

"One of them?"

"Are you fucking them?"

"So not your business."

"But you are."

"I'm a little confused. Exactly how would that make me 'one of them'?"

Why don't I deny it?

"The same way it makes them *them.* They are fucking each other, right?"

I'm proud that I don't show how that question torments me. I don't blink. I say, "So, to recap. In your little fantasy, I am either a fag-hag or their cum-towel. That the gist?"

"Ooh, you're so cold, so smart. I know that. Everybody knows that. Step outta that bubble a minute and look at yourself from out here. See what else everybody sees. You're always with them. Do they go anywhere without you? And! You look just like them. You're a mini-me version of them. You and Lowell have the exact same haircut. Are you wearing Lucas's hand-me-down jersey and Nikes or does it just look like that? Don't you see it? The only explanation, I mean, if you're really not fucking them, is that you're one of them."

I don't say anything, so she goes on. "I suppose you could maybe be the sister Maddie in a weird House of Usher gay S&M goth porn—" She pauses here, proud of her metaphor, and cocks her head. "But seriously, Darling, what?"

The south wall of the cafeteria is a floor-to-ceiling mirror. We are sitting right next to it, and I'm wondering if she's right. Do I look like them? Am I so self-unaware that I haven't noticed myself turning into them? I want to look at myself, but more than anything else I want not to. At least not in front of Carla. I'm afraid my head may be visibly shaking from the effort to not look. It passes. I continue to look at Carla, but I don't have an answer. In truth, maybe there's no need for a mirror. She's probably right. I could act all "this is none of your business, bitch," but I'm not sure who the audience would be. I am kind of paralyzed in an existential—what? Worm hole? Quicksand?

Carla stands up and pushes her hands up under her breasts and pulls on her bra straps. She sees me watching.

"Are you a boy too?" she says.

My mouth opens to answer her, but she cuts me off. "You're not their first pet, you know. Ask them about Laura Huddle."

When she's gone, I count to one hundred in French, and then I do look at the mirror. A cruel myopic might call me boyish. I'm not flat-chested, but from this angle, and given my posture and Lowell's old Bulldogs T-shirt, I see now I could be mistaken for a boy.

❧

It's probably time to tell this story. Filming and voyeuring and humiliating Carla was not our first foray into the "outer dark," as Lowell calls it.

We had driven up into Missouri, to Branson, where all the theaters are. I thought we were going to a country-music show, but we ended up at a Creationism place where we learned all about Moses and the dinosaur he rode in on.

In the car on the way back, the boys were still laughing about it. Lowell climbed over into the back seat and lit up a blunt. Lucas put on Madonna.

"What's this?" I said.

Lowell sighed audibly.

Lucas said, "It's Madonna."

I said, "I know it's Madonna. I have a father. He has CDs."

"Attitude from Darlin'," Lowell drawled, dragging out his Delta vowels, lingering on the caesurae. "Quite enjoyable." That was his Quentin Compson voice. Lucas calls it his stoner voice. Lucas doesn't smoke pot as much as Lowell does, which is all the time. He objects to it on aesthetic grounds. He told me once that marijuana is a synecdoche for everything wrong with the Boomer Phenomenon. When Lowell rolls, Lucas sings, "C'mon, people now, smile on your brother…"

"I understand retro," I said. "To quote Ecclesiastes, everything old is new again. But I think we have to use some discretion in what we excavate from antiquity."

"Antiquity," Lowell said.

Lucas said, "I like Madonna, *Darlin'*." Him affecting an exaggerated southern accent, striking two blows at once; one, putting me in my place, and two, mocking Lowell for whatever is going on between them.

"What are we listening to?" I said. *Blessed is the peacemaker.*

"The song is 'Holiday.' The album, *The Immaculate Collection.*" He might have been saying Mozart's Requiem, for all the reverence in his voice.

"I get it. Madonna. Immaculate Conception. That's cute."

Lucas ignored me. "This compilation pulls together hits from Madonna's early career, from 'Holiday' up until 'Justify My Love,' which is, in fact, the single from *Immaculate.*"

"So sayeth the oracle," Lowell said.

"Sure," I say. "But—"

"But?"

"Isn't she just ear candy? Dance music?"

"Indeed. Listen to what you're saying. Dance music. Like it's an abomination. So—what? You're going hit the clubs and throw down a full Dionysian revel to Ed Sheeran? You might as well try to dance to Ed Gein."

"Gein," Lowell said.

"Shut up, Donovan," Lucas said. "What kind of slave-morality, wind-facing cows, socially constructed fart ports could exist without dance music? Without dance? What did Nietzsche say about living without dance?"

"Something," Lowell said.

"Exactly. Madonna was a creature of the eighties. Now, I am very familiar with the standard criticisms of that decade. We might synecdochify the whole shitstorm in one word: cocaine. Yes, the go-go-go lifestyle so mocked today. The stupid clothes, the stupid hair."

"Maybe the word is mullet," Lowell said.

"No, it's coke. Everything speeded up, quick talk, quick dance, quick sex."

"The Zipless Fuck," I said.

"Did you just make that up?" Lucas said.

"Yes," I lied.

"Darlin'," Lowell said.

"Yeah, good one. Snorting coke and fucking in the restrooms. Dancing all night. Total disregard for any of the Apollonian prison house waiting for you in the morning, on the streets, at the jobs. That's Madonna. Just dance, fuck it all, and dance. *Carpe noctem*. It's genius. The music is genius."

"So, none of that Dionysian revelry in the clubs anymore?"

"The music's no good."

"The TV looks full of very danceable stuff."

"Not to put too fine a point on it, but you can get a danceable drum track off a machine. But what separates Madonna from our contemporaries is a voice and an enviable lyric."

"Enviable lyric," I said.

"When you hear her voice, you fall in love with her. To fall in love with a singer today is to fall in love with a Moog. No thanks."

"'Lucky Star' isn't exactly Keats," I said.

"Neither is 'Thunder Road,' but we're talking degrees of separation here."

"I don't think we are," Lowell said.

"Okay, look. I'm going skip to the next track." "Lucky Star" was playing. "Now this track is called 'Borderline.'"

"With a very similar drum track to 'Holiday,' I'm guessing, and not completely unlike even the very Bee Gees themselves, no?" I said.

Lucas sighed audibly, gathering himself, trying to stay calm with me. "Darling, I'm going to ask you to suspend judgment. Let's bracket the concomitant analysis."

"Let's what the what?" Lowell said.

"Let us push the pinhead-dancing particulates of real-time evaluation into the margins of the continuum for the four minutes it will take to listen to this song. What I'm saying, in my best Marsellus Wallace voice, is 'Let's get phenomenological on this shit.'"

"Marsellus Wallace," Lowell said.

"When I start this track, we don't talk, we don't think, we don't analyze. We don't scrutinize or criticize or critique or deconstruct. We experience. We loose ourselves from our constructed shells into the moment and lose ourselves in the music. Now shut up."

And he played the track.

We were quiet. Lucas was bobbing his head. I tried to be in the moment. Soon I was bobbing my head too. It was a good song. I could imagine myself in a club, with this song on. Then Lucas began to rock his hips side to side, like he was in a line dance or something, and I found myself rocking my hips in time with him and Lowell climbed into the front seat and just like that all three of us were rocking our hips, all kinds of front seat dancing and our hands in the air, windows down, scream-singing along, people staring, drivers getting out of the way, we were in eighties disco mode bigly, only without the coke.

"We need some coke," Lowell said when the song ended.

"QED," Lucas said. "Madonna—greatest pop star of the eighties and still relevant today."

"Q. Not necessarily ED," I said.

"Quid," Lowell said.

I said, "She's only the voice. That song is good. But isn't that on the producer? Isn't part of it on the arranger, the songwriter, the musicians? And her voice isn't that great. Any number of singers could've had a hit with that song and that backup."

Lucas shook his head. "Maybe, but not the point. She came from an earlier time. In the day, at least in the day I'm talking about, say the sixties and seventies, a singer had to have a unique voice, one that was instantly recognizable. And not necessarily a great voice. Hell, not even necessarily a *good* voice. Who would call Bob Dylan a 'good' singer? Johnny Cash? Mick Jagger? Ian Anderson? They have recognizable voices. Today most singers sound just alike. I can barely tell one from another. Are Chris Brown and Kanye West the same person? Not that it matters anymore. Everybody's auto-tuned. They *want* to sound alike. They're not creating art. They're creating revenue streams. The value of the unique voice in music was an anomaly of a particular time. Listen. All opera singers sound the same. In the forties and fifties, Frank Sinatra, Jerry Vale, Bobby Darin, Tony Bennett, their strength was in sounding alike, dressing alike, using the same arrangements. But, for a brief time, the unique voice was the ne plus ultra of popular music. And Madonna was the High Priestess of Disco."

"But the music isn't just her. She's not—"

"Fine. Let's posit that when I say 'Madonna,' I don't mean the person Madonna. I don't mean Miss Madonna Louise Ciccone, late of Michigan, New York City, and the world. Let's posit that from now on when I say 'Madonna,' you can understand me to mean the musical product called 'Madonna,' however that outcome is realized."

Lucas skipped a few tracks and landed on "Live to Tell," not a dance song at all, nothing of the Dionysian, but instead full melancholy and dejection and regret. He traced his finger down the scar.

We were back in Barnesville, closing in on the campus. The streets around Chandler are narrow residential streets, some of them brick, and you have to drive pretty slowly through there. And Lucas was no hot dog. He took it easy. About three blocks from the entrance to the school, a young man stood in the middle of the street. He was holding a bottle of liquor, Jack Daniels it looked like, drunk, talking to himself or to the world. There was no way around him. Two cars could barely pass on this street and the old boy was standing in the dead middle. Lucas stopped about a car length away. The drunk was wearing a Kappa Alpha sweatshirt and chinos. Lucas rolled down the window and hollered for him to get out of the way. The man squinted at us as if noticing us for the first time. He raised a most casual middle finger and smiled.

"Look at this guy," Lucas said and leaned on the horn.

Lowell stuck his head out the window. "Hey, KA, can you get outta the street, please?"

The guy did a little dance turn and walked off right down the middle of the street. Staggered, really. Unsteady on his pins, my father would have said. "Hit him," I said.

The boys looked across me at each other. Lowell shrugged and said, "Don't mess up the car."

Lucas brought the car to within a couple of feet of the man, followed along until the boy veered toward the left front bumper, then tapped the accelerator and knocked him up onto the sidewalk. He rolled into somebody's front yard. Lucas drove slowly to the next cross street and turned.

"How was that?" Lucas said.

"He survived," I said. "I think."

"Pull over," Lowell said.

Lucas pulled into a dark driveway. I was worried until I saw the sign that said Law Offices. The house next door was a dentist's office. The boys looked at the bumper and the front panel of the Escalade and then started walking back toward where we'd hit the guy.

We stood on the corner and looked down the street toward the yard where the Kappa Alpha lay. It was too dark to see much, but I guessed we were on the lookout for any sign of movement.

"No lights on in the house," Lowell said. "Let's take a look."

We strolled by on the other side of the street. I could just make out the guy lying, snoring, in the dark yard. We walked a little farther, crossed the street, and came back to where he was. The boys walked up into the yard. They went through his pockets and came up with his wallet and cell. We walked back down the street the way we came and got into the Escalade.

Lucas clicked on the interior light and read from the man's driver's license. "James W. Whitfield," he said. "From Memphis, Tennessee."

"Well, hell. I know that boy. We had—I don't know—some class together. I believe he's a senior," Lowell said.

"How many tries do we get at opening his phone?" Lucas said.

"I don't know."

I said, "It's a sliding scale. Depending on what model you have, it will lock you out after six tries. It comes back on later and gives you another go, but most models disable themselves at around ten."

"'Check out the big brain on Brad,'" Lucas said.

"So," Lowell said. "Six shots. Well, he's a KA. Something there?"

"Maybe the address of the house?" Lucas said. "That's probably four digits."

"Kappa and Alpha are both five letters. Maybe he uses Kapp or Alph."

I said, "One, two, three, four."

They stared at me for a long second.

Lucas said, "Too easy. Nobody's that dumb."

"What's my code?" I said.

In unison they said, "One, one, one, one."

Lucas said, "Yes, but you're pretty dumb."

"What about my big Brad brain?"

"Punch it in," Lowell said.

The code wasn't one, two, three, four, and it wasn't one, one, one, one, but it was two, two, two, two.

"He's got a folder full of dick pics," Lucas said.

"His?" Lowell asked.

"Like I would know? And, no. They're not all the same. It's a variety pack."

"Closet?"

"Maybe, but given the number of them he has sent to his female contacts, I think it's more along the line of advertising. False advertising at that."

"Caveat emptor." I said.

"Stop showing off, Darling," Lucas said.

Lowell said, "How do his contacts like the pics?"

"Not many replies. Let's see. 'Fuck off,' 'Fuck off,' and—that seems to be the general tone."

"Let's chuck it down the storm drain. Wallet too," I said.

"I don't know," Lucas said. "Some of his contacts didn't get pix. Maybe their phones need spicing up."

"Like for instance?" Lowell said.

"Like for instance, his mother?"

Lowell said, "Lord a mercy, boy. If his mama sees one of those thangs, she'll pitch a conniption. Now I ain't worried about him. But his mama might not deserve such as this."

Lucas made an exasperated sound. "I get it. I really do. You talk about Faulkner or Welty or cornbread, well then, you put on yo' southern accent, yo' charm, yo' fine manners. Okay. But I know you are not about to start pulling that shit on every issue of morality, are you? Turn all front-porch philosopher dispensing wisdom in your seersucker suit?"

"You cain't get at your mama through his."

Ouch. Lucas glanced at me. Hurt twisted his face, his scar deepened in the shadowy car. I didn't know the backstory of whatever they were talking about regarding his mother, but in that one look I could see him wondering whether Lowell had told me anything.

Lucas thumb-punched Whitfield's phone and then threw it out the window and down the storm drain. Then he got into the back seat and lay down with his arm across his forehead like a painting of a Romantic hero. I scooted into the driver's seat and cranked the SUV. I looked at Lowell.

"Home, I guess," he said. He turned toward the back seat and said, "A dick pic to every contact or every dick pic to his mama?"

But Lucas didn't answer. And I didn't get the mother of Lucas story until a week later, when Lowell took me to the library to prep me for an algebra test.

We had checked out a quiet room and spread my math stuff on the table. "This is moronically easy, Darlin'."

"Good. Stick the knife in first. You can't twist it until you do."

"Sensitive much? One might think you were in danger of failing this class."

"I don't want a B."

"Who are you trying to impress?"

"Can't I have a goal for myself? Can't I just please myself?"

"Of course you can. I just don't think you are."

"I'm a straight-A student."

"And that's a load-bearin' wall at your house, ain't it? Can we talk about something else first?"

"No. Will you please just talk me through this quadratic function graph thing? Use that sweet southern tongue of yours to impregnate me with understanding and application. Function-fuck me into comprehension."

"Impregnate you with my tongue? Maybe we should review the basics of sex and conception before you go on that date with what's-his-name."

"Who's what's-his-name?"

"You'd know better than me, sweetheart."

I let it drop. Of course, they knew. I hadn't told them, but they knew. I had accepted an invitation to go skating with Patrick Mitchell from my English class. I don't know why.

A lie. It was the way he looked at me. In his eyes, I could see myself wet and naked.

On the other hand, I do know why I didn't tell the boys.

Lowell's tutoring was kind and patient and encouraging. You'd think he was untangling the twisted relationships within the McCaslin family tree or something. When I'd successfully navigated five straight problems, he declared me ready. He was right. I would ace the test the next morning.

Lowell seems like a real savant in math, but it occurred to me while we were packing up our stuff that maybe he's not so naturally smart as he lets on, but actually studies super hard in secret and then feigns his savantitude for me. And for the world. "Where's Lucas?"

"He's still pouting. I broke the code. No mamas."

"That was a week ago."

"Yankees are every bit as sensitive on the subject of Mama as we are."

"Yankee? Since when is California a Yankee state?"

"It's not a matter of states, Darlin'. It's a matter of folks. Folks who are not from the South are Yankees. Pure and simple. You know it's true."

I can't say that I did.

"Anyway, Lucas is particularly sensitive on the subject of mamas. What I wanted to tell you is, his own mama left him and his father and his sister when the old boy was about thirteen. I think that was a really bad age for him to lose the mama. Lord, thirteen. Well, boys and their mamas. It's complicated, Darlin'. Not at all like girls and their daddies."

"Some kind of Oedipal thing?"

"Well, of course, that's a metaphor, you know. There is no 'Oedipal thing.' Just as surely as there was no Oedipus. But the love of the boy for his mama is a knotty problem, complicated by a desperate need for love that will never come from the father, and plus, a burgeoning sexuality muddied by a repressively Puritan society that sullies sex with guilt even while glorifying it."

"The sex or the guilt?"

"Both."

"So, what happened with his mama?"

"There are different stories, mythologies, if you will."

"Where did you hear 'different' stories from?"

"Freshman year, my parents decided to go on a Christmas cruise in the Caribbean. Well, as you might imagine, the whole idea went against my grain. It aggravated the shit out of me, to tell you the truth. I wasn't going on any cruise at Christmastime, especially not one that reeked of a second honeymoon for my parents. What the hell were they—sorry. Not the point. The point is that I was at loose ends for the holidays, so to speak, and Lucas said I could come with him to California."

"What was that like?"

"I'd never been to California before. And I haven't been back. Lucas is from a town, if you can call it that, called Sebastopol, up north from San Francisco. It's hard to talk about places out there in California because, at least from what I could tell, it's all one big-ass town stretched out along Highway 101. It's not like here, Darlin', whereby you leave one town and then it's full on country until the next town. Out there it's strip malls and convenience stores shoulder to shoulder up and down that coast as far as the eye can see.

"Lucas and I flew into San Jose and his father picked us up. Landon, his name is. He was a good ole boy, Yankee as all get out, but he treated me like a welcome guest. The sister, not so much."

"Really."

"She stared holes through me the entire week. It got off to a bad start. Somehow, I got left alone with her—"

"What was her name?"

"Leah."

"Leah and Lucas and Landon, huh?"

"Yeah, not great. I think the dog's name was Larry. Anyway, she's sixteen, in high school, and one evening she drops her hand high up on my thigh while we're watching television. Well, the tricks and traps out ahead of that particular road were too numerous and too obvious for me and so I lift her hand off my leg, place it back on hers, and she flounces out of the room—"

"'Flounces'?"

"Yeah."

"Is that even a word?"

"I think so. It's pretty visual. And visually pretty. Can't you just see her flouncin' away?"

"Kind of."

"So I'm thinking that she's figured me for gay or some such and for leading her brother out into the land of gayness and then you throw in the rejection and all, so she didn't care for me."

"Rejection is hard."

"So true."

"So—the mama?"

"I'll just go ahead and bottom-line you here. The old gal

took off with a boyfriend. But she didn't go far. At least not far enough. Just the next little 'town' up the road, I forget the name of it. But the sister, Leah, just before dropping her jail-baited hand on me, said that her mother left because she was done raising children. According to Leah, who was, I suppose, eavesdropping on one of her parents' fights—"

"I don't suppose you have to actually eavesdrop on a fight. They're generally loud enough for public consumption."

"I'm just trying to fill in the blanks here, Darlin', to create a more satisfying narrative."

"Sorry."

"Let it go. As I was saying, according to Leah, the mama told the daddy that she'd had enough of children and all the commotion that accompanies the rearing of them. Apparently, Leah and Lucas, in addition to the usual drama at home, had stirred up a fair amount of ire in the public school system so as to generate a steady stream of phone calls and emails from teachers and principals. Add to that a buttload of extracurriculars in the sex, drug, and rock 'n' roll vein on the part of both children, and, well, she'd finally had enough."

"So the mama let the child overhear that she was leaving—not the father—but the very children themselves?"

"If Leah's account is to be credited."

"What is Lucas's story?"

"You mean his version of the mama's departure? He put it all on the old man. Said his father ignored the mama, drove her off with a combination of indifference, alcoholism, and sexual incompetence."

"That's all kinds of TV movie of the week clichéd, huh?"

"I think what really got him was how close she stayed."

"What does that mean?"

"If she'd dropped off the face of the earth, hell, if she'd died, he might've handled it better. But what she did was, she moved, I don't know, twenty miles or so away and then proceeded to forget he existed."

"Ouch."

"Yeah. The point being, I shouldn't have said that about his mama."

"What did you say exactly? I forget."

"Something about not being able to punish his mama through what's his name's mama. The one he sent the pics to."

"Oh yeah. I don't get it, though."

"Well, if his old man drove the mama off, as Lucas tells it, why would he want to punish her? He'd want to punish the daddy."

"So he got the idea that you were taking Leah's story as the true one."

"Probably. Maybe. I don't know, really."

"Which one is true, do you think?"

"Doesn't matter. What matters to Lucas is that I believe him. Even if I don't."

We gathered up our materials and turned in the key to the study room, then Lowell suggested we go back to their dorm room and smoke a joint. We left the library, and I fell in step behind him on the narrow footpath worn into the grass south of the building. I wondered if this would be it. I could smell him, walking there before me: musky, sweaty, maybe Old Spicy somewhere in there. Old Spice? I imagined us smoking, our fingers touching as we passed the thing back and forth, his hand dropping onto my leg like unto Leah's on his, him turning, putting his hands on me for real, me lying back, opening my shirt, my legs.

The door to the room was ajar. Lucas was sitting on the floor by his desk. His face was bloody, his shirt ripped, barely hanging on him, pants torn at the knee, head thrown back, tissues hanging out of his nose. The proverbial bloody pulp.

"Holy fuck all, what is this?" Lowell bent down and tried to pull Lucas up.

"Fuh, k, k, aaaas," he said and spit on the floor. Blood. "Just let me sit a minute."

I pulled a washrag out of the closet and sprinted down the hall to the showers. A dripping naked football player, judging by the size of him, held the door for me. While I soaked the rag, I watched him over my shoulder. Big boy. Body out of a gay porn magazine. He didn't mind. He smiled. When I got back, Lowell had Lucas up into a chair. And Lowell stopped talking in the middle of a sentence when he saw me. I kneeled down beside him and washed Lucas's cheek and chin. Most of the blood had come from a cut under his left eye. It was clotted now, and I was just doing cleanup. I was thinking *stitches*, to tell you the truth. After a minute Lucas took the cloth away from me and thanked me. He dabbed at his knee through the torn britches and sucked his teeth.

"Darlin'," Lowell said. "I think you better get on home now."

"Why? What? Aren't we going to the ER?"

"The fuck ER," Lucas said.

Lowell leaned in and looked at the eye. "Well, this one right here could probably use a stitch or two, though I'm inclined to leave it be."

"It'll scar," I said.

"It'll scar in any event, Darlin'. But a nicer scar it'll be if we don't stitch it. Go on, now. Go home," Lowell said.

"Why are you trying to get rid of me?"

"That is not the case, sweetheart. I'm just gonna get him into—"

"Bullshit. What happened? When do we hear what the fuck happened?"

They didn't look at me. Lowell's mouth was open. But nothing, so I knew.

"He already told you?" I was pissed. "Fine. You don't wanna tell me. Fine. But don't treat me like a child. Are you fucking kidding me?"

Lowell said, "Well, it was, uh—"

"No, no, no. What? Do you think you can bullshit me, sitting there, stalling for all you're worth, trying to think up some bullshit lie, and then *not* be lying when you finally do open your lying mouths?"

I stood up and stomped around the room. "Why don't

you just tell me he ran into a goddamn door? Or cut himself shaving? Or fell down the motherfucking stairs? Are you trying to protect me? Spare my feelings? Hell, boys, I'm as about as pissed off right now as I'm ever gonna be. So whatever you've got to say, you might as well say it 'cause there ain't gonna be no hiding it from me."

Lucas managed a grin. "''Cause there ain't gonna be no hidin' it from me.' That's tough stuff. She's reverted to Helena Darling's old Confederate accent. What would Sylvia Plath say, Darling?"

I wanted to pout about it, I really did. But they were laughing now, and even though it was me they were laughing at, I ended up laughing too. We finally did decide on the ER after Lucas admitted that his head had bounced on the sidewalk.

The nearest hospital is Berryville and it took us twenty minutes to get there. In that time, I heard the full story. Maybe.

Lucas wanted to lie down in the back, but Lowell made him sit up front with us, not wanting him to fall asleep. Lowell's phone wanted to take us way the hell-and-gone down 62 and back toward Berryville on 412, but Lowell said he knew a shortcut. We were flying down one-lane country roads, the headlights illuminating the overhanging trees, busting out between open fields fuzzy with moonlight, passing houses and trailers darkened or lit with year-round Christmas lights. I could smell Lucas's blood and my mouth tasted coppery.

Lucas said, "I was coming around the back of the Christian Center—"

"From where?" I asked.

"Damn it, Darling. Let me tell it. I was coming from Murrah. I had a meeting with Dr. Bergman about my Trig project. I almost stopped at the dining hall. Fuck, I should have stopped at the goddamn dining hall. But I figured we'd all go out for something. I was about to turn the corner when—somebody hit me from behind."

But I knew from the way he said "somebody" that he knew who it was. What I couldn't understand was why he didn't say who. You can be sure he told Lowell while I was out of the room.

"I hit the sidewalk headfirst. And busted my knee. They started kicking me and I grabbed a leg and bit down."

"You bit him!" I said.

"Yeah, I bit the fucker. What about it?"

"Nothing. It's great. I love it. I just didn't know boys did that when they fight."

"I don't know about 'boys,' but I do whatever I have to. Shit, if I'd had a gun, I would have shot the motherfuckers." He looked across me at Lowell who never took his eyes off the road.

"So—what happened then?" I asked.

"The guy I bit screamed like a girl and kicked me in the face. The other one kicked me in the back a couple more times and they ran off. I rolled over onto the grass and lay there a while, contemplating the ruins of my life and watching the moon come up over the girls' dorm."

"Very John Keats of you," Lowell drawled. "'When I have fears that I may cease to be.'"

"Maybe so," Lucas said. "It may well have looked like posing. A couple of people passing by said hello to me."

"They didn't try to help you?" I said.

"In their defense, it was full dark, and I suspect my wounds weren't clearly visible. Also, my mouth was numb and full of blood so I didn't call out 'Good evening.' Eventually I got to my feet, and that was not easy, and staggered back to the dorm."

"Staggered," Lowell repeated.

"Yes. Staggered. What's wrong with staggered?"

"Just a tad melodramatic, don't you think?"

"Lord God, man. Can you let a person tell it?"

"Limped. Stumbled. Tottered."

"You're line-editing my story?"

"Fine. You 'staggered.'"

"Just let him tell it," I said.

"That's the end, Darling. I went to the room and then you two showed up. Where were you, anyway?"

"Library," Lowell said.

We rode in silence for a while. There was tension among us, but I couldn't tell if it was residual business between them or something about the library or something about who it was that had beaten Lucas. So, I asked.

"Who did this?"

Lucas took a deep breath. "Somebody with my dental impressions on his calf."

"I suppose," Lowell said, "if such a person turned up dead, the authorities could match the marks on his leg to your dental records."

"Let's hope, then, that nobody kills him before his leg heals."

"They wouldn't know whose dental records to look at," I said.

"Joke, Darlin'," Lowell said.

"Oh."

At the hospital, they did indeed put two stitches below his eye and shined a light in his eyes and passed a finger in front of him to follow. No concussion, they said.

"What happened?" the doctor asked.

"Ran into a door," Lowell said.

"And fell down the stairs," I said.

They all three laughed, though I don't know why the doctor thought it was funny.

I turned in my Dadaist poem. The boys had helped me. We used the refrigerator magnets. They roundly mocked me for having them. "They were a gift," I pleaded.

"And how many garbage cans have you passed since you got this 'gift'?" Lucas asked.

At the next class meeting Dr. Blackwell says she is going to review some of the poems right there in class. Right there in front of the predestinated damned. The air is quickly rich with the sour smell of panic. She flings one of the poems up onto the board via the overhead projector and points out its weaknesses. The usual suspects: sentimentality, banality, too many adjectives (the boys and I had carefully eliminated almost all adjectives from our Dada word-hoard). The unlucky poet is Siobhan O'Brian, and the name is no lie: she is uber-Irish, red hair, white skin, pale freckles. She has more than once shyly hinted that she is literally getting herself to the nunnery after she graduates. She cannot be nicer. Which is beyond off-putting, and I avoid her. Now she is blushing, for Blackwell has nothing good to say about the poem, which is all about God and the world and whatever, and it isn't that bad, maybe a little devout for the twenty-first-century post-postmodernism that infects literary studies at Chandler and a little derivative of the *Four Quartets*. Though I believe that she would have blushed just as carnally if Blackwell had been praising the poem. Needless to say, poker is not in this child's future.

Next Blackwell gives us a poem by the defensive tackle from the Chandler football team, the Pikes, the Fightin' Pikes. The poem is called "Ode to a Fumble." Every line is a mess of twisted syntax dragging itself like a run-over squirrel toward the bound and hostage and predictable rhyme at the terminus. She doesn't say anything. Just stares at it for a full minute in dead silence, then turns and looks at Jeremy, the poet. Still she doesn't say anything. The tone in Jeremy's voice is an irritating mix of entitlement, boredom, and suspicion when he says, "What?"

Blackwell sighs and puts up another poem and vivisects it with relish. That one is by Priscilla Tarwater and is actually pretty good. I say, "Dr. Blackwell, I like Priscilla's poem. All that moss and lichen imagery was really well done. Very Roethkesque."

Blackwell shakes her head. "Darling. Please." She reaches for the mouse. "And, for the record, Roethkesque is not a word."

I want to ask, *How can I say it if it's not a word?* but instead I turn around and shrug at Priscilla, but she is staring out the window at the clock tower.

Eventually Blackwell gets around to my poem. I cannot imagine she will find anything good in it. On the other hand, what does it matter? It has been conceived, designed, and realized to deflect—derision, attack, whatever. I am bullet proof. She puts the poem onto the overhead.

The Owl's Dream
by Darling Bramlett

you hum a thought and when
arms and yard cheek night there
the atoms of cars sweep low eaves
quit carbon down in no houses
after one fire watching when the street
is a night is bouncing trees such black
in the warm why of all cones crouched
and listening to the streetlight
how it folded in wonder intersecting
you to couples on the roof of one house
photons dark and no steps to boughs
of twilight, lights have bats stood up to
drinking TV, passing eyes up
in the moon, off the front gargoyle.

She reads the poem aloud. In its entirety. Her voice is—I don't know. Emotional, I guess? She lingers over certain words and pauses in strange places as if for line breaks or caesurae. I figure she's got to be mocking me, for there is no such emotion in the poem. It is as empty as a drum. Or a sociopath. Her voice is not unlike Lucas and Lowell's when they read aloud the selfsame lines in mocking poet voices. And I see it now: oh my God, she loves the ridiculous thing. I don't know what to feel. I do not look forward to being praised for a poem I didn't really write. Of course, one doesn't "write" a Dadaist poem, does one? One "finds" it. One finds it with the help of two boys who ridiculed the damn thing as fully as it deserves. How could she like it? I've heard of literary and philosophical hoaxes that fooled experts and made critics and editors look like idiots. Faux deconstructive stuff, ersatz postmodernist fiction, is that what we've done? Or is there really something in the poem, something that we weren't in control of? Something actually reaching out through Dadaist chaos to speak something true. Or meaningful? Or moving?

I feel the hate radiating off the other students. The class cannot end soon enough. Blackwell smiles endearingly at me as I exit. You have got to be kidding.

I feel pretty crappy about the whole poem deal for the next couple of days. Then I get a surprise call from ole Tommy Steele. He greases me up with a bunch of small talk, asking about college life and all that, and then gets down to it.

"I have a gig. We have a gig. It's at Lucille's, you know, that honky-tonk out west on 17, and I sent them a tape. We're doing a Friday and Saturday night kinda deal. But the thing is, they somehow got the idea that we have a female singer, and I was wondering if you might want to come over and do your thing for us. We've got nine of your songs in the playlist. So, like, you already know them. You know?"

"I'm not much of a singer, Tommy."

"You're good enough."

"How did they get the idea you have a female singer."

"I may have sent them the tapes of you doing the songs during rehearsal."

"May have?"

"Okay, for sure did. Don't hate me. I'm just trying to get somewhere."

"Uh-huh."

"Look, you could use a break, couldn't you? Studying, classes, cafeteria food. 'Sgotta be dull."

I picture Lucas and Lowell sitting at a rickety table, draining pitchers of beer and watching me onstage.

"Okay."

Tommy is delighted. "Great. Try to get there around seven. We probably won't start right away, but it's good to get the lay of the land. And I'm sure you want to look at the song list. This is great. This is good. Can't wait to see you, Darling."

Lucas and Lowell don't even blink when I ask them if they want to carry me over the state line so I can sing hard-rock songs with some guys I went to high school with.

"What time do we need to leave?" Lucas says.

"You reckon the joint to have a liquor license?" Lowell says, looking up from the book he's reading.

"I dunno. It's out in the country. Probably beer and bring-your-own."

"Then bring it we shall," Lowell says.

I sit on Lowell's bed. Since it's made. I pick up the *Alternative Press* he's left open, but I can't read anything. What was I expecting? Lucas is studying for a Trig test, his fingers flying over his calculator. I think Lowell is writing a paper for his lit class. He's thumbing and underlining *Gatsby*, a book I know he's read before and didn't like. It's nine p.m. They don't say another word.

Maybe, *Hey Darling. That's great.*

Maybe, *I didn't know you could sing.*

"I'm heading out."

Lucas grunts and Lowell says, "Love ya, mean it."

That's it.

At five on Friday, they pick me up at my dorm. I've dressed in tight black jeans, a black silk blouse, and my red boots.

They jump out of the SUV and walk around me whistling and high-fiving each other.

"Why, Miz Darlin', you are a vision," Lowell says.

"Pam Benatar is bouncing around in her grave with envy," Lucas says.

"It's *Pat* Benatar, and I don't think she's dead, doofus," I say.

Lucas says, "Do you want to drive? You know the way there, right?"

"No. You drive, I'll navigate."

"You're gonna end up driving home, you know that, right?" Lowell says.

"Of course. I assume you two will attempt to drink Alcoholics Anonymous under the table and outta business in one night."

"Whatever that means," Lucas says and goes around to get in the driver's seat. Lowell hands me up into the front seat. Little sister, all dressed up.

The last leg of the trip takes us on Highway 17, which parallels for some miles right up next to a wide brown river. *I don't know much about gods*, I think. We're headed east, running in the last of the sun, all the trees in sideways lighted bas relief. I wish we could stop, sit by the river, talk, in the darkening air. It occurs to me that I don't really want to do this thing tonight. It occurs to me that I'm just showing off for the boys. It occurs to me that I'm a full-blown idiot.

The place is called Lucille's, but Lucille and the sign that may have once borne her name have gone the way of all things. You'd straight up miss the place if you didn't know you were looking for it. The parking lot is next to empty, except for a dusty pickup and a sheriff's patrol car.

Lucas parks next to the sheriff's car and stares at it. Then he says, "Don't go all Jim Morrison on us tonight, Darling."

"What do you mean?"

Lowell says, "He means keep your britches on. He's joking."

"Why would I take my britches off?"

"To distract from your singing?" Lowell asks.

"Not funny. Not funny even a little bit."

"Relax, Darling," Lucas says. "How bad can it be? I mean, look at it."

Inside, the place smells like stale beer and piss-poor air conditioning. There is no sign of Tommy or his band.

Lucas and Lowell go over and say something to the sheriff's deputy and a couple of ole boys sitting at a table in the corner. I go up to the bar and ask the man there about the band.

"On their way. Just called my cell. Wanna Coke or something?"

"No, but these boys I'm with are gonna want some beer in a minute, I'm sure."

"Yeah, and I'm gonna want some ID."

"They're older than me."

"Honey, everybody in the world's older than you. Wait. You ain't the singer, are you?"

I nod.

He shakes his head and turns to his work, drying mugs.

Everybody laughs over at the deputy's table and the boys come over to the bar.

"So, what's the story, D?" Lucas asks.

"Band's late."

"I guess, a cappella then, huh?"

"Oh lord god, I think I just tasted my lunch."

"Let her be," Lowell says. "Don't worry, sweetheart. If those tapes you played me are any indication, you won't even be heard above the crashing 747 guitars those hometown boys are about to tear into."

"What tapes are those?" Lucas says.

Lowell raises a hand at the bartender, then leans back on the bar. "And so it was," he says, "in olden days, when Darlin' was just a lass, passing the salley gardens on snow-white feet, as it were, she wrote lyrics for this old boy what's performing here tonight. She has a couple of renditions of him and his group playing those very songs digitally preserved under her pillow."

"And when were you under her pillow?"

"She has a latent talent for lyrics, old son."

"And you heard her sing such on these 'tapes'"?

"No, some deep-voiced fellow was singing on the recording. Who was that, Darlin'?"

"That woulda been Tommy. Tommy Steele. The boy that wrote the music."

"Your friend," Lowell says.

"Yes."

"The one whose band we're seeing here tonight?"

"Yes. Okay. Him."

"Touchy," says Lucas.

"Nauseated," says I.

Half an hour later, Tommy and the band show. There is no time for introductions, the band is setting up as fast as they can, and as soon as they are ready, Tommy gets into a long discussion with the guy behind the bar. I'm thinking now that he's the owner too.

"Look at me," Lowell says. The deputy and his cronies have left, but other folks have arrived, and the place is about half full, mostly single guys, some couples. Two old men in VFW hats and checkered shirts.

Lowell lifts his chin and brushes a strand out of my eyes.

"You look good," he says. "Is there time to maybe double up on that eyeliner? What say, Lucas?"

Lucas looks at me and shakes his head. "Virgin, not whore." There must be a look on my face because he says, "It's more you, Darling."

I can smell my pits and wonder if I forgot to put on deodorant. I can't remember. I try to maintain an even countenance.

Feedback shrieks and Tommy waves me up toward the stage. No. Up is wrong. Stage is wrong. There is no up, no stage. They've set up against a wall on the same level with the bar and the tables and the dance floor. We're basically in the corner of the room. We could be in somebody's garage.

I step up to the mike and Tommy turns the back of his guitar toward me. He's taped the set list there. The first song is "Proximity Endeavor." He's written the first line of every song, too, which is good since I am not even about to remember any lyrics on my own. Tommy plays the opening licks of the song and the rest of the band comes in when I begin singing "You got no business rubbing up next to me...." It's not good. It's not exactly terrible, but the drummer is lagging and that's messing up the bass player who falls a little behind Tommy's guitar playing. It goes completely to hell on the chorus, which should be the easiest part, but now the drummer is a full half-beat behind. The bassist panics and just flat-out abandons him and catches up with Tommy. The crowd is pretty much laughing, those who aren't booing. Lucas and Lowell at the bar are falling all over each other in hysterics, taking turns air drumming. The drummer drops a stick—well, flips it really, and it hits on a table in the front, knocking over a beer. The drummer and bassist freeze and Tommy plays one more chord, then it's quiet. The young man sitting at said table looks from the drummer to his girlfriend, who has been beer-doused and back again.

Tommy says, "Oh shit."

"Sit down, bitch. You cain't sing for shit!" A full beer can flies past my head and hits the drummer on the shoulder. Tommy and bassist duck behind the drum kit. Lucas tackles a man who's about to throw something else at me and goes to punching him. Lowell is pushing through people trying to get to where I am. He pulls me toward the bar and puts me behind it. The boys square off against the guy Lucas knocked down and the guy's friends.

Lucas jerks his chin at the man he whupped on, as if to say, *Come on, bring it on.* Lowell raises his hands and says, "Let it go, boys. Chucking beer cans at a lady ain't exactly something your mamas would approve of, now is it?"

Three or four of them raise their hands likewise and back off, but the old boy that Lucas beat on is having none of it. He steps in close to Lucas, but he's too slow. Lucas punches him in the short rib and he drops like a sack of meal. Lucas shows the boy's friends the piece of carved wood in his right hand and Lowell pulls out a mean looking little pistol, though he keeps it pointed at the floor, and shakes his head in warning.

"Sorry, boys. We ain't really fighters, so when it gets right down to the nut cutting, we don't play fair," Lowell says. Lucas pulls me from behind the bar and toward the door. Lowell is backing up and saying, "Maybe take your friend there to the ER, make sure he's still got a whole spleen."

We drive in silence for a mile or so, then Lucas says, "Helluva show, Darling. Helluva show. I guess I'm okay to drive back since I didn't even get to finish one single, solitary beer."

"Who'd you throw it at," Lowell says.

"Throwing stuff at the stage is straight up white trash. Am I right, Darling?"

"So, what? Now I'm the expert on white trash or the representative thereof? Why aren't you asking Lowell this shit?"

"'Thereof,'" Lowell says, laughing.

I nudge Lucas and ask him about the wooden stick. He pulls the thing out of his jacket pocket and hands it to me. It's about six inches long, carved with ideograms and highly polished. It has rounded knobs on either end. Easy in the hand.

"It's a yawara. Japanese martial arts thing. However hard you might hit somebody, put that knob in their ribs and your power is multiplied—well, let's say many times."

"Where'd you get it?"

"Amazon, duh."

Lowell pulls out the pistol.

"Yeah, I recognize that," I say.

"Do you want to hold it?"

"Do I want to hold your gun?" I say, and they both laugh. "So—what? You just happened to have these violent and ferocious implements of destruction with you tonight? Or are you always carrying?"

"I think it was," Lowell says, "Havelok the Dane who said, 'Better safe than sorry.'"

"I'm stopping at the first 'Grab and Get' we see." Lucas is driving. "I am going to drink beer tonight. And you, Darling, *will*, in point of fact, be driving us home, for we are going to get drunk, drunk, drunk."

"And," Lowell says, "you owe us a show. So, I'm guessing that you're gonna be singing *wee wee wee* all the way home."

"Shoot."

"Do not pout," Lowell says. "You know I'm right."

We are on a long, straight stretch of country highway. It's

dark into the far distances. No telling where the first convenience store will be.

"But I don't have to sing until we have beer, right?"

They look at each other across me. Again.

"Right."

We don't find a store until we have been on the main highway for about twenty minutes. I wait in the car and they bring me a Coke and a Slim Jim. They have purchased a quantity of Milwaukee's Best, a bag of ice, a Styrofoam cooler, and a tub of pork rinds the size of a KFC bucket. They load the beer into the cooler and pour ice over it, then get into the back seat, pop their tops, and toast each other. I scoot over into the driver's seat and crank the car and pull out onto the highway.

For a moment or two there is only the sound of them crunching pork rinds.

"Anytime time now, Darlin'," Lowell says.

"I was just trying to decide what to sing first."

"Right. How 'bout that one y'all were trying to get going back at the roadhouse."

"'Proximity Endeavor'?"

"You're kidding, right?" Lucas says.

"I could do 'Transaction Traction.'"

"Do you mean 'Conjunction Junction'?" Lucas asks.

Lowell says, "No, do the Proximity one."

I sing all nine of the songs I wrote for Tommy. I have never sung them all before, not in a row like this. I realize that his music is pretty much the same from song to song, the difference being in his guitar work, I guess. I go through the whole set list, and the boys getting drunker and drunker, calling out requests, songs I don't know: "Send in the Clowns," "Return to Me," "My Kind of Town." So I sing Peter, Paul, and Mary songs. My father had some of their albums and liked to listen to them on Saturdays while my mother read. He played one of them more than the others. It had a song called "Stewball," and so I start with that one. The boys don't complain, and I sing every song I know until we get back to Chandler and they drunk-ass stumble off to their dorm. And I to mine to revel in the glory of my performance debut. Shoot.

Tommy calls me the next morning to apologize and to say not to bother coming for tonight's show.

"Am I fired? 'Cause if you're gonna fire somebody, I'm thinking you oughta be firing that drummer."

"Done and done, sweetheart. And, no, you were fine. Hell, I was fine, Darryl was fine, but Carl had some kind of breakdown, stage fright or some such. He quit anyway. Didn't have to fire him. But we won't be going back to Lucille's tonight. For that matter, we're not welcome back at Lucille's. Not even as customers."

"Well, shoot. That really was a bad show. I'm sorry, Tommy. Let me know if you find another drummer or another gig or something. I'll try to come. I was enjoying myself."

"Yeah. You looked it."

"What does that mean?"

"I saw a dead guy pulled outta the river once. You were about his color last night."

"I ate something bad."

"No doubt. And tell your friends not to go back to Lucille's neither. That old boy what runs the joint made several loud threats against them."

"For true?"

"Yup. Something about concealed weapons and IDs, I don't know."

"Got it. They're not going back. They only came for me in the first place."

"You have that effect on folks, Darling."

Since it's Saturday and the boys will sleep until noon, I walk over to the Student Union and get some coffee and the *Purple and Gold*, the student newspaper. There is a lake on the campus, Astor Lake, out past the tennis courts, beyond the new women's softball field. A walking path skirts the circumference of it and there are some benches and a couple of picnic tables scattered around for picnicking and such. I choose a bench on the far side of the lake, but I don't open the coffee or the paper just yet. I want to try to be in the moment: the wet, green smell of the water, the mockingbird running his medley, the breeze, cooler now, what passes for autumn in Arkansas drifting over me. Roger loved the Keats autumn ode, could recite it. Of course, he could recite all of the odes. How does it begin?

But this is not being in the moment. *Let it go*, I think. *You are capable of being right here, right now. Right? Season of mists and something, close-bosomed friend of the sun, maybe.* The full burning death-end of autumn of which old John Boy sang is unknown in the piney reaches of Arkansas. Even the very deepest depths of southern winter will not kill everything. And, thus, the cycle always feels incomplete. It may snow, yes, even here in the South, but the pines and evergreen bushes will shrug it off and glisten in unkillable joy, the permanence of the South. Death in life. Life in death. World without end, blah, blah, blah.

Yeah. This is not being in the moment. Maybe I am just not capable of doing that. Shoot, maybe nobody can. Maybe it's just something people pretend to do while they're really thinking about something else. I mean, who really knows what goes on inside folks' heads? Like them in churches when they go to shaking and shimmying and rolling on the floor. At least some of that's got to be put on, right? When I open my eyes, I see Carla and some boy on the other side of the lake. They are walking the path and will eventually pass right by me. I take off the lid and blow across the surface of the coffee. It smells like heaven, but it's hot and bitter. I relish it. What other animal on the planet deliberately seeks discomfort, pain? What dog or cat or raccoon would sit still for hot coffee? Or for Carla to get here? I mean, I could get up and walk away, not have to face her again, and her with somebody to berate me in front of. But I don't. In fact, I welcome whatever pain is to come. I open my arms to it. *Amor fati*, as Lowell says. And now, well, I guess I *am* in the moment, in each discrete second as they walk the gentle curve of the path around the lake toward me. I am not in the past, I am not anticipating, I just am. Waiting. In the moment. Coffee burning my tongue.

Carla is walking with Patrick Mitchell. Past, present, and future rush in on me like a wave of nausea. Patrick asked me last week to go skating with him, and I agreed. But he never called to set a time. I only accepted his invitation because I could feel him wanting me, sexually. And, well, I didn't plan to give him what he wanted any time soon. What I wanted, as always, was to be wanted and I was getting that already. Yes, I will let him lay siege to my body, let him claw at my impenetrable underwear, fumble at padlocked buttons and clasps, beg me for a taste, of my breasts, my pussy. Maybe he could smell all that on me and that's why he didn't call.

They come abreast of me and stop. Carla is staring at me with open hostility, but Patrick is looking away into the trees. Neither says anything. So I say, "I liked your poem, Patrick."

He doesn't look at me when he says, "Blackwell sure didn't."

Carla is staring a hole through me.

"She didn't like anybody's."

He looks at me now. "She liked yours."

"And what does that tell you, Patrick?"

"That she likes you."

"So, she pretended to like my poem because she likes me?"

"Or maybe it just means you're the better poet."

"Do you believe that?"

"I don't know."

"Did you read my poem?"

"Sure. I didn't understand it."

"Do you think that's because it's a really good poem?"

"What do you mean?"

"I mean, how could it really be a good poem if somebody as smart as you doesn't understand it?"

Carla says, "A lot of really good poems are hard to understand."

"So they say," I say. To Patrick I say, "I took some icebox poetry magnets and chucked them against the side of a car and wrote the words down in the order they randomly stuck there, and I turned that in for my poem."

"You're kidding."

"It's called Dadaism."

"I know what it's called, Darling. I just can't believe you did that. That poem did not make one lick of sense. I mean, she could have really called you out. I mean, seriously, mocked you. You put your grade on the line there. That's pretty brave."

"Or pretty stupid," Carla says.

"It was an act of cowardice, Patrick. There was no part of me in that poem. Literally nothing she might have said about it could have touched me. You, on the other hand, you put yourself into your poem and then laid it out there for the world and for her to judge. That's guts."

"Well, everybody in the class did that."

"All but one."

"So why did she say she liked it? She must have seen something in it."

"What? There was nothing in it. I put nothing in it. So how did she get something out of it? And—how do we judge her taste in poetry since she likes a poem that some magnets and a door panel wrote?"

"She likes Yeats too," he says and smiles.

"Everybody likes Yeats." His eyebeam crosses the distance between us and I am disturbed like dust on rose petals; I feel like flowers that are looked at. And I remember why I agreed to go out with him. He licks his lips. *Yes. By all means, want me. As much as you can. With everything you've got.*

Carla takes my newspaper and opens it and drops it onto my lap. "Well, Patrick," she says, though she's looking at me, "try not to end up like Jimmy Whitfield."

The headline reads, "Student Expelled."

Carla sneers. "Somebody stole his phone and sent all his personal pictures all over the internet."

I scan the article: genitalia, female students, the College President's secretary. *What was she doing in his phone?*

I show nothing. "I guess Jimmy shouldn't be sending unsolicited dick pics."

"Somebody else sent them!"

I look down at the newspaper again. "I don't see that in this article anywhere."

"He *told* me. Somebody took his phone."

I say, "You're upset, Carla. What is it? Fear? Guilt? Did you steal his phone? Did you send the pictures?"

"You know damn well who sent them."

"How would I know?"

Patrick says, "You told me Darling had something to do with it? Did you, Darling?"

"She said *I* had something to do with it?"

"I didn't say she *did* it."

"Uh, yeah, you did. When I told you that I was going out with her, you said she got Whitfield kicked out of school."

"I didn't mean *her* her."

"What the heck is 'her her'?"

"I mean those friends of hers."

"Lucas and Lowell? What do they have to do with it?"

I say, "They're your friends too, Carla. At least one of them is." Her mouth is open. "So if they did it, though I don't see how they could have, and I'm guilty by association, then so are you, sweetie. So are you."

She walks away saying, "Watch yourself, Patrick. You don't want to get on the wrong side of those sociopaths."

She's about fifty feet away when she stops and turns around. "Darling. Did you ever ask them about Laura Huddle?" I just stare at her. "I didn't think so."

I watch her walking away and when I can't see her anymore, I look at Patrick. He says, "What's she got against you anyway?"

"Who's Laura Huddle?"

He comes over and sits down on the bench by me and stretches out his legs. His jeans are giving off a sour smell, like he let them sit in the washer too long. Over that, Skin Bracer, the same aftershave my grandfather used. He's ginger light. Golden-red hair, pale freckles, clothes in fall colors.

"Freshman year, that was two years ago, she was a girl that disappeared."

"That's it?"

He hesitates. There is something he doesn't want to say.

"What?"

"She ran with Lucas and Lowell's crowd."

"Crowd? They don't have a crowd."

"Not anymore. You see, you only know the 'new and improved' Lucas and Lowell. Freshman year they hung out in a group with—well, let's see, Jimmy Dale Whatshisname, Steve Marshall, Sarah Somebody. A couple of others. And Laura Huddle."

"And she disappeared."

"Vanished off the face of the earth."

"But—there's more. Right?"

"You know. I heard some things."

"Like what?"

"Like Lucas killed her."

"Bullshit."

"You don't think he could?"

"No, yeah. I mean, I find it hard to believe anybody was saying that about him. Who would believe that Lucas just up and killed some girl."

"It's not like it was all over campus. It wasn't the rumor of the day or in the paper or anything," and here he rattled my newspaper at me. "After she disappeared, that group scattered. Jimmy Dale dropped out and Steve moved off campus. That Sarah girl pledged a sorority. That left Lucas and Lowell, like a black hole after a star's explosion. I don't know what happened, but the effects can be read. You can't see a black hole, only its effects on other bodies. Whatever blew that group apart, Laura running away or eloping or whatever, didn't, in and of itself, seem powerful enough to fire that supernova."

"Leaving Lucas and Lowell spinning around each other like a neutron star."

"Well, you're shifting the metaphor a little, but yeah."

"And they never found her?"

"No, they did not."

"And that's what Carla thinks. That Lucas killed her. Not that she eloped or ran away. And she's sorta sarcastically warning me that I could end up like Laura Huddle, pushing up daisies in a shallow grave or bubbling up in some swamp—"

For a second I can't catch my breath. There's a pit in my stomach. A big one. I close my eyes. The smell of the rotting leaves at the edge of the water yanks me back to the river, under the trees, the dark hole, my face superimposed in their cameras against the black of that opening. I see it now.

They already knew the place.

❧

The next day I skip Sociology and go to the library. A Lexis-Nexis search of Laura Huddle gives me a brief AP story that says nothing beyond the fact that she disappeared and two longer pieces from the *Northwest Arkansas Times* and *Arkansas Democrat Gazette*, both of which say basically the same thing: Laura Huddle, graduate of Union Christian Academy in Fort Smith, parents Jim and Adele Huddle, sisters Maxine and Laurel, brother John Paul. Disappeared from Chandler College in 2014. No sign of foul play. Roommate says some clothes missing. Roommate says she was unhappy at school, not doing well in courses. Parents say happy child, no reason to run away, suspect the worst.

I swallow the frog in my throat down to the pit in my stomach where they knock against each other like bowling pins. What are the possibilities? *One*, she ran off with somebody. But nobody else from school turned up missing. So maybe she ran off with somebody from town. Or from Fort Smith, somebody she knew from before. That seems the most likely.

Two. She just left. Forget the somebody. She just went by

herself. To start over. Just enough clothes to stay clean awhile.

Who does that?

Three. Somebody took her. Kidnapped her. But no ransom demands.

Four. Somebody killed her. Hid her body so well no one could find it. Who? Serial killer? Sex maniac? Some enemy she made at the school, some boy she rejected, some girl whose boyfriend she stole? Or?

Five (extension of four). No reason at all. Somebody killed her just for the hell of it.

No reason at all. Is that even possible? *Of course it's possible. You know it is.*

And who was saying that Lucas killed her?

"What's the worst thing you've ever done, Darlin'?"

We have driven out west of Barnesville to a place the boys call The Deeps. It's a swimming hole of sorts, an abandoned gravel pit that over time filled with water. I've never been here before, but I've heard people talk about it. The boys like it because not too many people know about it and they can run around naked. Not, I suppose, that people being here would stop them from running around naked. Tonight they have brought me here to swim under the full moon. The water is warm and little fish nudge and nibble at me as I tread water and watch the boys to see if they notice that I too am as nekkid as four o'clock in the morning. I walk out of the water like Venus out of the foam, but they're arguing over who gets the PB and J and who gets pimento cheese.

I plop down next to them on the blanket, three naked people, apparently devoid of sexual curiosity. *Little sister, don't you kiss me once or twice.*

I pop the top on a beer and watch the rippling reflection of the moon on the surface of the water.

"Well? Darlin'?" Lowell asks.

"Huh no. What is this, confession? I'm not Catholic. I was

reared up in the Baptist church. We do our confessing on our knees, in the dark, under our breath, with the door closed. You tell me: What's the worst thing you've ever done?"

Lowell thinks a moment.

"I tripped a boy on the stairs in high school, Jason Chadwick, and he broke his jaw and a whole passel of his teeth come flying out too."

"Why did you do such a thing?"

"He was dirty. We played basketball together in gym class and he was a dirty player. He had, the week before, elbowed me in the head. Right on the ear. Stung like the devil. So, I tripped him."

"Did you get in trouble?"

"No. I fell too, only a couple of steps, but everybody thought we just got our feet tangled up, even him. I did bang my knee a little on the step, so it wasn't perfect. Close enough. So, Darlin'. You?"

"No." I laugh. "Lucas. You?"

"Showed my mother some pictures."

"Of what?"

"That's the worst you ever did? Really?" Lowell said.

"Pictures of what?" I ask.

"I think, well, yeah. That's the worst thing I ever did," Lucas says.

"Of course, self-analysis is the toughest kind. Not to mention the hardest to get right," Lowell says.

"Pictures of what?" I repeat.

"Her boyfriend, Billy."

"Her boyfriend?"

"The dumbfuck was cheating on her with a girl in my school."

I look at Lowell. He cocks his head.

"Everybody in the whole school knew. I mean everybody. And somehow, it was all on me. Like I was doing something wrong."

"Did you know the girl?" I ask.

"Everybody was all, 'Hey, dude, your mom's boyfriend. Can you believe that shit?' Like I was supposed to do something about it. How the fuck did that turn into my responsibility? What was I supposed to do?"

"Obviously, you did something," I say.

"I did know the girl, Jennifer Baldwin. She was a senior. I mean, she was eighteen, so he wasn't actually statutorily raping her, but she was way too young for him. And you know what? Forget that. Who cares? Grown woman, she can do what she wants. But that son of a bitch was making a fool outta my mother."

"And you," Lowell says.

"Apparently."

"What did you do?" I ask.

"I borrowed a camera from the school newspaper. I got my friend, Tomás, to drive me around for a couple of weeks and we followed him. Took pictures. It was easy. Ridiculously easy. That boy was a dumbass of the first water."

"And you gave the pictures to your mother."

"Yes."

"That's it?"

"And to Billy's mother."

"Ouch!" I say.

"I sent the worst of them to his boss. Billy worked at a Sears Outlet store selling dented washing machines. I wrote on the back of the pictures, "Your employee and a seventeen-year-old high school student. Somebody's daughter."

"Seventeen?"

"Yes."

"Good one."

"I thought so. They straight up fired his ass. Straight up."

"He deserved it," Lowell says.

"On the other hand, my mother didn't."

"She would have found out anyway," Lowell says.

"Not the point. And don't try to parse the moral implications, Bentham. Don't play outcomes. Don't play inevitability.

Don't offer me the variegated cones of future possibilities. What might have been is an abstraction, only there in a world of speculation. In the end, one thing happened. She got hurt. I did that. I took those pictures and I showed them to her and she was hurt."

"If you say so. If you want to own that, I have nothing but love for you. Myself, I didn't own tripping that ole boy. But I did enjoy it. Truth now, old son. Did you truly take no enjoyment in the ruination of the fallen Billy?"

"When we were following him around and taking pictures, I enjoyed that. Not the private eye stuff, but imagining his future pain. I did enjoy that."

A little wind picks up and chills me. Out somewhere in the dark an owl hoots, and that chills me too.

Lowell says, "That's good. That's a good story, I mean. But I'm gonna have to disagree with you here. This cannot be the worst thing you ever did."

"Really? You're suggesting I've done something worse than hurting my own mother."

"I'd rather say I've heard this story before and I don't recognize it as a story of evil."

"Okay, you've got my attention, Quentin."

"I tripped ole Jason, busted his ass. What was I tryin' to do. What was my ultimate goal?"

"Hurt him," I say.

"So is that Good or Evil?"

"Evil. Maybe," I say.

"Maybe? Oh, well, the human prerogative. Choice. No sin without it. So, our boy Lucas here catches out the cheating Billy and his wicked, wicked ways. His goal?"

"Hurt him?"

"Nope."

"Get him away from my mother."

"Right. Good or Evil?"

I wait. To give Lucas the moment.

After a minute he says, "Mere intentionality."

"Not 'mere,' my friend. You were trying to do good."

"And did evil."

"But not on purpose."

"Intentionality—"

"—has gotten a bad rap. Like self-interest. And casual sex."

"Okay. So what?" Lucas asks.

"And you haven't answered the question: what's the worst thing you've ever done? What evil have you set out to do and done it?"

Will Laura Huddle's name come up now? Would they discuss it right here in front of me? Is that where we are? Do they trust me that much?

Or is the Laura Huddle story just so much bullshit?

Of course it is.

"You know my whole life story. What do you say?"

"Let's start with, I don't believe for a minute that I know your whole life story."

"What don't you know?"

"'What don't I know?' Did you just ask that, Mr. Epistemology?"

They laugh.

"So, think. What haven't you told me? Something, maybe, you think would embarrass you. Or lower you in my eyes."

He looks at Lowell a long minute. The owl hoots again.

"Maybe. We should let Darling tell her story first."

And whatever it is that Lowell is digging for or trying to get Lucas to say out loud he decides to let go. "But Darlin' was a good girl. Is a good girl. I predict there is no story forthcoming from her. At least none what will be ethically clarifying. What say, Darlin'?"

"You're right. I was a good girl. Cheerleader, don't you know. Sang in the choir. Made home visitations to old folks and the sick and infirm. I ran the March of Dimes campaign in junior year."

"What did I tell you?"

"Nobody's perfect, Darling," Lucas says.

Lowell says, "Did you enjoy it? Doing your good deeds? Did

your heart swell with nobility? Did your cheeks burn with the inner fire of a job well done and a god well served? Or—did you run up on the highly vaulted problem of altruism? And then find, to your regret, some of the intrinsic value of your good deeds buffered, deadened even by your pleasure in them?"

"I didn't know about all that back then. The tricky nature of the perfectly selfless act. I thought you were supposed to enjoy doing good."

"So, what was your problem?" Lucas asks.

"Doing good grows tepid. Sin burns."

"Oooh. Good one, Darling," Lucas says.

"Tell me your sins, my child," Lowell intones.

"Give it a rest, padre," I say.

"Darlin', it's your turn."

"Fine. So, this one time—"

Lucas says, "And I don't want to hear, 'I broke his heart,' or 'I led him on and never let him fuck me,' or 'I blackballed her from cheerleaders,' or any of the other run-of-the-mill shit girls do every day of every year in every high school in the history of the world."

"I wasn't going—"

"And no punishing your parents either. 'I wrecked their car on purpose.' 'I let the cat pee on their bed.'"

"May I continue? Now, if you'd asked me two months ago what my worst sin was, it wouldn't've been this story I'm about to tell you. You see, I've been thinking about what you said that day on the river. I had to look up Leopold and Loeb, by the by. And I have come to believe that the killing of someone you don't know, and for no reason, just to do it, just to say no to the Judeo-Christian ethical tradition—and I know, Lucas, that you don't think much of that option, lacking a certain heat, as it does—killing the stranger, well, I've come to the conclusion that that's worse than killing your cheating husband. I believe some little mitigation might be due the wife who had to put up with his shit for twenty years. So, old Leo and Loeb thought they were doing the ultimate evil act, worse than just a regular murder. Anyway, I've been thinking about it, about that scale. The scale of evil—"

"None of this is to the point, Darling," Lucas says.

"Hang on. So anyway, where we went to church, my parents and me, The Rockbridge Baptist Church, the preacher had a son. An only child he was, and if you're thinking that that is an ungodly combination, preacher's kid and only child in one package, I can only say that the boy was spared, as were we who knew him. Instead of the amoral, narcissistic bully that such a conjunction would seem to betoken, Sandy Hewitt was a shy, kind, introverted kid. We took Sunday school together."

"What did you wear to Sunday school, Darlin'?" Lowell drawls.

"And so it came to pass that during a break at cheerleading, ole Sandy walked by and I happened to notice Liz Herbert watching him. Staring at him, really, and then she saw me looking at her. All I did was raise my eyebrows a tad. Seriously, it was involuntary. She kinda ducked her head and said that she'd always liked ole Sandy, even if he did have a girl's name. That's what she said, a girl's name. And didn't I go to his daddy's church? I confirmed that I did indeed attend that selfsame church. She asked me what I thought about it. I didn't have to ask what 'it' was. She was sweet on the boy and wanted to know did I think she had a chance with him. I clucked my tongue, believe it or not, and shook my head and told her she was wasting her time, that he was all tore up over some other girl, and she should just forget about him."

"Oh lord, you broke somebody up?" Lucas says.

"No."

"Darling. I said none of this high school drama shit."

"It's not."

"Boy meets girl. Darling sabotages girl. Girl cries. Oh my god, Darling, you've shaken hell itself."

"Ask me why."

"Why is obvious. She was a cheerleading attention whore. You wanted to punish her."

"She wasn't."

"She was rich."

I feel Lowell shift his position on the blanket.

"No."

"You wanted the boy for yourself? You hated the boy and didn't want to see him happy?"

"No."

"No? Let's see. What's left? She owed you money. Somebody paid you money."

"She was just a girl. I barely knew her."

"Then why'd you do it?" Lowell asks.

"See, that right there's the problem. Why? That's the question that makes us unique, isn't it? Motive. Us humans, I mean. Any animal might on some level think *what* or *who* or *how*? But could an animal even conceive of the question *why?* But we, oh, we always think, what gain is there in it? Things make more sense when there is gain. Everything falls into place where there is gain. 'He killed for the inheritance.' 'She robbed for money to buy drugs.' But—no motive? A person acting without motive, without a why? Lowell tripped a boy on the stairs. You hurt your mama. You explained your reasons well."

Possibility five: for no reason at all.

"See, I don't think most people can even imagine that option, and thus when it does happen, as it sometimes must, we construct motives where there are none. For our understanding and our reassurance: he was crazy; she was drug addled. But 'just for the hell of it'? Too remote. But there is reason that that phrase even exists. Even if it's used metaphorically most of the time. That was part of the horror of Manson. Those murdered people—no reason."

"He was trying to start a race war."

"Yeah, maybe, but I doubt it. It's so stupid. You tell me that and I think, 'Those folks died for no reason.'"

"What's your point here, Darlin'?"

"I didn't know about the problem of altruism when I matriculated up in here. Or rather, I didn't have the words to express it. But I do now. In a nutshell, boys, the P of A says that no act is purely good if it has an even remotely selfish motive. If you do what you do so you can feel better about yourself or look better to your neighbors, then it doesn't count. Or it's tainted, it's not purely good. For that matter, feeling good doesn't have to be the motivation. You could do good just to do good, but if afterward you feel even a tinge of pride or well-being, then it doesn't count. Everybody agree?"

The boys look at each other. They have to agree. But they don't want to. They know I'm baiting them, but they can't see the trap.

"Fine. We agree. So, let me offer this. If no act is purely good when it has an even remotely selfish motive, *then no act is purely evil if it benefits you in any way either.* Or satisfies your sense of justice or decorum or aesthetics. An evil act that benefits you, even a little bit, is merely utilitarian. Or pragmatic. Or enriching. But not purely evil. Not the tippity top of the ladder of evil. Leopold and Loeb were right."

The boys are quiet, so I continue.

"See, if I had seen Liz looking at ole Sandy on a different day or maybe just later on that same day, I might not have done it. Not have peed all over poor Liz's hots for the preacher's kid. What was the difference? Why that moment? But my point here is that *there was no why.* I didn't do it for a reason. I just did it. That's what makes it purely evil and not just some rising action in a soap opera."

"Ouch," Lowell says.

"I think she just called us dilettantes. Tourists in the Garden of Good and Evil."

"I think she might just be right."

"That'd be a first," Lucas says. No surprise.

"And," I say and look at Lucas, "doing it for no reason also eliminates one leg of the stool."

"What stool?" Lowell says.

❧

The next day is Wednesday and I have three morning classes in a row. The boys have class in the afternoon, so I skip lunch and head for the library again. It's a beautiful day. Sun, hard blue sky, the black tupelo flaming in the quad. I need to talk to somebody, somebody from two years ago. Patrick said their group was Laura Huddle and then Jimmy Dale something who dropped out. I don't suppose I'll be able to find him. Steven Marshall is still at Chandler and Sarah somebody may be too. I need Sarah's last name, so I dig out the yearbooks for 2014, 2015, and 2016. If they were a group, I'm hoping that there'll be a picture of them in there somewhere.

What am I thinking? What am I doing? Is Carla to be taken seriously? The boys don't want to hurt me. Right? There is no way they did anything to Laura Huddle. At least nothing serious. I'm sure. And even if they did do something to Laura, which they didn't, it doesn't mean they'll do something to me.

What's this "something" shit?

I mean "kill." They didn't kill her, they won't kill me. Not without a reason.

That's what I mean.

Did I just last night convince them that they don't need a reason? That it's better not to have a reason?

I look at lots of pictures on lots of pages before I find the one I want. And there you are: Lucas and Lowell right in front, six people draped around them. The boys, my boys, the gravitational center of their group, like stars spinning at inconceivable speeds around a supermassive black hole at the heart of a galaxy. List of names: Lucas Susskind and Lowell Alford. Also pictured, Jimmy Dale Williams, Steven Marshall, Sarah Jackson, Aaron Dillard, Thomas Smith. And Laura Huddle.

She's dressed just like the boys. My boys.

Prettier than me.

What am I even saying?

In the Registrar's office I have good luck. There is a boy working there, so when I touch my chest and softly rub the top of my breasts, he just hands over Steve Marshall's off-campus address and tells me in which sorority house Sarah Jackson lives: Delta Delta Kappa. Shoot. Of course.

I can hit the sorority house today without Lucas and Lowell noticing. They are in class all afternoon and intermural basketball after that. But going off campus will have to wait until—when?

At 5:30 I walk over to the DDK house. Girls are trailing in and out, going to the dining hall, coming back, talking, flipping their hair, smiling. How much smarter are they than I to be so happy? I'm in Lucas's Kings jersey and I didn't wash my hair today. Or yesterday. Or. Still, I stroll in like I know what I'm doing and ask a random girl, *Where's Sarah?*

"Johnson or Jackson?"

"Jackson."

"Upstairs, second on the left. Funny, their names so alike, Sarah Jackson, Sarah Johnson," she says and giggles.

"I know, right?" I say in a voice I heard on television.

Sarah's door is covered with posters and cartoons: Bitch Planet, Monstress, Steven Universe, old marriage-equality stickers, other stuff.

She gasps audibly when she sees me.

"Darling. Lord God."

I'm as shocked as she is. Turns out that Sarah is the girl who hung back when Clarissa tried to recruit me for Delta Delta Kappa, the French movie-star girl. Who stared at Lucas and Lowell the whole time. And—well, no wonder.

"Yeah. You got a minute to talk."

"I was just about to leave for the dining hall."

"Me too."

"All right. Well, then."

I don't need to be an empath to know that Sarah doesn't want to be within ten miles of me. Outside it's chilly and the air smells woodsmoky, a backyard fire somewhere. The east sides of the buildings are in shadow, but the sky is a blazing blue smeared with the finest wisps of cirrus.

"How are they?" she says, her voice, soft, tender almost.

"They are how they are," I say. "I've got no frame of reference for comparison."

"And that's why you're here. Yes. I understand."

We walk in silence a minute or two. The dining hall is just ahead. I can't imagine she'll sit with me.

"It was a cult, Darling. Lowell lured us in and Lucas proselytized us."

"With or without a condom?"

She stops dead in the middle of the walkway and gives me a long look.

"I'm sorry," I say. "Stupid joke. Shoot. I don't know why I said that. I really don't. I don't know what it is that I want to know. Or how to ask for it."

"Come on," she says, and we go into the dining hall. We get our food and I lead us to seats close to the windows. Away from the mirror wall.

I have gotten the mystery meat and what looks like canned pear halves smothered in cottage cheese. I hope it's cottage cheese. Sarah has selected a salad. She eats with great delicacy. I'm self-conscious about my food and how hungry I am and how I want to eat it with my fingers and gulp it down. Am I really just a boy after all?

"We were freshmen. What we had in common? I don't know. Not loners exactly, but none of us fit in anywhere, really. I mean, Lowell is at home in the world, isn't he? He could have pledged the best fraternity or run for student office. He could have taken over the drama department and starred in every production. He was born to be looked at. Lucas? He's a loner."

"A loner? He's virtually in bed with Lowell. I've never met anybody as close as those two."

"Yes. But if there were no Lowell for Lucas, he wouldn't be here. He'd be in a cabin in Montana or somewhere building bombs out of matchsticks and bedsprings and coal oil."

"So, you think he could kill somebody?"

"Oh. Laura Huddle. How'd you hear about her?"

"Well, um."

"Never mind."

"No, no. It was, well, it was Carla. Carla Dowell."

"Really. I just heard a rumor about Carla. Did you hear it?"

"I don't believe I have."

"If you say so. Somebody taped her having sex."

"I gotta go with 'so what?' Who doesn't have a sex tape floating around somewhere these days?"

"Me. You. Everyone we know. This isn't a television show, Darling. This is our actual lives. If there is a tape of her somewhere, it's potential dynamite. She's an Arkansas girl. Not a reality show whore."

I wince. "Whore? Really? At this late date?"

"No judgment. Just a useful term."

"So. A cult. Tell me about that."

She shakes her head and doesn't say anything for a minute. "I know what I look like. Like I'm headed for a stable, boring husband, the Junior League, the country club, well-groomed children smiling in sunny photographs. I don't know if that will happen or not. It's definitely not where I was going when I arrived here. I wanted to be painter. I saw myself someday in a huge loft in New York City, in paint-splattered overalls, canvases hung all around, a wiry, bearded, shirtless lover at my beck and call. But things got so weird with Lucas and Lowell and Jimmy Dale. And when it all fell apart, I went looking for something else—I don't know, more structured. Stable. More normal. I know you don't think so now, but it is possible that you will want some normal soon."

"What makes you think I—" My voice trails off. I can hear it as well as she can.

I cannot claim to want "normal" and still sit between Lucas and Lowell. She knows that but lets it lie. I like her for that.

"I had algebra with Lowell. I fell in love with him. Or in lust with him. You know what I mean, I'm sure. He's so beautiful, isn't he? That mouth. That lower lip of his, I don't know, it's pornographic. Don't you think? I threw myself at him.

"Sort of. Truth told, I'm a little shy. I guess one of the great questions of my life is, how do you ask someone if they like you when you desperately don't want them to know how much you like them? So I—let me put it this way. I got in front of him. I tried to be where he was, you know, in the caf, in the library, at the same table in chemistry. Finally he did notice me. He got very friendly. He's got a way, have you noticed, of making his friendliness sexy. His 'pass the salt' sounds like 'I want to lick you like the inside of a ripe mango.' Don't you think?"

"He's sexy."

"Yes! So sexy! I don't know what I was thinking really."

"You seemed sort of pissed at him that one time."

"That one time? Oh, you mean when Clarissa was hitting on you."

"Hitting?"

"Recruiting, I should say. She stands a little close, don't you think? It's kind of intimate."

"I didn't really notice."

"She's like that."

Sarah eats a piece of lettuce and looks out the window.

"So. You were pissed that day?"

She shifts her gaze to the salad. She stirs it around, separating elements: green pepper south, lettuce east. She's bouncing a cherry tomato back and forth between the north and west poles.

"I was."

"Why? All that stuff was so long ago. Did they hurt you that bad?"

Now she looks up. Kinda surprised, kinda curious.

"I was pissed at you, Darling."

This is not what I was expecting. I won't lie, it takes me aback. I lean back in my chair, putting distance between her face and mine. I am taken aback, as I say. Way aback.

Ah, Darling. The girl of the quick comeback, the rapier wit, as my daddy calls it, but I'm starting to think it has not served me so well, for so many reasons.

Me? Are you kidding? What the hell? These words are out on the tip of my tongue, trying to jump off. Words that will call into question her right to be angry with me. For I have done nothing. Nothing to her. A kid's words. Defensive, deflecting, passive-aggressive. Holding those words in my mouth gives me just a quantum speck of the moment I need. Maybe I'll carry pebbles around in my mouth from now on, spit 'em out in my hand when I need to say something. When I truly need to say something.

Finally, I say, "Yeah, sure. 'Course. I'd be pissed if you were sitting between them and I was in a sorority."

"It was just him, really. Lowell. Lucas is kind of a dud. I never understood what Lowell saw in him. He's pissed off all the time, constantly hitting up Lowell for money, jealous as hell of me or anybody else that got Lowell's attention even for a minute."

I am about to say—but I stuff some pebbles in my mouth.

"Don't you think?"

I shrug.

The dining hall is about to close. We don't have to leave but they're about to stop letting people in. Five guys run across the quad, probably headed here. Two girls with guitars sit on a bench under the black tupelo playing chords, watching each other's fingers. The long shadow of the clock tower bisects the quad and I wonder for the first time why the clock never sounds. It's a clock tower. I almost ask Sarah about it. Pebbles.

"I guess that's it?" She tilts her head when she says this. She wants to go.

"Wait. I want to hear about Laura Huddle."

"Yeah. Okay. So Laura was the last to come into our group, such as it was. She was, well, I think she was Jimmy Dale's girlfriend. At least that was the impression I got."

"The impression?"

"We weren't a group the way you might think. We hung out. We listened to Lucas and Lowell preach at us. We got drunk and high and—we did a couple of things."

"Like what?"

"But when it came to who was with who, you know, we kept that private. Secret, really."

"What did y'all do?"

"I didn't know if she was Jimmy Dale's girlfriend, if they were sleeping together or what. For all I know she was sleeping with Steve or Aaron or Tom Smith. Maybe even Lowell. I think Lowell may have slept with her. Like, I sure didn't want anybody to know about me and the boys."

"The boys?"

"I wanted to be with Lowell, but what I ended up being was with Lucas and Lowell. I thought I was a wedge, splitting them apart, but there was no splitting them apart, you see. I was more like cement, I think."

"Wait. Are you saying that you were sleeping with them? Both of them?"

"Yeah. Aren't you?"

I don't know what to say. My first instinct is to say, *No, fuck no, what do you think I am*? Then the full force of the fact that I'm not sleeping with them, that they slept with her and not with me, hits me. And why have they not slept with me? She thinks I'm the new her. I'm not the new her. I'm the less-than-her.

My second instinct is to lie. To say, *Of course. Yes. I'm the meat in their sandwich, the cake frosting on their nipples, the pussy hoard of all time.*

But it's too late. I've choked on my pebbles. Her expression changes. She sees the truth.

And she smiles. Just a little.

And now I don't like her so much anymore.

Neither of us says anything else. She gets up and takes her tray back and leaves. I turn my head and look at the mirror wall across the room. My eyes are a little blurry. I can't read the expression on my face.

❧

I have begged off a road trip with the boys, pleading with them to give me time to write a paper for Blackwell, a paper which I have, in fact, already written. They're going to Fayetteville to some Thai restaurant they hope will meet with Lucas's prohibitively high standards for Asian cuisine. The look on his face says nothing is going to satisfy him, and Lowell blows me a kiss.

"Stay out of trouble, Darlin'," he says, wiggling his fingers and putting up the window. I wait in the lobby of the dorm for half an hour, watching the parking lot. When they don't come back, I head out.

Steve Marshall is a senior. He lives in a house off campus and drives a station wagon. His fiancée peeks at us from the kitchen. He is the grownest man I've ever gone to school with.

"You're writing an article for the *Purple and Gold*?"

Steve and his girlfriend (I don't get introduced. She goes into the kitchen as soon as I'm in the door, flounces maybe) live in a duplex, an old home that got turned into two smaller homes, way out in a neighborhood west of campus. It's nice. Little fireplace, furniture looks like it's out of one of their mama's attics, comfortable, homey stuff, tchotchkes on every flat surface. Twelve-foot ceilings. I can see an old concert poster on a wall in the kitchen. Place smells like cinnamon. One of those cinnamon-smelling brooms is standing in the corner, so yeah.

I'm determined to fill my mouth with pebbles. Not easy when I'm supposed to be asking him questions.

"Not so much," I say.

"No? What then?"

"I'm curious about the people around Laura Huddle before she disappeared."

"Ah. Detective work." He leans back on the couch and crosses his legs. "Don't you imagine the police have been over this ground before? Surely they considered every option, every outcome?"

"I'm not trying to catch anybody."

He looks at me for a long moment. Then over his shoulder toward the kitchen. He lowers his voice. "Lucas and Lowell?"

"What about them?"

"Well, I'm guessing you're involved with them?"

"I'm not fucking them, if that's what you mean," I say too loudly. Kitchen noise from the kitchen.

He winces and says, "Why don't you go now?"

"No. No, I'm sorry. I'm sorry," I repeat louder and toward the kitchen. "They're my friends. I care about them. They care about me. But this Laura Huddle thing. I'm just trying to find out—I don't know. Some people think Lucas might have killed her."

"No kidding. Maybe you should be thinking that too."

"Did the police interview you?"

"They interviewed everybody on campus, I think. President to gardener."

"But there must have been more focus on her immediate group, right?"

"Not from where I sat. They asked me about her mood and any boyfriends—was I her boyfriend?—drinking, drugs, anything she might have said about leaving Chandler. I'm sure they asked everybody those same questions."

"They didn't suspect you?"

"I don't think they suspected anybody. I don't think they suspected foul play. My take was that they figured her for a runaway."

"What do you think?"

"About what?"

"What happened to her."

"No idea."

"Do you think Lucas could have? That they could have?"

In the kitchen, the fiancée turns on the radio. Smooth jazz. Some singer repeating, "Stay close to me, stay close to me."

"I was in Katrina."

"You're not from New Orleans."

He's surprised. "What did you do? Look me up?"

"A little."

"I'm from Bogalusa."

"New Orleans took the brunt, right?"

"No."

"You're kidding?"

"You're using the word 'brunt' wrongly."

"Wrongly?"

"Brunt implies an amount, as in New Orleans took the most of Katrina's power and left less for other to suffer. What you're trying to say, Darling (he says the name as if he doesn't think much of it), is New Orleans was hurt the worst. And that is true. By far the worst. But it's degree of suffering in no way mitigated the amount of suffering that others endured."

"All suffering is not equal."

"I'm not remotely suggesting that. What I'm—you know what? Forget it. My point is that in Bogalusa that day, with Katrina bearing down on us, I was scared. I was eleven, but I was old enough to understand what dying really is, old enough to be totally scared of dying. Even now I can still feel those emotions, the physicality of them. If I were a poet. QED, you want to know why I left that group. I had to step out from in front of Lucas and Lowell. If a hurricane is coming your way, there's no dealing with it, there's no reasoning with it. You're just going to have to get out of its way. You're going to have to get out from in front of the thing. Well, for me at least, there was no dealing with Lucas and Lowell. Chandler is a small school, and there's not room enough on that campus to hide in. I decided to get completely out from in front of them."

His girlfriend comes in right then and cocks her hip. The motion is—I don't know—pointed. Steve stands up. A clear indicator that our time together has come to an end. At the door she smiles at me. The smile says, *Fuck you, don't come back, you little bitch.* She shuts the door behind me. So much with zero words. Yeah, I'm thinking pebbles. She's the queen of pebbles. I aspire to her reticence. I hope I can stick to my pebble vow. I talk too much.

❧

My head hurts. When I open my eyes, the world is an Impressionist painting, *Starry Night over the Rhone* or something, and every light is halo ringed and every line gone non-Euclidian on me. So much Impressionism in the world and so little time. I try to sit up, but my head throbs so badly that I just lie right back down. The stars bob in bags of water. I turn my head and see the observatory. I'm on the Hill. What am I doing on the Hill?

Every time I move, a jagged pain drags itself from the back of my head around to my eyes and sets off an M-80.

I lie still. High-pitched whistle. Flashes of light in the corners of my eyes. The smell of gunpowder. No. Pancakes. Or lavender. Sweat? Am I wearing deodorant? So. Olfactory hallucinations. I'm thinking concussion. Brain tumor?

"Oh shit."

"What?"

"There's somebody already up here."

"So? We don't have to do it right next to them. It's a big hill, Jonathan."

"No, it's just one person. Who is that?"

I open my mouth, but that changes the pitch of the whistle which hurts more. So I shut it again.

"Look. It's Darling Whatsit. What are you doing, Darling? Star-gazing all alone?"

He steps closer.

"Oh shit."

"What now, Jonathan?"

"I think there's—this is blood. There's blood on her face. I think it's blood."

"You are quite the date, Jonathan. I'm so glad we decided to come here instead of my cousin's house."

It feels like an hour since they got here. I fumble for Jonathan's hand and whisper, "Help."

There's more talk, some more people show up, stand around, but I can't get their features to focus. I hear the ambulance, the girl holding my hand now smells of cinnamon. Maybe. Cinnamon again? The EMTs hoist me onto the gurney; I wish I would pass out.

In the ambulance I throw up and apologize. Rainbows glow on the edge of my vision and darkness right behind.

The previous afternoon, Patrick picked me up in front of the Christian Center. *Why not at the dorm?* He was driving a big black pickup truck, a Chevy, lavishly waxed and polished, with oversized tires so that the whole thing sits up higher than everybody else. Maybe he didn't want anyone to see him picking me up at the dorm. So what was that about? Was he embarrassed to be dating me (somewhat understandable)? Was he afraid of running into the boys (not entirely ridiculous)? Maybe he didn't want to drive his big, beautiful truck around into the crowded parking lot behind the women's dorm where it might get door dinged. We headed over to Fayetteville and drove around town for a while. He seemed to be looking for something. When he'd asked me out, he suggested we go skating, so I figured he was looking for a roller rink, but instead we went to the fair. We parked in a grass field and then walked around on a couple of acres of sawdust strewn with carnival rides and food carts. Kids everywhere, the wonderful, memory-tingling smells of corn dogs and cotton candy, the merry-go-round, tilt-a-whirl, Ferris wheel. We rode rides and ate fat hamburgers and played arcade games until after dark. Patrick drank beer all afternoon, not a crazy amount, but steady. He did good by me, as my daddy says, because I do love the fair. Every year back home the fair would come and set up just off the highway halfway between Helena and Darville. For weeks afterward, every kid in school had pockets full of saltwater taffy, which the teachers were delighted to confiscate and eat when they caught us with it. I really enjoyed myself with Patrick at that little carnival. It was corny, but he didn't say that it was, and he took me on every ride. I got a box of taffy too. Though I never got to finish it. In fact, I barely got it open. It probably ended up on the floor of his truck.

Afterward, we drove back through town and got on 412 back

toward Barnesville. I expected him to pat the seat beside him, to tilt his head in invitation. I was ready. He took his eyes off the road a couple of times and looked at me. I met his eyes. *Pat the seat, dude. Here I come.* Where was that look he gave me when he asked me out? Those eyes wherein I could see myself naked? Instead, he reached under his seat and pulled out a bottle and shook it at me, invitationally, I guess. I said no thanks and he told me to pour him a drink into my empty Coke cup. It was dark and I'm no whiskey expert, but it smelled hot and bosky like bourbon. The passing headlights threw his features into high relief and he looked satisfied and pleased with himself. We didn't say much. He had three drinks on the way home. On top of all that beer.

When we got on campus, he didn't drive to the dorm, but parked at the bottom of the Hill. So. Finally.

"Let's take a walk," he said.

I didn't say, *About goddamn time.* Pebbles.

The Hill, of course, is a make-out place. Who doesn't know that?

We neared the top and walked all the way around the observatory, and there I let him lean me back against the burned and blasted wall and kiss me. That's when I realized how drunk he was. He handled it well, on his feet, behind the wheel, but now, kissing me, he was staggered, bleary, reeking of whiskey sweat. I stepped away from him and walked to the top of the Hill.

Here's what I was thinking: I'd never been in this situation with a drunk man before. Or with a man at all, for that matter. I had been with high school boys and the boys I'd been with were so desperate for me, so eager for my body that they were entirely pliable. They were under my thumb, putty in my proverbials. I could hear him huffing behind me up the last few feet to the top. I considered running, but I was afraid of looking foolish to him. *Oh, Darling.*

He grabbed me hard from behind, whirled me around, and took hold of my arms. Up close, his eyes bleary and unfocused, a stupid, drunken grin. Then he sorta crumpled to the ground, dragging me with him. He rolled on top of me and started kissing me again. The ground was hard there, not much in the way of grass. I kissed him back and he fumbled at the button of my jeans.

And then it got not fun. He was too heavy, the ground too hard. I had no intention of us doing it here. On the Hill. In fact, I didn't intend for us to do it at all. At least not tonight. My plans were to hold him off for a good three or four dates. Maybe more. Tonight was going to be the good part, the foreplay, the kissing, the touching, the begging. But now his breath was bad and he was all slobbery and smelly. He didn't care that I was under him. Me, I mean. I could've been anybody, any wet warm vagina. He didn't want me. He wanted to get off. And I wanted him off me.

I tried to roll him over, but he was heavy and strong. I yelled in his ear, *Patrick!*—and he pushed up onto his elbows so that I was able to slip out from under him. Before I could get to my feet, though, he caught hold of the waist of my jeans and yanked me back. I swung my arm behind me to try to knock his hands away, but my elbow caught him right square on the nose. I felt the cartilage give and I knew I had hurt him bad. He roared in pain and let me go.

I got up to run but he caught my foot and I tripped. This time when I got up, he was already on his feet and he hit me with a closed fist in the stomach. I couldn't breathe. It was as if all the air in the world had rushed into the cold of outer space and I was in a vacuum. He grabbed me by the hair and swung his fist into my jaw. I staggered, but didn't fall. My daddy had told me if I ever needed to defend myself, I should remember that there's a column of soft and painful places to hit a person, running in a straight line from throat to crotch. "But really, Darling, run. If you can run, run. But if you can't, then throw your fist at his third shirt button, and try to push it out through his backbone." That's what my daddy said.

Patrick and I both reared back at the same time and threw our punches. I was aiming at that third shirt button, but that's the last thing I saw so I'm guessing he hit me before I hit him.

That's all I remember. Gathering from what the hospital folks told me, he must have hit me at least twice more in the back of the head or maybe banged my head on the ground because they had to put some stitches in back there. I was kinda in and out of it for a while. Thirsty as all get out. The nurses wouldn't give me a whole lot of water for some reason.

At one point a man came into the room and asked me what had happened. He said he was a policeman. He wasn't in a uniform. He was in a nice suit. And he was good looking. I thought the suit was too nice for a cop and that only cops on television wear suits that nice and are so good looking and maybe there was a joke in there somewhere I could say, but I couldn't put it together coherently, so I told him I wasn't sure what happened, that I couldn't remember everything, that I thought I must have tripped and fallen down.

"That's a pretty good knot you managed to knock on your own head," he said and smiled kindly.

"I won't deny I'm a klutz."

He leaned in close. Aramis. Hint of coffee. He spoke softly to me now. "If you want, I can just talk to your boyfriend. It doesn't have to be anything official. You won't be putting him in jail or anything. But, Miss Bramlett, and please understand that this is gospel. I can make him leave you alone. For good."

"I don't have a boyfriend. Seriously, I was up there by myself. I appreciate what you're saying, but everything is fine."

He didn't believe me. It was right there on his kind face. "I'm going to leave you my card," and he put the card on the table next to the bed. "Call me."

"Thank you. Really, though, I'm all right."

He nodded and left. His back was stiff. His shoulders looked angry from behind. No question: he really, really wanted to "talk" to whoever had done this to me.

My parents come the next day. My father seems to have no

trouble believing I have done this to myself. My mother sits by the bed signing for me all the gossip from the neighborhood and about a show she is binging on Netflix and anything else she can think of.

"Mama. You're giving me a headache."

headache-you-before-me-sign

"Yes, and you're making it worse."

My father goes outside to the parking lot to call the school. He's telling somebody that they are taking me home for a few days. I cannot complain. I feel like a half-eaten sandwich that's been dropped on the asphalt in the hot sun.

The hospital won't release me until tomorrow, so they are spending the night in the Ramada Inn just up the highway. Mama wants to stay in the room with me, but I tell her that I'm not dying, that she doesn't have to spend our last few minutes together before the Lord calls me home.

"Don't be a smartass, Darling," my father tells me. And he takes my mother and they leave. I don't know why I am so grouchy with her.

Bullshit. I do know. *Where are Lucas and Lowell? I've been here forty-eight hours. Where are they?*

And then, sometime during the night, I wake and find Lowell sitting by my bed.

"Where's Lucas," I say. Lowell's holding my hand just like my mother did.

"'Where's Lucas'?" he says. "Really?"

"Sorry. Dulled by the butter knife of poppies."

"Don't say anything. If this is going to be your level of discourse, please, say no more."

"My parents are taking me home."

"They told us the very same. It's a good thing, Darling."

"Will you come too?"

He laughs. "Brain smashed. Sense of humor the only survivor. No, sweetheart, we can't come with. We've got school. We have classes to go to. No brain-damage-two-week free pass for the likes of us. We'll have to muddle on. You just go home and get some rest and then come on back when you're feeling better."

"Where's Lucas?"

"Lucas, Lucas, Lucas. He's out in the hall talking to a handsome doctor, if you must know."

"My doctor?"

"Could be. I 'spect he's really just greasin' the wheels of our being here at four a.m. in the morning. You know, sweet-talkin' the Socratic oath out of him."

"Hippocratic."

"Oh yeah. So is there even such a thing as the Socratic oath?"

"I don't think so."

"Your servers are down, sweetie. I'm gonna look it up, if it's all the same." He lets go my hand and pulls out his phone and starts tapping.

"And will you swear the Socratic oath?" Me. Not knowing what I'm saying.

"Maybe. Remind me, what's the Hippocratic oath?"

"I don't know. First, do no harm?"

"So, what then the Socratic? First, answer a question with a question?"

"Sounds good to me."

"I will not take that oath."

"Why not?"

"I'll forget to do it."

"True. Much too confining. Don't you agree?"

"Agree to what?"

"You're doing fine so far."

Lowell walks around my bed to the window. I don't know what's outside there. I've only gone from the bed to the toilet and back, and that nursing-home wobbly.

"If twilight is the crack between the worlds, why isn't dawn also the crack between the worlds. They are the same things, just in reverse."

"Reverse. That would make dawn the world between the cracks."

"That doesn't make any sense."

"Sorry. Brain damage and all that."

He looks out at—the parking lot, a lake, interstate, 7-Eleven? "'The world between the cracks.' Yeah. May be."

Lucas comes in and kisses me on the cheek (first kiss, from either of them) and takes my chin in his hand and looks into my eyes. It's more doctorly than loverly.

"Fell down, did you?"

"I think so."

"Uh-huh. What do you think, Lowell?"

"What do you mean by 'think'?"

"What?"

"He's doing a thing," I say. "He took a Socratic—"

"—I don't think she fell down," Lowell says.

"Yeah, me neither. The doctor's of the impression that you'd have to fall down several times in several kinds of directions to do the level of damage that sweet Darling has done to herself. Is that what you did, love? Fall down, get up, fall down again. Over and over until you're nigh on to concussion and expansive contusion?"

"I'm not sure."

"She's not sure, Lowell."

"So I see."

"Odd thing, Darling, us right here calling you a liar and you just lying there taking it. Where's your outrage, your southern honor?"

"I'm guess I'm just not at my best right now, Lucas."

He leans in and puts his lips close to my ear.

"Say his name."

Lowell says, "You don't have to whisper."

I turn and kiss him on the cheek (yes, the first). My feelings are raging. My heart is pounding so hard it's making my head hurt even more. The easy thing would be to say that I love him, that I love him more than anything I've ever loved, that I love them both the same way, that I would do anything for them, *be anything for them*, and to say I love knowing they love me enough to pay Patrick Mitchell back in spades, if they could only get confirmation of his culpability.

Of course, it's more complicated than that. But right now, I don't care anything about Patrick Mitchell. I don't want revenge or payback or even justice. I love them. I love them both. I love the fact that they want to find him, they want to find him and beat him. Their want is everything. Their desire. It's like, I don't care if they never fuck me. I just want them to *want* to fuck me. *Desire me, desire to fuck me, desire to avenge me.* That's what I want. Right now, though, it's all little-sister stuff. They love me, I know that, just not the way I love them, not as much as I love them. But maybe, once in my life, somebody loved me that much. It's possible. You don't know.

The next day my parents pick me up from the hospital. I sit in the back seat with my suitcase, which my mother has packed for me. If I could think straight, I'd probably be worried about what all she might have found contraband-wise in my room and when she'll bring it up. But right now everything is too difficult. Too bright, like the eye doctor dilated me. Too loud. It's all making me a little nauseated, as is riding in the back seat.

I tap Mama on the shoulder and sign *sunglasses-yours-bright-hurt-head-me*

"Here, baby, take mine."

My father grabs his off his face and reaches them over the seat to me. They're way big, but that's all right. Great coverage. Then my mother tries to give him her sunglasses and he says he's not transitioning yet.

"Daddy!" I don't think my mother caught it. She wasn't looking at him. He didn't take his hands off the wheel.

"If you need to stop, just holler," he says.

Daddy switches on the radio. Talk. I don't try to listen to it. It's all bee-buzzy in the background of my thoughts. Then he turns off the highway.

"Where are we going?"

"We're going to your grandma Jean's."

Grandma Jean is my father's mother, distinguished from my mother's mother who is Grandma Ruth. I spent a part of every summer I can remember at Grandma Jean's. She lives out in the country, as they say. Daddy turns off the county road onto a dirt road, then another turn, then another. What they should call it is the deep-ass country. The land's hilly out here and Grandma Jean's house is on top of a little ridge. We park right up in the front yard, next to a sun-faded blue pickup. The ground slopes away behind the house, and down the hill a little ways are the two chicken houses and beyond them, a small pond. Past that is Jean's pasture and then somebody else's pasture and out on the horizon, a line of gray-green woods.

Grandma Jean comes out the front door, smiling, arms open to me. She's short and wiry, looking for all the world like Georgia O'Keefe in bifocals. She hugs me tight and kisses me three times on the cheek. Then she stands back to look at me.

"Big girl," she says and looks at my parents.

"Too big for her britches," my father says.

I give my father a look, but Jean whispers, "That doesn't mean what you think."

She hugs my mother and makes the few signs she knows: *welcome, love you.* She gives my father a kiss, and says, "Y'all come on in the house. I got some dinner ready."

Grandma Jean's husband, her second husband, Ed Moore, is perhaps the most cheerful and decent person I have ever met. And he just loves my mama to death. He knows zero sign language, but whenever we go out there, Ed grabs a yellow legal pad and sits Mama down at the kitchen table and the two of them take turns writing back and forth to each other half the day. Today he leads my mama into the dining room where he has a stack of pads and a handful of rollerball pens and they get right to it. Jean has to call them to dinner three times before Ed pays her any mind.

It's an old shotgun-style house with that long hall down the middle of it. At the back of the house is the kitchen, and it is five kinds of country cooking aromatic heaven. The table is spread with fried chicken and green beans and mashed potatoes and corn casserole and some kind of pie for dessert, maybe apple, maybe peach, hard to tell without cutting into it. I find I'm hungry, really hungry for the first time since those Fayetteville hamburgers.

After dinner, Jean and my father and I sit on the front porch and talk. I mostly listen. Ed and Mama are back at the dining-room table, flipping yellow pages and filling them with God knows what. I don't think Ed even talks to Jean that much. And what does my mama have to say to him? It cools off as the afternoon progresses, and my father brings out a blanket for me. My head nods and I jerk it up quickly.

Jean says, "Put your baby to bed, Horace."

"Just tell me what room, I can put myself to bed." But Ed and my mother have come out and, seeing what's what, Mama puts her arm around me and leads me to my cousin Janie's old room. I strip to my underwear and climb in between sheets that smell like wind and wildflowers. My mother lays a nightshirt across the foot of the bed and leaves. She signs something to me that I don't completely catch: *rest-love-something-something*

It's the middle of the night or thereabouts when I wake up. I can't find my phone. *Who is it I would call?* I pull on the nightshirt and go out into the hall. There's a soft light coming from the living room. Grandma Jean's left a lamp on. I open the front door and go out onto the porch. Chilly. It's all cicadas and bullfrogs and the thick scent of some night-blooming something somewhere. I sit in a rocking chair damp with dew. I won't be able to stay out here long.

When I was twelve, I spent the whole summer with Jean and Ed. Something was going on between my parents. It seemed to me like they might be headed for a divorce. They didn't fight or anything. At least not out where I could see it. But everything felt gritty and off balance with the tension of the unspoken.

The unsigned. Without much discussion about it, my father drove me up to Jean's, and my mother stayed home. He told me stories and sang songs the whole way. He was almost certainly trying to avoid any talk about whatever was up between him and Mama. We got to Jean's and I was sent on into the house, but I stood by the window and watched mother and son. Everything seemed perfectly normal between them, but she gave him what I thought at the time was a meaningful look as he got back into the car to drive home to my mother. And then she leaned in through the window and wouldn't let him drive off until she had said some more things to him. In the car, he had given me a book. It was titled *Oh, Promised Land*, by some Mississippi writer, and it turned out to be about early settlers in the state. It was a pretty good read, at the time and for a twelve-year-old, lots of towering trees and red dirt and brave, good-hearted men and women, but I didn't just read it. I scoured it for hidden meanings related to my parents' marriage and my status thereto like some absinthe-addled, deconstruction-maddened literary critic. Waste of time, it turned out. Daddy just liked the book and thought I might too. And to tell the truth, I did.

Every day Jean and Ed and I rose early and ate breakfast in the still, pale light of dawn, with the windows open and the leftover cool of the night seeping in. I followed Ed or Grandma Jean around all day as they did their work, trying to help or trying to stay out of the way. We ate a light dinner around noon and then napped under ceiling fans through the heat of the day. Around four, Ed would sometimes take off in his truck and be gone until after dark, doing who knows what. Other times he'd pull cane poles out of the barn and he and I would fish the still pond past the chicken houses and watch the light fall out of the woods in the distance. In the evenings, we sat on the porch and Grandma Jean told stories and sang old songs, and every once in a while Ed pulled out his autoharp and played "The Old Rugged Cross" and "Just as I Am" and other such hymns as he remembered from his strict Baptist upbringing until Grandma Jean would cluck her tongue and make him put it away.

One day, three boys knocked on the front door. They looked to be about my age, a little older maybe. Grandma Jean said they were the Henley brothers, Zach and Cody, and Jimmy Harlan. They showed up every now and then, she said, looking for cookies or a piece of pie or cake or anything else that Jean and Ed might give them. Jean enjoyed being the lady who gave out treats. Also, Ed told me later, what Jean really enjoyed was aggravating Mrs. Henley, who didn't believe in giving her young'uns sugary snacks. Jean handed me a Tupperware bowl full of oatmeal cookies she'd made the previous day and pushed me out the front door.

The boys were surprised to see me, and for a moment it looked like they might turn and run, but each took a cookie and mumbled his thanks and backed down off the porch and stood in the yard eating them. They stared at their feet, shuffled said feet. I sat in one of the rocking chairs and asked them if they didn't want to come up on the porch and take a seat. Sit a spell and talk. They looked at each other with puzzlement as if I'd given them a particularly knotty math problem. Finally, one of them, Zach it turned out to be, did come up and sit. I offered him another cookie and he took it. I shook the bowl at the other boys and they came back up onto the porch to get another one, but turned around and sat on the steps eating them, whispering, and looking over their shoulders at their boon companion and at me.

I was thinking that Zach was a shy boy who didn't talk much. Then he asked me if I liked fishing. I told him that Ed and I sometimes fished his little pond.

He snickered and said, "Don't catch much, I bet."

"We don't catch anything," I said. "But maybe some minnows."

"So, anyway, me and the boys here are going fishing tomorrow down to the Widow's Creek, if'n you cared to come along."

I said I would, and he said it was a date, and he stood up and tipped an imaginary hat and tapped the other boys on the shoulders and they all waved and ran off down the road. The next morning Ed took me out to the barn to get a pole. He gave me the best one and winked at me. Then we dug up some worms and put them into a little bait bag he'd fashioned out of an old sock.

"Don't stay out there all day," he said kindly. "Try to make it back for dinner, if you can. And watch out for them boys."

"Why?"

"Shucks, one of 'em's liable to propose matrimony to you and I don't want to have to explain to your folks how you done run off to the Niagara Falls."

I giggled and ran down to the road where the boys were already waiting for me in the creeping dawn. We walked down the dusty road for a mile or more and then lit out across a fallow cornfield. By and by, we stepped off into some woods, and half an hour of traipsing among tall, dark trees put us at the creek. It smelled cold and green and wet. Orange sun twinkling through the dark leaves. Zach led me to a spot I guess he liked and he laid out his implements.

We baited our hooks and dropped them into the swirl. Cody and Jimmy went downstream a bit, out of sight. We could hear them talking and laughing.

Zach and I fished with basically the same poles and the same bait, but in a couple of hours he had caught five nice crappies and a decent-size trout. I had caught one crappie. We put them on a stringer and dropped them into the water, then I followed Zach upstream about a hundred yards to a kind of hangout place I guess he and his friends had: an old coffee can half full of cigarette butts, some empty Coke bottles, candy wrappers, and a couple of broke-ass lawn chairs, where we sat down. Zach pulled off his T-shirt and opened a paper bag. He had a peanut butter sandwich, cut in half, and two apples. He handed me half the sandwich and took the other half and leaned back in the poor chair and chewed with his eyes closed. His skin was smooth and brown as a berry and his eyelashes were long and black. When we had eaten the apples, I began to wonder what time it was and if I should ask him to take me back to Grandma Jean's.

The other two boys came scrambling up, carrying their stringers of fish and ours. They'd had even more luck than Zach.

"Y'all ain't swimming yet?"

I stood up and looked at the creek. And, indeed, there was a perfect swimming hole right there: wide, slow, and, I guessed from the look of it, deep.

"I don't know about that, Jimbo," Zach said, looking at me out the corner of his eye.

"What?"

Zach tilted his head toward me and shrugged.

Jimmy and Cody looked at each other and laughed, then stripped naked and jumped into the water. I walked down to the bank and Zach followed me. We watched the boys splashing and laughing and diving deep and coming up sputtering.

"Sorry," Zach said. "Let's go."

The boys in the water were whispering and glancing sidewise at me.

"Don't you want to go swimming?" I said.

"We don't have to."

"It's hot," I said.

"That it is," he said.

I pulled off my shirt. My chest wasn't that much different from the boys'. I dropped my shorts and stood there in my underpants. The boys in the water were quiet now and no longer pretending not to look at me. I took a deep breath and stepped out of my panties. I started to jump into the swimming hole, but I hesitated. Every eye was on me. I turned toward Zach so that he could see me, and I said, "Are you coming too?" Then I jumped into the water.

It was shockingly cold. I was breathless and goosebumpy, but the water was silky and slow, and then Zach jumped in. I didn't see him come out of his clothes. The boys horsed around, dunking each other and racing, but no one bumped me or brushed up against me. We swam for a while and then Jimmy and Cody got out and ate the little dinners they'd brought with them. Zach and I swam some more, and he asked me about where I was from and what I was doing at Ed and Jean's house. I told him about Helena and where I went to school, about some of my friends, but I didn't mention the ongoing troubles of my parents.

Cody hollered at us: "Let's go home!"

Zach looked at me. Then he said, "Y'all go on. I'll catch up."

The boys laughed and turned to go. When they were out of sight, one of them called, "Zach's got a girlfriend."

The trees overhung the river and fashioned a ragged canopy so that the sunlight fell dappled and bouncy onto the water. I had gotten used to the temperature of the river. I had never swum naked before. I felt—something. I want to say "liberated" or "free," but that's not quite right. I think what I felt right then was "grown." I felt like I was an adult, which, of course, includes such things as liberation and freedom, but also contains, I don't know, let's say, power. I felt powerful. I felt in control. Which, I guess now, was a weird thing to be thinking, inasmuch as I was butt nekkid and far from home and with a boy I didn't really know. Looking back, I suppose I was right there on the verge of victimhood, if Zach had turned out to be a psycho or some such.

I wasn't really swimming, just treading water, pushing myself against the water. Amazingly different, to swim without pants, to feel the water between my legs. How did those few micro-millimeters of bathing suit fabric hold off this sensation of water right on my pussy? I was thinking I never wanted to wear a bathing suit again. I turned and turned with my eyes closed like a water ballerina entranced. Zach kept his distance, but I felt him watching me.

Power. Right there under the surface. He wanted something. Something of me. I tried to picture how far and into what reaches his imagination was wandering.

I moved a little closer to him and he moved a little closer to me. We circled each other like boxers. We were within inches of each other. Inches. Less. He stared into my eyes. He was looking for something in there. His breath came quickly. Of course, it could have been the effort of treading water for so long. I closed the distance between us and I felt his cock against my leg. It was small, of course. He was twelve, but it was hard. He kissed me. Our lips were tightly closed, like we were kissing our parents, but he kissed me nonetheless. He wanted something, but maybe he didn't yet know what it was. I liked him.

I let myself sink under the water and pushed myself down, down, but I couldn't find any bottom and the water got colder and colder until I frightened myself and came rushing to the surface, gasping.

"Ain't there no bottom to this?" I said.

He smiled and said, "Not none that I ever found, but to tell you the truth, I don't wanna be going that deep noways."

We climbed out and chastely dressed without looking at each other. At least, I didn't. We gathered up our poles and grabbed up the stringer of fish and headed back. When we got to Jean and Ed's, they were on the porch, waiting, I realized later, for me to get back instead of napping like they shoulda been at this time of day. Zach held up the stringer of fish and they applauded him.

"Did you catch none yourself, Darling?" Grandma Jean said and winked at me.

"One of them," I said, though I didn't take her meaning at the time.

I had, in fact, caught Zach. We spent the summer together.

And it was the great ballyhooed Golden Summer of legend. We ran the fields and prowled the greeny woods and the glens and the dales and all that other Wordsworthy kind of stuff, except that in all our traipsing and traveling about the countryside, we weren't driven to poetry. I think we were driven to love. At least, I was. Cody and Jimbo grudgingly left us mostly alone. We did go fishing with them a couple of times a week (though we did our swimming without them). Running the fields, rolling down hills, lying on our backs under the burned-out white sky of full summer. Sometimes he would lie on top of me and he would kiss me with that tight-lipped hard kiss we had. Sometimes I lay on top of him. And I did kiss him, but mostly I just looked at his face, the scatter of freckles, that little button nose, those lashes black as split silk. In the heat of the day we sheltered under the trees where the silver voices of the birds and the sawing of crickets lulled us into a green drowse.

One night toward the end of the summer, after Ed and Jean had gone to bed, I crept down the long hall and creaked open the front door and Zach was waiting for me in front of the house. I don't guess Jean or Ed would have minded all that much that I was going out of a night. With Zach. But the tiptoeing and the sneaking and the squeaky front door jacked up my level of excitement and enjoyment in the enterprise. I didn't know what Zach had in mind, but he was proving to be a fine guide to the elemental pleasures of country life. And I had placed all my trust in him to be that guide, and it was my intention to follow him, like unto the very love-struck puppy that I so resembled.

He took my hand and we headed for the road. We walked in the fine powdery dust, like walking in talcum. When we reached the crest of the ridge, he pointed at the horizon and the moon that was almost gone, the fine white edge of it, a fingernail clinging to the rim of the planet, falling now as we stood there in wonder, like Adam and Eve, curious and willful children in an empty world.

Then we climbed a rail fence and headed toward a barn, dark and looming in the night. A ladder leaned against the side, and up we went. I was a little scared, that the roof wouldn't support our weight, that we would fall off, I don't know. The roof was tin, maybe. Some kind of metal anyway. Zach lay down and put his arms behind his head, so I did the same. The sky was clear, and the stars were bright and hard like the tips of spears. The blackness of the space between the stars looked more like substance than emptiness, velvety, almost like you could touch it. I moved the back of my hand against his hand and he took it and squeezed it. I thought he would kiss me now. Wasn't that why he brought me up here?

Yes, I know we were only children, but I thought we were on the trembling verge of adulthood, of sin. We had kissed, we had touched, we had lain atop one another, he had pushed against me in what I now suppose was an instinctive way of simulating sex. Dry humping, I guess you'd call it. I don't know. Maybe the lizard part of his brain knew how to fuck before the front part of his brain did, or maybe boys just know this stuff instinctively. Or maybe country boys see things town boys don't, cows and such going at it. Shoot, maybe his parents had already explained it to him. My father had. In any case, I kept expecting him to push our making out to another level. I was ready to follow wherever he wanted to lead. That night, as I lay on the metal roof of that barn, with the heat of the day's sun leaching out of it through me into the night, I hoped he would climb onto me and do something we could never come back from. Almost every night that summer I had masturbated in Grandma Jean's spare bedroom, and even though I understood the mechanics of intercourse, they seemed unreal to me. I couldn't imagine what actually doing it would be like. But I was there. I was right there and ready. I was a more-than-willing participant in whatever he might make happen. I was a Stockholm-syndromed victim of love.

What happened instead was that great blazing stars fell on Arkansas.

It was a meteor shower, and for hours we watched rocks from outer space tear through the hard atmosphere and burn up like angels falling out from the doors of heaven. It went on and on and forever, and eventually I drifted off to sleep. It was close to dawn when Zach shook my shoulder and said we needed to climb down now and get on home. On the porch, just before I went in, he kissed me. Of course. But this time, before his lips touched mine, he gently thumbed my bottom lip down so that my mouth was slightly open, and when he did kiss me, his mouth was a little open too, and I felt like I was on fire, like hot stars were falling on me, piercing me with their hard points, sticking into my body, and I was like a Christmas tree, struck by lightning, burning, shining like a spinning galaxy rushing away from the world out into the emptiest of spaces, beyond any imagination. His hands were on my shoulders and I wanted him to move them over me, to explore me, to spread me like a map, to find the undiscovered countries and untapped rivers and lakes within me.

After he turned and was walking away, it occurred to me that he would probably go home and get in his bed and masturbate. And that he probably masturbated every night. He was a boy, after all, and while I might be a strange and unusual girl who sometimes did it, boys did it all the time. At least that was what I'd heard. Many nights that summer, I lay in Grandma Jean's spare bed and rubbed myself against my pillow, picturing Zach, remembering him kissing me, lying on top of me, feeling his hard little dick against my leg, my stomach, and now I wondered what he pictured or remembered as he touched himself. As he kissed me that night, I thought I had felt his tongue close to my lips, my open mouth. Would he ever go any further?

A few days later I ran out the front door and jumped off the porch holding the last biscuit with butter and jelly dripping out of it onto my hand, and I gave it Zach. We walked around to the back of the house while he ate it. He bent down to the spigot and took a long drink. He wiped his mouth with the back of his hand and pointed south across Ed and Jean's cow pasture.

In all the days of our summer wanderings, we had never gone out in this direction. Today we hugged the edge of the woods and at one point found a tangle of blackberry bushes pushing out into the pasture. I ate two good handfuls. Eventually we came to a dirt road and headed off east. By and by we arrived at a little settlement of tarpaper houses. Chickens and children pecked and played in the dust. Not much was going on, no grown-ups were out and about. At a house at the end of the road, a man sitting in tattered lawn chair in front of the place stood up and waved a hand at Zach.

"How are you, young man?" the old gentleman said.

"I'm fine, Mr. Fennel. This is my friend, Darling. She's been staying up to Mr. Ed and Miss Jean's place this summer."

"Mr. Ed and Miss Jean. That's nice," he said. "How are you, Miss Lady?"

"Tolable," I said and curtseyed.

"'Tolable,'" he said and laughed. "She's a sharp one, Mr. Zach."

"I believe you're right, sir," Zach said.

"'Darling.' That's a right nice name you got yourself there, young lady. You just wait here a minute, I'm gonna show you something."

He went into the house and in a short minute came back with a fiddle and a bow. He settled himself into his chair again and slapped the bow against the strings a couple of times, wrenched the tuning knobs some, and lit into a lively number. All the kids gathered around and went to dancing. They were joyous and their braids flew and flashed with colorful ribbons and pieces of cloth. The tune was bouncy, it might be called a reel, I think, and then, to my eternal surprise and great joy, Zach started dancing too. His was a strange blend of sixties hippie-style arm flailing and downhome country foot stomping that together were somehow both happy-making and heart-rending, and I thought right then and there that I loved him, that all the kissing and skinny-dipping and empty-wanting-to-be-filled feelings I had notwithstanding, I loved him. I mean, I *love* loved him. Because he was a good kid, a genuinely good soul, a decent and lovely person with a heart of pure gold, and I was right then struck as if by lightning with the quite real fear that I'd leave this place and never see him again, and never again find someone so pure and so open and so enamored of me.

When the song came to its abrupt but satisfying end, the children all jumped and shouted and called for Mr. Fennel to play another one, but a woman came out of one of the houses and yelled at the children to get gone and stop scaring the chickens, and the kids scattered and Mr. Fennel set the fiddle on his knee and bowed his head. The woman gave me a particularly hard look, I thought, and went back in, letting the screen door slam shut.

Mr. Fennel looked up at us and his smile was heartfelt and his eyes were sad. He raised the fiddle to his chin once more and played a slow tune and it was full of so much—I don't know—longing? Sweetness? Sadness? My heart was full; I felt like I was on the verge of tears. Zach stepped up to me as if asking me to dance and I put my arms around his neck and he put his hands on my hip bones and we rocked in place, barely moving our feet, and looking into each other's eyes and I know mine were brimming with tears and then he pulled me to him and my face was in his neck and the tears fell and the dust and salt mingled on his shoulder and I thought I would never again be so miserable and so happy.

The song came to its sad end, and Mr. Fennel stood up and shook Zach's hand and he bowed to me and he went into his little shack. Zach took my hand and we walked back through the settlement the way we came. The children looked up from their play and a couple of them wiggled their fingers at us in goodbye.

We spent the rest of the morning wandering the hills south of Ed and Jean's. We found some high spots from where we could see the late summer landscape spread out before us, brilliant green alfalfa and corn under the blazing sky. Honestly, I felt like we were the lords of all creation, at home in a beautiful world just for us, an Eden. In the prettiest places, the deep greeny-black shades of the trees, Zach kissed me with our new open-mouth kisses and held me so tightly against him that I wanted to put my hand down his pants. Even now I wonder what formidable, unspoken, subliminal constructions of girlhood stopped me.

It must have been close to noon because I was getting hungry. Zach's house, it turned out, was closer than Jean's, so we went there looking for some dinner. Zach's mother was standing on the porch with her arms folded across her chest when we got there. She looked all kinds of pissed off.

"Mama, this is—"

"Shut yo mouth." She pointed at me. "Is this the little hussy you been runnin' around with these past few days? And nights?"

"Mama—"

"Don't bother. Get yo behind in the house, right now. And you, you go on back to town where you belong, you little tramp. I'm not gonna have my boy traipsing all over Baxter County with some floozy. Go on! Get yo nasty little butt outta here before I take a switch to you!"

I turned and ran and didn't stop until I was on the road to Jean's. I walked slowly, crying and thinking, hoping really, that Zach would come after me, walk me home, say nice things to me. But he didn't. He wasn't a grown man, he couldn't just tell his mother to go to hell, defend me, take my side against her. He was a kid, my age, ridiculously caught between childhood and—whatever came next.

When I stepped up onto the porch at Ed and Jean's, I was still sniffling, and I didn't want them to see me in such a state, so I sat in one of the rockers and tried to compose myself. I didn't do so well. Remembering Zach's mama and the things she'd said to me, I started crying again, and that gave way to some straight up wailing, and then Ed and Jean were out there, asking me what was going on, looking me over and patting me down for injury. They took me inside and to the kitchen where Ed pulled me up onto his lap and Jean went to wiping my face with a wet cloth.

When I finally stopped crying and could talk, I told them what Zach's mother had said to me and the names she'd called me and that I didn't know if I'd ever see Zach again and that I loved him so much, and then I cried some more against Ed's chest.

Jean, who'd been squatting by me, went to stand up, but Ed took hold of her arm and they struggled comically against one another, she trying to stand, he holding her down. She finally tipped over out of her crouch and sat smack down on the floor with Ed still grasping her arm.

"Let go of me, you old fool."

"I'm not gonna do any such a thing. You listen to me, Jean Moore. You're not going down to that woman's house and start nothing."

"Finish it, is more like it."

"And do what? What Christian thing will you do, huh? What godly thing will you say? Are you going over there to turn the other cheek? And what will Darling Jean here learn about how to deal with the raging heathen?"

"Please don't go, Grandma Jean. Please," I said.

She stopped struggling and sat there on the floor, looking up at me in Ed's lap.

"No, child, I won't go. I promise." Then she looked at Ed and something passed between them that I, as a child, was not privy to.

I didn't see Zach for a week. The summer was coming to an end. It was probably the most miserable seven days of my entire life. And then, like out of nowhere, it was the last Friday of my visit. On Sunday, my parents would drive up to get me and I would go back home and start getting ready for the school year, shopping with Mama, picking out outfits and shoes and binders and notebooks and such. After breakfast, I sulked around the house, following Jean while she worked until she shooed me outside. I walked down to the pond and dropped biscuit crumbs into the water and watched the littlest of the fishes come up to the surface, bumping their heads together trying to get them.

I stared out across our pasture and Mr. Henderson's to the line of trees beyond. I'd like to say that I was conflicted, but I wasn't. There was no conflict: I absolutely did not want to go home. I did not want to go back to school. I did not want to see my friends. It wasn't like I wanted my friends *and* Zach. My parents *and* Zach. I just wanted him. I wanted to stay here, with my feet in the dust and my hand in his. I was in the tight fist of a breathless crush and I wanted more than anything to languish there. No Romantic poet ever loved the land and the boy more than I.

I walked back up to the house and in through the kitchen door. Grandma Jean smiled at me and said that my boy was out front. I ran down the hall and busted out through the screen door onto the porch. Zach and Ed were out by Ed's truck with their heads together, talking something over. I didn't like the look of it, but Zach smiled at me and I knew everything was going to be okay. Ed clapped Zach on the shoulder and headed over to the barn, giving me a distracted wave. Zach had a small, soft-sided cooler which I assumed had some dinner for us, and we ran off down the road. When we climbed the embankment up to the blasted old cornfield, I knew we were headed for the creek. I thought it would be nice, one more dip into that cold, cold water with Zach, once more to feel him hard against my leg.

We took a different route there than before and ended up at a spot way far upstream from the swimming hole. There we met Cody and Jimbo, who were just arriving. They were lugging two giant inner tubes, like out of tractor tires or something. The boys all slapped hands and Zach gave them something I couldn't see and the other boys turned and headed out through the woods, calling to us to have a good time and not get drownded.

"We're floating today," Zach said.

"To where?"

"To wherever."

"Sounds good to me." I was fine floating away with him and maybe never coming back, following the snaking trail of the creek down to the ocean and then off the edge of the world, if that's where he wanted to take me.

We manhandled the tubes down to the water and got situated in them. Zach held the cooler in his lap, and the current tugged us southward. The tubes bumped against each other and drifted apart and then together again. We talked. About nothing. About everything. Sometimes we would hold hands and float together, sometimes one of us would get farther downstream than the other, under canopies of overhanging trees, in the bright sun where the creek wandered out through somebody's pasture, past cows watching us curiously.

After a couple of hours, we came to a huge sandbar at a turn in the creek. There we pulled the tubes up onto the sand and took the cooler and sat under a clutch of willow trees and ate. Peanut butter and jelly (Zach's favorite, I'd learned) and overly ripe pears.

Zach walked down to the water and washed the pear juice and peanut butter off his hands, then came back and tapped me on the shoulder, saying, "Tag, you're it," and ran. I jumped up and took off after him. He made several good moves around a fallen and rotting tree, but I caught him and took off myself.

Turns out I was faster than him. And finally, I had to let him catch me so we could continue to play.

We got really hot running in the sand, and so we stripped out of our clothes and got in the river. There was no deep place for swimming so we had to just sit on our bottoms in the current and cool off. We'd been sitting there a few minutes, me trying to catch my breath from the icy water, Zach staring off into the trees on the other bank, when he started singing, soft at first, shyly, then full-voiced, echoing off the trees and filling the countryside with music.

The song was all about being alone on a lost highway, about a sinful life full of cards and wine and women's lies. He had a clear, sweet voice. I think there were four or five verses. He knew them all. When he finished, I clapped and said it was good.

I told him I didn't know the song. He said it was by Hank Williams, that his mama had a number of record albums by Hank and that he'd listened to them all many, many times. He said that sometimes his mama asked him and his brother to sing the songs off the albums instead of her just playing them on the record player, and that they obliged her. His brother Cody, he said, had the better voice, but they enjoyed singing together and entertaining their mama.

"We know all the words to just about ever song ole Hank ever wrote."

I asked about the song he'd just sung, and he said it was called "Lost Highway," and that like most of Hank's songs, it was sorrowful and that it predicted, according to Zach's mama, his early demise at the hands of alcohol and drugs.

"He died of alcohol and drugs?"

"From what I hear tell."

"Just how young was he?"

"In his twenties, I believe."

"Wow. That's bad."

"Wrote a lot of songs, though, in that time."

"Will you oblige me by singing another?"

He grinned and sang a tune called "I'm So Lonesome I Could Cry," and the title was no lie. It was powerfully sad and Zach could a put a real hurt-sounding twang in his voice. When he concluded, we got out of the river and went and stood over our clothes, waiting for the sun to dry us. Zach gave me a look and then fell down in the sand and went to rolling. He was still river wet and the sand stuck to him all over, and when he stood up again, he looked for all the world like a sugared doughnut. I shrugged and then got down in the sand and rolled and rolled until I was dizzy. I stood up, a little shakily, and we stood there looking at each other. He crossed the short distance between us and put his hands on my shoulders and kissed me. I stepped into it, pushing my gritty body against his. We kissed a long time and rubbed against each other, but the sand took a fair amount of the pleasure out of that. I stepped back and said, "I gotta wash this sand off." He nodded and we walked down to the water and splashed ourselves clean.

Without waiting to dry, we put on our clothes and Zach dragged some dry branches together and lit a fire. We sat across the fire from each other and fed it little sticks and pine cones and dry leaves. Zach stepped off into the woods and came back with a branch off some evergreen bush. When he put it on the fire, it smoked like crazy, a wild, eye-stinging, but fragrant, smoke that even to this day when I smell it carries me back to that sandbar and to that boy.

We lay back on the sand, and I fell into what I can only describe as a waking dream, neither asleep nor awake. Then I heard Zach calling to me. He was down by the creek, getting the inner tubes into the water. I walked down there and I caught him to me and kissed him. He gave me a look and I thought he was about to say something. What?

We lay down on the soft, wet sand next to the water and kissed like there would be no tomorrow.

As indeed there would not be.

And I thought, *Now.* Now he will do that which he must have dreamed so many times of doing with me. But he just kissed me and pushed against my belly, as he'd done before. We weren't going there, wherever *there* was. I didn't care. I just wanted him. Not what he'd do, not what he wanted or what I'd fantasized about. Just him. Just Zach.

We floated the rest of the afternoon until I thought we must be in Louisiana. Maybe it was true and we were never going back, to Ed and Jean's, to his mother's, to the bittersweet longings of childhood. The shadows were lengthening across the creek when I saw Ed standing on a bridge up ahead of us waving. We pulled the tubes out of the water and up to the road, where Ed and Zach loaded them into the back of Ed's pickup. Then we drove back, Ed and Zach talking the whole way about the creek and the relative differences in tube and fishing boats for navigating the trip. Every mile toward home filled me with despair. Is despair too strong a word for a child's fears of losing everything? Everything? Ed dropped Zach and the tubes off just down the road from his house. I guess he didn't want to face off with Zach's mother. I know I didn't. Zach shook Ed's hand and thanked him for his help in arranging the float. He came around to the passenger side and leaned through the window as if to kiss me. I turned my face to him, but he just said goodbye.

I fought tears all the way home. Ed drove in silence. He was a good man, a better man than I knew at the time, I think.

On Sunday, both my parents drove up to get me. They were smiling and happy and talking out of my earshot with Jean and Ed. At least my daddy was. Mama was peeking over Jean's shoulder at me, a little smile on her face, almost like she knew. About Zach. Which she didn't. Which she couldn't have. Whatever had been bothering my parents looked to be done. But so was my summer. So was—he didn't come. To say goodbye. I was thinking maybe he saw my parents' car and knew—what? Our summer was over? Our—whatever—was over? That's what I knew. I loaded my stuff into the car, kissed Jean and Ed goodbye, and climbed into the back seat. I tried to maintain a good disposition, but I heard my father say to Jean that I must have had a great summer because it was clear that I didn't want to go back home. Jean didn't reply, but looked at me, kinda sadly. I had to turn away from her. We drove off down the dusty road toward the highway and home. I didn't watch the side of the road going by, didn't look for Zach standing in a field or among some trees watching my passing, my passing out of his life forever. I stared at the back of the seat and fought tears.

Grandma Jean mostly leaves me alone. Every day I look into the mirror and every day the bruise on my face fades a little more, from blue-black to a sickly yellow. She won't let me help much, a little in the kitchen, turning pork chops or stirring beans on the stove. We sit on the porch in the evenings and watch the color drain out of the world. I have trouble distinguishing the buzzing in my head from the cicadas, but I do feel more steady on my feet as time goes by.

One evening I say, "Whatever happened to Zach?" And then add, "And his brother?"

"Well, let's see. Cody, the brother, is still home with his

mama, of course. He's a mite younger than you, still at the Consolidated high school over in Mitchell. Zach finished school and last I heard he'd gone into the army, up to South Carolina for training, then overseas somewheres."

"The army," I say. "That doesn't sound good."

"The country is a hard place to get away from, Darling. It's easy to get trapped here. I don't suppose ole Zach was as good at the books as you are, so college wasn't his road out."

"I guess. But the army. A body could get killed there."

"True enough, I reckon. Let's hope the Good Lord is looking out for him, wherever he be."

"Let's do hope that."

"He was five or six kinds of sweet on you that summer."

I let that hang in the air between us.

"Well, I was pretty sweet on him too."

"You don't say."

"Don't tease an invalid, Grandma Jean."

"He was a good boy, Zach. So was his brother. They came around all the next summer, looking for sweets and such. I think he was still looking for you to come tearing out that door."

"You're gonna make me cry, Jean."

"I'll hush then."

I cry a little bit anyway, quietly, in the soft twilight.

Late Sunday afternoon, we arrive at Chandler and my daddy and mama walk me into the dorm.

"I can get in by myself," I say, but kindly.

Daddy says, "I know that. Can't a man spend a few more minutes with his poorly daughter before that long drive home?"

"It's not that long. And I'm not that poorly."

"Give me your key." He opens the door to my room.

The aroma is overwhelming. The room is filled with flowers: roses, honeysuckle, gardenias, stuff I don't even recognize. "Oh my," says my father.

"Understatement, Daddy."

Mama walks around smelling the flowers and signing *look-look.* On the bookshelf, clematis droops, and I walk over and put my face to them.

The boys have put a new blanket on my bed. I am assuming there are new sheets under it too, 1,500-thread-count Egyptian or something equally crazy extravagant. The blanket is, in fact, a quilt. White. Stylized crimson branches with long pointy thorns stretch from a clover-shaped center and birds on the wing impale tiny creatures on them. Or wait to. Weirdest pattern I ever saw. *Where did they even find such a thing?*

Two-liter Coke, spicy pork rinds, five or six Slim Jims, and a dozen or so three-packs of Ferrero-Rocher have replaced my lamp and alarm clock on my nightstand.

Mama picks up the Slim Jims and says, *Somebody-know-you-like.* She looks around and adds, *generous very.*

I want them to leave. I need them to leave. I hug them. I tell them that I'm feeling so much better now, that this show of support from my cohorts has really buoyed my spirits. I talk in clichés. What is wrong with me? I don't say that what I want more than anything, what really would make me feel that God is up in His Heaven and all right, is that the boys are out there somewhere in the unfolding twilight, waiting for my parents to leave.

So that they can come get me.

I take my mother's arm and walk her through the door and out into the hall, hoping my father is following, signing and talking the whole time, as if they won't notice me getting rid of them. I talk all the way down to the car and I put her in it and kiss her before I shut the door.

I look over the top of the car at my father. He says, "Come around here and give me a hug. You can run us off, but not without my hug."

I hug him as tightly as a body can. He holds my shoulders and says, "Bye, girl. Try to be more careful with my daughter, would you?"

And he gets in the car, and they head off for home.

I turn 360 degrees in the parking lot, but I don't see them anywhere. They don't show up at the dining hall nor are they waiting for me at my room when I get back. *Where are they*?

The next morning I lie in my new sheets and stare at the ceiling. I reach over and grab a Slim Jim and peel it. Not much of a breakfast. Maybe if I run to the dining hall, I'll see them there. No, breakfast is surely over by now. *Why didn't they come to me last night? Or this morning? Why is it so urgently and vitally important to me? Why am I such a girl?*

I get up and dress. I need a shower but have overslept. I wash my face with a wet wipe, so now I'm feeling every kind of white trashy, but I have to get out of here and find them. When I open the door, Lucas and Lowell are sitting in the hall right across from my room, leaned up against Pamela Richardson's door. They get up and pretend to brush themselves off.

"Beginning to think you'd never get up, girl," Lucas says.

"We've been sittin' out here for two hours," Lowell says and pushes past me into the room.

"Do you not make your bed of a morning, Darlin'?" he says.

He and Lucas start arranging the bedclothes. "Whoa. Look at this." Lucas is holding up the empty Slim Jim wrapper.

"Lord a mercy, Darlin'. Seven-eleven trash for breakfast is one thing. I think we're all guilty of that oncet in a while. But just dropping the leavings of such right up here in the bed? I think you might be hopeless."

I fling myself onto the bed before they can get it made up. I love them. I want them to fall onto the bed with me, roll up with me in the sheets and quilt. I say, "These things are so beautiful. I just want to lie here all day."

The boys look at each other over me. Then they reach down and pull me up off the bed and finish making it up.

"You need to get your butt to class, girlfriend. You are so behind. Taking a week off." Lucas shakes his head.

"Can we hit the caf first? Is it open? I'm starving."

Lowell chucks me the pork rinds and says, "Closed. We're barely gonna make it to Whitman's class as is. Try to keep your mouth closed while you're chewing. He doesn't need the distraction."

"The distraction?"

"We're talking about abortion today," Lucas says and smiles at Lowell.

"Oh lordy. What are y'all up to?"

In the hall outside Whitman's classroom, Lowell opens the pork rinds for me. We trail in and find our usual seats by the windows. A lot of eyes are cutting at me. Some folks are openly staring. They're all curious about where I've been and I'm sure there have been stories about what happened. I'd love to hear all the variations and permutations of all the rumors that must be swirling the campus, since nobody really knows except Patrick and me, though I'm sure everyone has a pet theory. Lucas and Lowell haven't mentioned the incident this morning. They are acting as if everything is just like it was before. The whole thing is fading, I hope, like the last yellow of the bruise on my cheek.

"How you feeling, Darling?" some girl says from behind me. I turn to answer but can't distinguish who spoke, and so I say to the back of the room that I'm fine and thanks for asking. As I sit down, it occurs to me that the question may have been sarcastic. I look over my shoulder to see if I can figure out who asked. There are four girls in the back two rows. I know their faces but not their names. *How do they know mine?*

Dr. Whitman comes in and drops his briefcase on the desk and writes the word "Abortion" on the whiteboard. Then he turns and looks out over the class. When he sees me, he smiles and nods. He says, "I'm hoping you have given our topic some thought. And I hope you have been working to separate the emotion from the reason surrounding this issue, as we discussed. Nothing wrong with emotion, with passion. I encourage you to bring both to your life and to your purposes and goals. But here, in the classroom, we seek to dispassionately examine hard issues and difficult, controversial topics with an eye to establishing a firm foundation of logic and evidence and reason on which to carry our passions."

"What does abortion have to do with the history of philosophy?" I whisper to Lucas, who shushes me and takes a pork rind from my bag.

A boy who wears a white shirt and black pants every day raises his hand. He has, by my count, four ties that he wears in rotation on the white shirt. Shirts, I hope. I mean, of course, shirts, plural. He's not wearing the same one every day, surely. Today he has knotted up his paisley tie, maroon and blue swirls, like psychedelic sperms lost in a fallopian wilderness. Did he wear this one on purpose? Or am I reading too much into the paisley? And—do I read too much into everything? I think his name is Henry.

When Whitman acknowledges him, might-be-Henry rises from his desk and says, "I think everything hinges on the moment of conception."

No student has ever stood up to speak in this class, or in any class I'm taking. It seems like a gesture out of the past, something out of an old movie, an English movie, like the wearing of the white shirt and black pants thing. Might-be-Henry speaks up regularly in this class and yet he has never risen from his seat to do so before. Something is different about today? Or about this topic?

Henry—I'm just going to go ahead and call him that—lets that assertion hang in the air until Whitman asks, "Where are we going with this, Harold?"

Fine. Harold then. Harold says, "The crux of the argument seems to be the point at which life begins."

Someone behind me says, "After graduation, I hope," and the class laughs. Harold looks around the room, a little hurt, I think.

"People, please," Whitman says and nods at Harold to continue.

"If," Harold says, "we could determine with precision the

moment that life begins, we could intelligently discuss the issue of whether or not abortion is murder."

Several students murmur, *Murder?*

"That's a loaded word, Harold," Whitman says.

"I think it's accurate though. Don't you, sir?" Harold is pretty sure, it seems, that Dr. Whitman is solidly pro-life. He's looking for affirmation.

Whitman deflects. "Does anyone else have an opinion?"

Several hands go up. Whitman points at a young woman I don't know, though she has sorority written all over her.

"You can only murder a person," she says. "A tiny mass of cells is not a person."

"What about late-term abortion?" This comes from a boy that's in my algebra class. Stan? Sam? I don't know.

"What about it?" the girl says.

"That baby is not a 'tiny mass of cells,' now, is it?"

"It's not a baby either." She fairly yells this.

"Let's keep it civil, folks," Whitman says.

"Why not? It looks like a baby when they tear it out of the womb."

The girl flinches but says, "Can you hold it? Nurse it? Rock it to sleep? Take pictures of it? No. Thus, not a baby."

"That's the stupidest thing I've ever heard," Algebra boy says.

"Stop right there," Whitman interjects. "If we can't discuss this in a civil manner, we have no business being in a college classroom. We will not make this personal."

Algebra boy says, "I'm sorry. I didn't mean to say you were stupid, just the argument you were making."

"Better," Whitman says. "But not much."

Lucas and Lowell are hanging back. What are they waiting for?

Algebra boy says, "I'm just saying that, yeah, maybe forty-eight hours after conception all you have is a bunch of cells, but at some point, a month or two down the road, those cells become a baby. You can see the baby on a sonogram. Eventually it looks just like it will when it delivers in a couple of weeks. You're saying that as long as it's inside the mother, it's not a baby. That somehow the act of sliding down the birth canal confers personhood on the baby. And I'm just saying that makes no sense."

"Yeah," someone says. "By that logic you could abort the child during labor and it wouldn't be killing a baby."

Harold stands again and says, "This is exactly my point. If we could know for sure the point at which the—let's say, entity—goes from being a bunch of cells to a baby, we could solve this."

"Such a determination may not be possible," Whitman says.

Harold seems to want to say something but sits down instead. There's a moment of silence. Then Lucas speaks up.

"In truth, there really is no point in our discussing abortion at all in this class."

Oh, the look on Whitman's face.

Lucas continues. "If I've been paying attention this semester, and I think I have, in this class we work in a Socratic method. That is to say, in the process of argumentation. Can I assume we all agree on that?"

No one disagrees. Though it should be noted, no one agrees either. At least not out loud. Lucas continues. "Argumentation is not about winning an argument, which, frankly, sounds like what all of you are trying to do. Argumentation, and I think Dr. Whitman will back me up here, is designed to reduce conflict. Argumentation should lead, by its back and forth dialectical method, toward compromise." And here Dr. Whitman nods his agreement. But he doesn't look happy. Whatever else he knows, he must surely know that Lucas is not a peacemaker. And that this is not going to end well.

Lucas says, "But this topic, this discussion, is a complete waste of time. There is no compromise possible in the abortion debate. Let me repeat that: *there is no compromise possible in the abortion debate.*" And here Whitman tries to cut him off, but Lucas raises his voice, not yelling exactly, but more like commanding.

"Let me posit something I believe to be axiomatically true: if you truly believe in your heart of hearts that abortion is the murder of a baby, *the murder of a baby, I say*, then you should, by god, fight against it every day with everything you have. Debate? Compromise? On murdering babies? Are you kidding me? Are you fucking kidding me? What kind of person sits around politely debating baby murder? Baby holocaust? You're just gonna sit here and allow this abomination to continue? You should be out in the streets fighting—politically, physically, if necessary—with everything you can bring to bear."

Several people look uncomfortable. Maybe they do think abortion is murder, but what are they supposed to do about it? Stand in front of women's clinics with signs? Bomb abortion clinics? Kill gynecologists?

And now, to my total and everlasting surprise, Lowell stands up and says, "Now now, my little California boy, lend me yo ear for a moment."

As if. As if they haven't planned this, composed it, rehearsed it, tweaked it. Rehearsed it again. Now let me say that at this point I imagine Lowell's standing up may have been improvised, prompted as it were by Harold's standing. Nevertheless, it is effective.

"I am, by no means, a libertarian." By the time he hits the word "libertarian," Lowell is in full Quentin Compson southernese. "But I do find governmental overreach intolerable." He turns and smiles down on me. And I get it. In a blinding, road-to-Damascus flash, I get it.

Lowell has donned his black silk shirt, tucked tightly into his tightest faded jeans. When he turns away from me toward class and I have him in profile, I can see the bulge of his cock. Shoot, he may very well have a sock in there too. In fact, he must have. Of course he does. I've seen his cock. This is not it. This is a kielbasa or something taped to his leg. And him standing up—*hello, clearly not improvised, Darling.* And he reeks of Versace Eros. The whole room must smell it. He's making a slow turn, a full circle, almost but not quite doing his Gladiator thing, making eye contact with everyone in the room. I'm sorry. With every woman in the room. I turn in my desk and look toward the back. The four women there have fixed their eyebeams on him, two of them staring at his movie-star face, the other two, I don't know, sausage shopping?

"Let me be perfectly clear. The United States government (he pronounces it Newnited States Gubmen) has absolutely no business whatsoever intruding into the medical affairs of its citizens. Who would ill agree? The idea of some governmental, sinecured, goat-sniffin' weasel sticking his snout in between doctor and patient. Well, it's just ludicrous. On so many levels. But it's nothing compared to this notion. Hear me now. Hear me right now. That the government, whether located in Washington DC or in the statehouse at Little Rock, would tell a woman that she will have a baby—*will have a baby, will she or nil she*—is absolutely and unequivocally insufferable. It is egregiously insufferable. And overreaching. And more to the point, it is my contention that anti-abortion politicians are, at this very moment, attempting to retrograde women into their former status as male property, through enforced childbearing. Forcing a woman to have a baby!—why, that's something a plantation owner would do with a slave. Myself, I do not intend to stand by and watch women subjugated into property by a recalcitrant patriarchy that just can't let go of its privilege and power. I'll fight them with everything I have. Nor can I believe that there's a woman in here who doesn't agree with me." And here he turns and shows himself again to the women in the back of the room. They look like hungry refugees at a buffet. Well, you know. A summer sausage buffet.

Then he sits down. And Lucas—and, oh, I get it now—dressed as poorly as he is able and smelling like dirty laundry, says, "So to recap, if you believe abortion to be murder, then you should fight that policy, fight that government. And if you think there is no place in the contemporary world for the enslavement of women into the role of government broodmares, then you should do everything you can to keep abortion legal.

QED, no middle ground. There is no compromise toward which we can argue."

"So we can't talk about it," a girl in the front of the room, turned in her desk, says, clearly wanting to save babies. I know her. What's her name?

"Yeah, we can talk about it, Alison," Lucas says. *Alison. Where does Lucas know her from?*

"So where do you stand?" Alison says.

"Well, I don't know. What are my choices?"

"There's pro-life and there's pro-choice."

"Surely that is not all," Lowell drawls. "It's so, so—binary. Aren't we past all such as that?" He looks at Whitman, who shrugs, helpless.

"What do you mean?" Alison says.

"How about pro-abortion?" Lowell says. "Is that one of my options."

"I think you mean pro-choice," she says.

"Oh, no doubt. I'm thoroughly pro-choice," Lowell says, "but I'm thinking that maybe I'm also pro-abortion."

"That doesn't make any sense. Even pro-choice people admit that abortion is a terrible option. They just believe a woman should be able to make that choice."

And here Lucas takes over again. "Yeah, I'm familiar with that mantra. But listen: we can all agree, I'm sure, that the world is overcrowded. This planet simply does not have the resources to continue to support the billions of people already here, much less billions reproducing themselves ad infinitum. And, more to the point, the world seems to be crowded with mostly morons. Cretins. Mouth-breathers. I'm sorry if this sounds callous, but for my money, if you can't figure out how to use birth control, maybe you're not smart enough to reproduce."

"So you kill an innocent child?" Alison is near tears.

"What does 'innocent' mean, Alison?" Lucas asks. There is a particularly cruel tone in his voice.

"You know what it means. It means the baby has done nothing wrong. It's innocent, not guilty."

"Well, in a court of law, innocent and not guilty are not the same thing. Am I right, Darling?"

I'm caught off guard. I didn't think I had a part in this frolic. I say, "Yeah. No, courts don't find people 'innocent.' They find them guilty or not guilty. The defendant may well have committed the crime, but if the state doesn't prove its case, the defendant is found not guilty. He's never found innocent." *Law and Order*, don't you know.

Lucas says, "When you say 'innocent,' Alison, I think you mean innocent like Adam and Eve in the Garden. You mean 'ignorant.' You mean the child has no knowledge of Good and Evil. That's what innocence is. That's what we mean when we say that life is a journey from innocence to experience."

"That may be, but I'm saying the child is good. That's what I mean by innocence."

Alison is nigh on to hysterical. I half expect Whitman to ask her to calm down.

Now Lucas stands. *What is this about?* "Fine. I'll accept your definition. So, Alison, are you 'innocent'?"

Alison stares at him with her mouth open.

"And I don't mean 'ignorant.' Because you are not ignorant. You know your options, don't you? You know what your choices are, right?"

Something is really wrong here.

Even Whitman senses it. He says, "Where are we going with this, Lucas?"

"Only saying that an 'innocent' Alison, ignorant of Good and Evil, like Eve in the Garden, would be one thing. She's not that."

"We're not going to make this personal," Whitman says.

"I don't see how we can avoid it." Lucas is calm. His voice sounds like someone talking a jumper down off a roof. "The child in the womb may be innocent in both senses of the word, but you're not innocent at all, are you?"

"I don't know what you mean."

"Lucas—" Whitman begins.

"Let me just ask her one question, okay? Alison, did you take off half of your junior year to go away to have a baby?"

Alison turns in her seat so that she is not facing Lucas anymore.

"No. You didn't. So what happened to that baby? Jerry Richmond's baby? Please tell me you didn't abort that innocent child."

Alison stumbles from her desk and runs out of the room. Another girl grabs Alison's backpack and follows her. The class is out of control. People are talking, loudly, and some are yelling at Lucas and some are yelling at Whitman. Whitman dismisses the class and spends some minutes herding people out, including Lowell and me, but he keeps Lucas behind.

In the hall, people are still talking, some of them glaring at Lowell (and me), one guy actually shouldering Lowell angrily out of his way.

Lowell says, "Well, that was interesting, don't you think?"

"Good God. Did y'all just out Alison for having an abortion?"

"What's this 'y'all' stuff? Did you hear me say one word to sweet Alison?"

"Horseshit. Y'all planned this from the git-go. How did you find out?"

"Carla."

"Carla? You mean Carla Carla?"

"How many Carlas do we know?"

"Wow. Just, just wow. Are you crazy?"

"What?"

"Lucas. He's going to get—he's going to be in trouble."

"Well, maybe. But not much. I mean, if he'd lied about innocent young Alison, that would be one thing. But apparently Carla was telling the truth. Judging from Alison's reaction."

"Where do I know her from?"

"She stands outside the Student Union every Saturday morning screaming about the murder of babies."

"Right. And so that's why—"

"In a nutshell."

Lowell walks me to Murrah Hall for my Music Appreciation class. He tells me to come to their room as soon as I'm out of class so we can get some dinner. Professor Dunbar is on Stravinsky today, *Le Sacre du Printemps*. Apparently, this music caused something of a riot in its Paris premiere. Dunbar says the reaction of the audience was to the music, new, shocking, icon-breaking, but I wonder if it might not have been the stylized sacrifice of a young woman to the gods of spring. Poor Alison. I wonder if she'll be on the quad Saturday morning.

Lucas and Lowell are waiting for me outside Dunbar's classroom. They don't say anything. We just head across campus toward the men's dorm. People are turning and looking at us, sometimes pointing. I feel so self-conscious. Finally we get to the parking lot where we climb into the Escalade and head off down 62. I feel better, out of the public eye, so to speak.

Lucas says, "Dairy Queen."

"Lord oh mighty," Lowell says. "Chili dogs?"

"Yes."

"They're better at the Sonic, old son."

"Maybe. I want a milkshake too. Don't even try to tell me that the Sonic makes a better milkshake."

"Y'all are too much," I say. "When are you gonna tell me what Whitman said?"

"Are you worried about me, Darling?"

"Of course I am."

He takes my hand and puts it on his heart. "Oh, Darling. Sweet little Darling. Everything is going to be fine. I have to go and speak with the Dean of Students. But I don't think he's going to kick me out or anything. It's a formality. Whitman, on the other hand, will never forgive me."

"And so it goes," Lowell says. *Where have I heard that?*

Lucas says, "Remind me. Why did I bite the bullet on this one?"

"It was your idea," Lowell says.

"It was you Carla told about Alison."

"Still your idea to use it."

"True. But next time, you pull the trigger."

"We'll see." Lowell smiles.

Lucas decides we need another vehicle. He calls it a "forensic countermeasure" and he puts quotes around it with his voice, mocking me, I'm sure. He tells Lowell that we need an older transport, a small pickup truck, maybe, something that will blend in to the surrounding redneckery more easily than his Rich Boy Car. He tells Lowell he should buy such a truck. We should go out and hit some lots on the edge of town, he says.

I hesitate. The problems with this plan are obvious. If I point out these obvious problems, Lucas is not going to like it. But more to the point, what does Lucas plan to do with the truck? What is he planning, what are they planning, that would require forensic countermeasures? They sure haven't told me anything about it.

Why not? Does it have something to do with Patrick Mitchell? Or with whoever it was that pounded Lucas?

Or is it something else?

Lowell says, "Where would I get the money for another car?"

"Fuck all, Richie Rich. The same place all your money comes from."

"Yes, Lucas. Of course, Lucas. My parents. What do I tell them I need another car for, Lucas?"

"They're not watching you that closely."

"Oh, but they are. I might could go and buy another watch and they might not ask why I need another watch even though I have ten already. But a car? A fucking car, Lucas?"

"You can stop saying my name now, bitch."

"Or what?"

"Maybe y'all don't wanna hear this," I say to them both, to avoid singling out Lucas, "but buying a car right here in town might undermine the forensic countermeasure characteristics of such a move."

Lowell says, "Explain."

"So, we roll up to Gomer's Used Cars, or whatever, right here in Barnesville. They'll know we're from the college. And Lowell's car is the most easily recognizable vehicle on campus, probably in town. So whatever it is we use the truck for, it'll be traceable to us right here." I emphasize the words *whatever it is we use the truck for*, thinking maybe that'll spur some explanation. It doesn't.

"So, we go to Little Rock and buy the truck," Lucas says.

"No," Lowell says. "She's right. Same problem. Traceable right to us."

"We need another fucking vehicle!"

"Yes," Lowell says. "You're right. But we need something that can't come back on us so easily."

"You have an idea?" I say.

"That I do. That I surely do."

We pack up the Escalade and get on Highway 65. Thirty minutes later Lowell turns off onto some farm road that isn't even marked and we are in the deep country. Lucas grumbles and climbs over into the back seat and goes to sleep. I get it. There is an easier and quicker way there, and Lucas thinks we should take it, but Lowell always insists on doing it the southern way. Or the "southren" way, as he'd put it. By midafternoon, the sky is lowering, black and gray thunderheads scudding across the horizon, their interiors sometimes lit up by lightning as I imagine brains lit up by electrical impulses. Rain spatters, fields and trees darken. I comment on how nice it all looks. Lowell says it's something we can appreciate that Yankees cannot. Thus, we in the front, stirred by what we see, and Lucas in the back, dreaming of California, all sun and beaches and tanned bodies, the brainless bonhomie of those who never fell into history the way southerners fell so hard into history.

It's a full three hours or more, Lucas asleep in the back seat the whole way, or pretending to be. Lowell's parents live out from Tunica, Mississippi. The delta is flat, wet, gray under the marbled sky. We don't approach their house. It's not what I pictured. I was thinking plantation home, but this is a long, low building, more in a ranch style, planky looking exterior, weathered gray or made to look so. A line of smoke rises from the chimney and I imagine how nice it must be inside, inside all that comfort and money, soft white clothes and red wine in crystal glasses, Bartok from hidden speakers, quiet words and long looks across warm rooms. Lowell skirts the house on a dirt road and we approach a crumbling barn a good mile away.

Lucas and Lowell drag open the huge door and inside is an old Chevrolet pickup truck, got to be from the sixties, faded red, dusty, with a flat front tire.

"You have the key, I assume," Lucas says.

"Get the pump."

Lucas hauls the battery-powered pump out of the back of the Escalade and sets it up next to the flat tire. Lowell crawls under the old truck to drain the gas tank. There is a lot of cursing and grunting. Lowell climbs out and Lucas gives it a go. Much more cursing from Lucas. They spray the stubborn bolt with WD40 and eventually break it loose. They replace the little bit of old gasoline with new. Then Lowell eases the front end of the Escalade into the barn until it is nose to nose with the truck. He pops the hoods of both vehicles and stretches jumper cables between them. Shortly the antique truck is running and the tire is inflated and they are loading their tools into its dirty bed.

Lowell says, "Darling, you drive my car. The gas card is in the glove box. Lucas and I will take the truck.

"And how, Columbo, is this truck not traceable to us?" Lucas says.

"You mean traceable to me?"

"Yes. Traceable to you and then ultimately to me."

"And me," I say. Actually, it's more of a question.

"The truck has no registration. It belonged to a series of deep woods folks and was ultimately bought by my grandfather without benefit of title, for cash."

"No registration. What if we get stopped?"

"I'm not sure. I've never been stopped. Have you?"

"Yes. Several times."

"You, Darling?"

"No. Never been stopped."

"Have you ever been in the car with me when I was stopped?"

"No," I say.

"And why is that?"

"I don't know. I guess you don't break the speed limit. And you never seem to take a main road," I say.

"Or perform any other foolish, testosterone-driven excesses of automotive masculinity."

"No."

"So, we drive carefully. Just as we always do. We stick to back roads all the way to Chandler. Did we see even one cop on the way here? No. And we won't see any on the way back."

"We might," Lucas says.

"And, as we have agreed, there is an element of risk in everything we do. So—do we want this truck or not?"

I cannot remember agreeing to the element of risk in all we do. I don't even remember a discussion about risk. Maybe he wasn't talking to me.

I leave first. I don't even try to remember the route Lowell took on the way here and just drive the main highway back to Chandler.

I park the Escalade in the lot adjacent to Lucas and Lowell's dorm, and I walk back to Stetson Hall in the purple dusk and lock myself in my room. For three days now I haven't seen or heard from Lowell or Lucas. They cut Whitman's class, they haven't come to the dining hall, no one has seen them.

From my dorm window, I can see the Escalade still parked in the south lot. It occurs to me that maybe they broke down in that old truck on some country road. Outside of cell reception. Or that they got stopped by the cops with no registration and a muddied tag decades out of date. I fight the overwhelming urge to go and knock on their door. Because. If they were here, they'd call me. Or come get me.

Or.

Maybe they wouldn't. Maybe they have turned me loose. Let me go. Deserted me, abandoned me. Got whatever it was they wanted and kicked me curbward.

And if so, what was it they wanted from me?

Am I the toy that the child has grown bored with? The puppy that turns out to be too much trouble to take care of? The too-innocent, too-reluctant girlfriend on whose favors the teenage boy can waste no more time? The best friend who has grown too familiar, too staid, too boring?

They're planning something. Something with the truck. Something that doesn't include me. Or doesn't seem to include me. At least, something they haven't clued me into yet.

Will they? Finally?

Or am I done?

I try to imagine what I would not do for them. Where are the limits of my loyalty, my devotion, my desire?

I sit in the window and dangle my feet. It's only the third floor. Falling wouldn't kill me. Being left behind might. Might kill me. Might ruin me.

I think maybe they have ruined me already. I don't want exile. I don't want to be left behind. If they had fucked me, fucked me and told everybody, fucked me and posted the video on YouTube, I don't think I could be more ruined. If they had slapped me and made me suck their dicks, I couldn't be more ruined. I think I would stay with them anyway.

Why do I think that? Surely that's not true. I'm a person, yes, a social construct, but a person nonetheless, and not defined only by them. I do exist apart from them.

Don't I?

What other friends do I look to for self-image, self-worth? And it occurs to me, terribly, that I don't have any other friends. Not here, not at home. I have cut myself off from everyone. For them. To be with them. I have closed my eyes to the judgments of others, the entreaties of others, the offers of friendships, the offers of dates, of cute fraternity boys, of pizza in the TV room with other girls in the dorm.

For them.

The sky is orange and gray, clouds stretched thin, the light failing. My emotions, my feelings, my interior seem to cast the objective world into a numinous state. I mean, the world seems alive, driven, guided. Purposeful. And thus are the beginnings of religion, I suppose. And now my heart, independent of my mind, my will, asks this world, this living world, *Who are these travelers, so much more fleeting than even I, twisted, wrung out, by a will never satisfied, a power that tosses them like ocean waves senselessly pummeling a drowning man?*

Or girl.

❧

I'm paranoid.

The next day they're waiting for me outside the dorm, ready to walk me to breakfast. "What happened to you?" I say.

"Truck broke down halfway back."

"Sucks."

"We had to walk into the next town and get a new water pump. It took us a full day to replace it."

"Yeah."

"It's running fine now. We stashed it behind that abandoned elementary school out on the edge of town. I don't think anybody goes out there. And we took out the spark plugs, so—"

"It won't get stolen."

"Right."

"It already looks vandalized, so why would anybody bother?"

"Good point."

So now. Now I will say it.

"What do we need the truck for anyway? What's the plan?"

Lucas turns away, ignoring me. Lowell hesitates. Then he says, "You never know, Darlin'. Something might come up."

I feel a giant pit in my stomach. Because that is a lie. They're planning something. And it doesn't include me.

Or more terribly, it does.

Halloween. Many of the independents in the dorms are dressing up and going out into the neighborhoods around the college. I suggest that we go to the Hill. Lowell wants to dress up and crash the Greek ball. Lucas wants to dress up and wander the streets of the neighborhood with the indies. I don't want to dress up.

"What girl doesn't want to play dress-up?" Lowell says.

"May I suggest that I'm not really a girl?"

"How old, Darlin'?"

"You know how—"

"Eighteen. Eighteen, Darlin'."

"Eighteen is grown. Shoot, Lowell. Thirteen is grown. When you're a girl."

"I'm guessing you mean 'When you're a *woman*.'"

"You know exactly what I mean."

"Do I? Maybe, but, Darlin', you're not a woman yet."

"That's bullshit. Just because you treat me like a little sister doesn't actually make me a little sister. There's a reality beyond your construction of me."

"If you accept the premise of your argument, then you just lost it. You posit my ability to construct you. Ipso facto. I've constructed you."

"Independent reality!" I'm yelling.

"You're yelling, Darlin'. It's just a thought experiment."

"You treat me like a child and you know it."

"And when have we left you home with the babysitter?"

He is equivocating. They are hiding something from me.

"She's poutin'," Lowell says.

"Fine," Lucas says. "Let's go to the Hill."

"If that's what she wants."

I want to say something cutting, but that would just prove their point that I'm pouting.

"Let's take some wine," I say.

"Do you have any wine?" Lowell says.

"As a matter of fact," I say.

"Let's go," Lowell says.

"You two go get the wine and I'll meet you on the Hill," Lucas says.

Lowell and I walk to Stetson and he waits on the ground floor while I collect the wine. I start down the stairs, then turn around and go back to get the corkscrew.

Lowell inspects the bottle as we walk along the sidewalk. He stops under a lamppost and says, "Mouton Cadet. Oooh. Top shelf."

"Give it a rest, Quentin. I'm just a poor girl, from a poor family."

"Scaramouche, Scaramouche."

We walk out from under the lights of the campus and into the dark and trudge up the Hill.

"Shall we sit by the Eye of Sex and Death or climb to the top?"

"You're never going to let that go, are you?"

"Top it is."

We sit and watch the lights in the town and the lights in the sky. Fifteen minutes later I say, "Where's Lucas?"

"Lucas, Lucas. If I didn't know better, Darlin', I'd say you like that Yankee boy better than me."

"I'm just wondering about opening this wine."

"Open it," he says. I work the corkscrew. Then he says, "So, where exactly was it that you got your ass beat? I'm sorry. I mean, where was it you tripped and fell down? Over and over? On a fist-shaped rock?"

Ouch. "I'm trying to open this wine."

"Give it to me."

And he pops the cork and offers me the first pull. We swap it back and forth a couple of times and then he pushes the cork back in and stands the bottle in the grass.

Lucas surprises us by coming over the Hill from the opposite direction. He is carrying a plastic bag. "I got some beer," he says.

"We brought the wine," I say.

"Yeah," he says. "One bottle."

"Point taken," I say.

Lucas opens a beer and Lowell and I pass the Mouton. I'm just beginning to feel the wine trilling in my veins, when Lucas points toward the campus. It looks like a fire.

"Is that a bonfire?" I say. "On the campus?"

"What do you know," Lowell says. There's something in his voice. "That's an interesting turn of events."

"Y'all want to go see it?" I say.

"And stand around watching a bonfire with a bunch of drunk Greeks, no thanks," Lucas says. Is he being extra sarcastic to me?

And then we hear sirens. And then we see a fire engine rushing down Monument Street and turning into the campus.

"That's no bonfire," I say.

"Nope," Lowell says. "Probably not."

"I hope it's not Stetson," I say. "My laptop is in there and I have a paper on it that's due next class."

"Not to mention all your clothes."

"More clothes I can get. But the Goodwill doesn't have any essays on Durkheim I can walk outta there with."

"Spoken like a true scholar." Lowell says.

I say, "So what do y'all reckon is burning?"

The next day is buzzy with news. Turns out it was the Kappa Alpha house that burned. The KAs were all out celebrating the holiday and thus there were no injuries or fatalities. But the house is a complete loss. I stand outside the police tape next to Sally Jenkins from my English class and watch the firemen digging in the ruins. "Hell of thing, huh?" I say.

"You bet," she says and points at the Kappa Alpha parking lot. "Look. There's one car that's burnt up too."

"That's a truck, I think."

"How come just one car burns?"

"I don't know. Maybe—I don't know. Something blew up in the house and landed on it?"

"I guess. Or maybe the truck burned first and set the house on fire?" she says.

"Right. Could be. It's weird."

"The cops think it was deliberate."

"Really. Why?"

"That's what I heard anyway. Maybe it's just too coincidental, you know, it happening on Halloween and all. A lot of mischief goes on of a Halloween night."

That's when I notice Patrick standing by the smoldering truck. And I recognize that it is, in fact, his truck that has burned and his fraternity house burned to the chimney.

He's waving his hands around and talking to a uniformed policeman. They are pointing from the truck to the house and back, as if tracing a line of cause and effect.

Then he sees me.

He stares at me as if he's putting something together in his mind.

I stare at him as if I'm putting something together in my mind.

Does he think I did this?

Who do I think did this?

Patrick gestures in my direction and the officer looks over. I step behind Sally and peek over her shoulder. They're not looking at me, surely. Maybe I am getting paranoid.

"Let's go," she says. "We're going to be late for English."

Blackwell is going on and on about Byron. I can't concentrate. I keep seeing Patrick pointing at me. Or toward me. Or in the general direction of me. I'm overthinking it, for sure, but I can't stop. Did that officer look right at me?

After class, I go back to the dorm. I'm cutting French today. I'd be more than useless anyway.

Relax, Darling. You didn't do anything.

But who did?

Do the boys know it was Patrick who beat me up that night? They knew I was going on a date, but did they know it was with him?

I don't go to the dining hall either. I eat most of a bag of Fritos and drink out of a warm two-liter Coke. I'm hiding, I realize. I feel like every eye is on me. That can't be true.

There are some knocks on my door from time to time during the afternoon, girls wanting to study or go somewhere or eat. I ignore them. On toward evening, a more aggressive knock.

"Miss Bramlett."

Shoot. Who is that?

"Miss Bramlett. It's Detective Somerset. We met at BCMC? The night you were brought into Emergency?"

This cannot be happening.

It's like that movie moment when the camera zooms in on somebody's face as the rest of the world falls away.

I open the door. I step back and let him in. He's still cute. Again with the Aramis.

He's too big for the room. He sits in the chair at my desk and takes a notebook out of his jacket pocket. It's like television. I feel like I'm on television or something, you know, abstracted from my body, like I'm watching myself—on television? I'm freaking.

He flips through a couple of pages and then looks up at me and smiles.

"Are you feeling better? You looked pretty wobbly that night at the hospital."

"My parents took me home for a while. I feel a lot better now. In fact, I'm all good now. I'm just trying to get caught up with my classes now."

How many times did I say "now"?

"That's good."

"Yeah."

He looks at me for a long minute. I can't read him. I must be seriously rattled because if this were any other situation, I would swear he was about to hit on me. He's smiling and looks expectant. If he put his hands on me right now, I wouldn't be totally surprised. In fact, I'd be relieved. Greatly relieved.

"I guess you heard about the fire."

"I did."

He doesn't say anything. So I say, "Terrible thing." *Why? Why am I speaking?*

He nods. But still doesn't say anything.

I gotta pull it together. What is he doing here?

"Are you just checking up on me? Because I really am feeling better." *Shut up. Pebbles. For God's sake, pebbles.*

"I'm glad. Do you know Patrick Mitchell?"

I feel my face change. Does he see it? *Of course he fucking sees it, Darling.* "We have English together."

"And?"

"And what?"

"Do you have a personal relationship with him?"

"I know him to say hello, talk about class."

"But that's it?"

"Pretty much."

"Never went out with him?"

"Like a date? No."

"No? Are you sure?"

"What does that mean?"

"So where were you the night of the arson?"

"Wait. Arson? Are you saying the fire was set deliberately?"

"Yes."

"And you think—I started the fire?"

"No, no. Of course not. I'm just gathering information."

"So somebody burned down the KA house? On purpose?"

"Looks that way. We know the truck was set afire deliberately. Patrick Mitchell's truck."

I flash on the night Lucas got beaten up. What did he say? Something about the KAs?

The detective says, "The fire from the truck spread to the building. That part might have been accidental, though. Hard to tell at this point."

I'm so very pebbles right now. I'm trying to look him square in the face, right in his depthless brown eyes. I'm trying not to blink.

"So. On the night of the fire, you were where?"

"On the Hill."

"Yes. The Hill. Where you got beaten up. I mean, where you fell down."

"Yes."

He writes in his notebook.

"You don't believe me?"

"That you were on the Hill. Of course I believe you."

"I mean, you don't believe I fell down."

He fixes me with those eyes, so brown they're black, for a couple of long seconds before he says, "Me? Well, don't take it personally. I'm suspicious by nature. Police work, you know. But, in point of fact, I don't think your friends believe you fell down."

"What friends are those?"

"The ones who visited you in the hospital that night." He flips the pages in his notebook and says, "Lucas Susskind and Lowell Alford."

I don't know what to say, so I keep my mouth shut. Finally.

"They were having a pretty intense discussion that night in the parking lot of the hospital."

"You were watching them?"

"Coincidence. I just happened to be there."

That's a lie. I can see that's a lie. I need to find his tell.

"They were worried about me."

"I would think they would be."

"I'm telling the truth."

"So. The night of the fire, you were on the Hill. Was anyone else there?"

"Lucas and Lowell."

"Yes, Lucas and Lowell," he says, writing in his notebook. "And they were both there with you the whole time?"

"Yeah, I guess so. We all saw the fire from there."

"Got you. Okay. Well, that's all I have for now." He stands up, pockets his notebook, and looks around the room. Everything is dwarfed by him. I feel like I'm in the room with a giant. "Take care of yourself, Miss Bramlett."

He pauses at the door, staring out into the hall, then turns back to face me: "Have you ever been to Muskogee? You know, over in Oklahoma?"

I'm stunned and sit there with my mouth open. Finally, he just nods and leaves.

I'm pretty sure he didn't believe a single thing I told him. How many lies did I tell? Where did Lucas go that night? Did we see the fire before or after he got there? I'm having trouble remembering what is a lie and what is the truth. You tell a lie often enough, picture it in your head while you're telling it, and it becomes like a memory. How many lies am I living at this point?

I sleep fitfully. My dreams are all running, hiding. Fear.

I wake with a start around four. My heart is throbbing and I'm crying: what if Somerset talked to Patrick? Would Patrick tell him we went out, that he was with me the night I got beat up? Is it possible he's that stupid? If so, then Somerset knew before he asked me and only asked in order to catch me in a lie. To find out, am I a liar.

And Muskogee?

The next morning I decide to forgo the dining hall and breakfast at the 7-Eleven instead. I'm just stepping into the parking lot when the Escalade pulls up next to me.

"Get in," Lucas says from the passenger seat.

"Can't. Gotta eat. Class at nine."

Lowell parks the car and they follow me inside.

Lucas rummages in the microwave breakfast sandwiches and Lowell fiddles with the Slurpee machine. I can't decide what I want. Finally, I get a Coke and a large bag of beef jerky. Peppered.

When I go outside, the boys are sitting on the curb. I drop down between them and struggle opening the beef jerky until Lucas takes it from me and slits the top with his pocketknife.

"The cops came to see us last night," Lucas says.

Now I've got a pit in my stomach. Again.

"What about?" I say.

"About the fire at the KA house, I think."

"What do you mean 'you think'?"

"Well, he asked about the fire, but—"

"Yeah?"

"He asked about Patrick Mitchell too."

"Who?"

The boys lean forward and look at each other.

"'Who' she says," Lowell says. "To tell you the truth, Darlin', I got the feeling from that old boy that he doesn't believe you fell down up there on the Hill."

"What old boy?" I ask. Maybe I can take this in a different direction.

"Officer, um, oh, what was his name, Lucas?"

"I don't remember, but he definitely doesn't believe you fell. He thinks you're a liar."

Lowell says, "Somerset. Officer Somerset."

"*Detective* Somerset," Lucas says. "And I think, Darling, that he is under the impression that somebody kicked your ass up on the Hill."

"I fell. You know I fell, right? Why would I lie about that? And what does any of this have to do with the fire?"

"Good question. That's a good question, isn't it, Lowell?"

"What did you tell him?" I ask.

"We told him that we didn't have any knowledge of anybody beating you up. We said that we took you at your word," Lucas says.

"But you don't take me at my word, do you?"

Lucas turns and looks me in the face. He's pissed off. "No, Darling, I don't. I think you have lied to us. What do you think, Lowell?"

"Yes, I think she has lied to us."

I look at Lowell, hurt.

"But," Lowell continues, "that is her prerogative. That is your prerogative, Darlin'. You don't have to tell us the truth. Truth's a notoriously slippery concept anyway. And you don't for a minute imagine we always tell you the truth, do you?"

The pit in my stomach has swollen. And I am put in mind of nothing so much as that dark tunnel we saw at the river. I see it in my mind's eye. Superimposed over Laura Huddle's yearbook photo.

Lucas says, "And then the detective man wanted to know if you had ever dated this somebody named Patrick Mitchell. We told him we didn't know. I said that you might have gone on a date recently, maybe skating."

"I never told you that."

Lucas says, "You told somebody that, Darling, because somebody told me that. You did go on a date, didn't you?"

I should answer but I don't.

"You see," Lowell says, "it turns out that it was a certain Patrick Mitchell's truck what burnt of a recent Halloween night, and what ultimately caused the burning of the KA house."

If they burned his truck, how easily they can shift the blame to me. Have they set me up?

"He asked me if I'd been to Muskogee," I manage to say.

The boys look at each other. Lowell pales.

Lucas says, "What did you say?"

"Nothing. He asked me that and walked out the door. He didn't wait for an answer."

"He was telling her he knows something," Lowell says.

Lucas gets up and opens the passenger door of the Escalade. "Get in."

So I do. We head back toward campus.

It's really tense in the car. Finally I say, "Why are y'all mad at me?"

Lucas wants to say something, but I guess he can't find the words. He's driving, so he doesn't have to look at me, but something—anger, frustration, fear—is radiating off him. It's like sitting next to a space heater.

Lowell says, "You're like a cat, Darlin'. You know, like really smart and really stupid."

"Maybe we should call her Pussy," Lucas says.

That hurts. On so many levels, that hurts.

Lucas pulls the Escalade into a parking spot behind the men's dorm and jumps out almost before the car is stopped good. He stomps off toward the dorm without looking back.

"Why is he so mad at me?"

"Go to class, Darlin'. There's nothing to be done about it now."

Here's a story I didn't tell before. Maybe I should have. I don't know why I haven't included it in the overarching narrative of the boys. This happened less than a week after I first met them, after our ride out into the country, where we ate barbeque and I saw them naked for the first time. Was that an innocent time? Something to look back on and ache for, though it be lost now to time? Lucas once told me that the Nostalgia Ratio was shrinking. He said that back in the day nostalgia was a once noble idea, old people remembering the deep past, looking back with a quiet longing. Then the baby boomers found nostalgia in their thirties, and cynics called it Premature Nostalgia. Lucas suggested it had to do with the rapidity with which boomers sold out their revolutionary dreams and aspirations. And now I'm looking back on a time less than four months ago? Calling it innocent? A day when two boys exposed themselves to me as casually as you would say good morning and me wanting nothing so much as to be fucked by them both? What contrast makes that seem innocent? What binary?

It was the very next weekend. Saturday morning they beat on my door and I let them in. They wanted to breakfast at Turl's. I'd never heard of it. Of course, I'd been at Chandler all of a week. Turl's was a small restaurant in a strip mall on the edge of town. Family joint. Food was good. I was seriously thinking of sending back for another order of bacon, when they told me that we were, this very Saturday morning, driving over to Muskogee.

"As in 'Okie from Muskogee'?"

"Given that the town of Muskogee is, in fact, within the borders of the great state of Oklahoma, I'm reckoning that every cowboy and Indian there is an Okie," Lowell said.

"Sounds hobbled."

"Regardless," Lowell was pulling out the drawl here, "we are going."

"You know, I'm not your little sister. Whose mama has left her with her badass brothers while she makes groceries. You can't tell me what to do."

They looked at each other. I didn't know then how many times I'd see this. What I said was, "You're children."

"Except ye be born again. . . ." Lowell said.

"Quoting Biblicals at me? What have I signed on for here?"

"Well, paraphrasing, you understand."

"Okay. I'll bite. What's in Muskogee?"

"It's the place where three rivers meet," Lowell said.

"Why does that sound familiar?"

Lucas said, "There is an old theater that Lowell wants to see."

"A theater," I repeated.

"Yes."

"That's it?"

He shrugged.

Lowell lifted his coffee cup and nodded at the waitress.

"It's only about three hours," Lucas said.

"You've got to be kidding."

"What?"

"So, three hours there, three hours back, whatever time it takes to look at an old theater. That's the whole day."

"Did you have plans, Darling?" Lucas asked. Kind of sneery.

I didn't. He knew I didn't. I didn't know anybody, well, besides them and my roommate, Delores, who, already in the second week of school, was spending every free moment impaled on her boyfriend in his apartment off campus.

I had a good time, of course. Riding with the boys was never boring. And on this first road trip I really got to distinguish them: Lowell and his Late Romantic Vampire Existentialism and Lucas and his Distant Thunder/Music Nietzschean Hard-On.

Of course, I may be too close to the phenomena to be label-making.

While Lowell stood at the counter paying the check and flirting with the cook's wife, Lucas asked me if I needed to pee before we got on the road.

"Seriously, not your little sister."

"Go pee."

They enjoyed the long ride. They were intrepid travelers. They had endless music of incredible variety. If your taste runs to ancient blues and country, early Rolling Stones and Beatles, eighties disco, and psychedelia of the forgotten.

"What are we listening to?" I asked.

"The Chocolate Watch," Lucas said.

"The huh?"

"No," Lowell said. "You mean The Strawberry Alarm Clock. And this ain't them neither. This is The Electric Prunes."

"Lowell, Lowell, Lowell. The atheist who can't let go of God," Lucas said.

"This is their album, *Mass in F Minor*. Back in the day they were long-form prog-rock precursors."

"Outta all of that, I understood the word *album*," I said.

"It's time to interrogate this blunt, Mr. Jones," Lowell said.

"Get in the back seat, hippie," Lucas said. "And crack a window."

"I'm driving, son."

"So you are. Darling, take over for this tired old sixties loving spoonful of crapola."

I grabbed the wheel. Sitting in the middle, don't you know. Lowell popped his seat belt and wriggled over the seat back. I scooched behind the wheel. Lowell had the cruise control set to seventy. I backed it down to sixty-five and settled in. The sweet acrid smell of pot filled the car.

"Window?" Lucas said.

"No such," said Lowell. "Drown out the music."

We rode in silence for a while. I wanted to hear whatever it was that Lowell heard in this music, a music that predated even my parents.

I couldn't. It sounded like a parody of sixties music in a beach movie except the boyish voices were singing in Latin.

"What do you hear in this, Lowell?" I asked.

"We are dying animals on a flickering cinder rising up out of a fortuitous cosmic fire."

"That must be the new weed, huh?" Lucas said.

"We are but the briefest of things. Stretch out your imaginations to see us within the range of physicality: A hundred years ago we thought that the farthest reaches of the Milky Way were the farthest reaches of the entire universe. Then we stumbled onto the fact that some of those stars we were looking out at weren't stars at all, but galaxies, billions of them, all holding billions of their own stars. And we saw that our galaxy, once unthinkably large, is only one of hundreds of millions of galaxies in a small cluster of them near a much larger cluster and beyond that galaxies reach out in quadrillions of light-years. And where are we, what are we? We are nothing. As the smallest quark in the quantum world is the Milky Way, even less are we to reaches of the universe. There is no point to any of it. There are only the games that we play before our cinder cools and falls."

"Wow," I said quietly.

"Wow is right. How much did you pay for that weed?" Lucas asked.

"I haven't even touched on Time."

"Lord, please. No Faulkner today," Lucas groaned.

"Faulkner?" I asked.

"Talking about Time always leads him to back to old Billy goat-boy."

"Surely, surely. Old Bill was as fully imbued with Bergson as I am with this, the choicest of the American marijuanas. The wisdom of the earth reaching up through the plant into me. The elasticity of Time bending and shaping the curve of narrative in Bill's typewriter."

"I don't think he had a typewriter," Lucas said.

"Did too. Remington Model 12. I've seen it."

"Bullshit."

"Not at all. You see, California Boy, we have a thing in the South called history. And we keep up with it."

"You're an idiot."

"'Full of sound and fury.'"

"Sound anyway."

We hit Muskogee around dinnertime and ate in a faux-fifties diner, all chrome and candy colors. Afterward, we walked around and hit the tourist spots. There weren't that many. Finally we came to the great ballyhooed theater, and it was very nice. A restored neon front, plush red seats, huge screen. There was no movie showing that afternoon. We listened instead to a panel discussion on Oklahoma writers. It was five or six kinds of boring. Lowell seemed entranced, but Lucas stared at his phone the entire time. I tried to listen, but the only name I recognized was Sarah Vowell and the panelists mentioned her only briefly.

"Vowell?" Lowell said to me as we walked out. "You're telling me you don't know Jim Thompson?"

"Nope."

"Lord a mercy, Darlin'. He invented the hard-boiled detective genre."

"Uh, no," Lucas said. "Dashiell Hammett. Raymond Chandler. Hello?"

"Oh. Right, of course. The detective novel was invented in California, is that it?"

"Basically, yeah."

"So, the Beach Boys and the detective novel are the high points of California culture, am I hearing you correctly?"

"Yeah, you beat us to the KKK and Jim Crow."

"Ouch. Fine. But, Darlin', you need to have read at least one Thompson novel, if you're gonna be truly educated."

"I don't know," I said. "I haven't even read, whatsit? Dashboard Hammer or Raybone Chandelier."

Lowell stopped in his tracks and stared at me.

"She's fucking with you, Lowell."

"You think? Let's head back to school. Should we eat something first?"

Lucas said, "I'm still processing that cheeseburger from lunch in the fifties. Let's hit the road."

"I'm hungry," I said.

"We'll get something on the way," Lucas said and that was the end of that.

I got into the front seat, but both boys climbed into the back and bent over a library book and snorted coke off the plastic cover. I looked over the seat and said, "What about me?"

Lucas said, "Do you want some?"

"No."

"Pfft. Duh."

"It would be nice to be asked."

"I don't have any cocaine manners. You don't even smoke pot, Darling," Lucas said.

"Do too."

"When?"

"Try me sometime."

"Whatever. Who's driving?"

Lowell said, "You. Or Darlin'. I'm firing up this joint. Darlin'?" he said invitationally.

"Not right now." And they both laughed.

Lowell got behind the wheel anyway, I think mainly to have control of the music, which was some kind of—I don't know, Indian meditation thing, dreamy, rhythmic, like getting-a-massage music, maybe.

An hour and a half later, I said, "Okay, hippie-disco boys, I'm starvin' now."

Lowell said, "Next place we see."

The sun had just gone down. Dusk, twilight, the sky blue and orange, the land darkening, the colors falling down out of the sky and into the ground. Lucas commented that a gray pickup was coming toward us on this two-lane blacktop and that since they didn't have their lights on, they were a menace.

"You're telling me you can't see that car coming straight at us." Lowell pronounced it "cain't."

The car was still a quarter mile away.

"Twilight is the most dangerous time to drive."

"Darlin', don't you like how he passes off his own Californian opinions as if they were facts?"

"It *is* a fact, you, inbred, corn-cob-eating redneck."

"Is this the 'road rage' one hears so much about these days?" I said, trying to allay all the attitude.

"Shut up, Darling." To Lowell he said, "You know goddamn well that it's harder to see at dusk than at night, even though there is more light remaining."

"I don't know that." Lowell was deliberately antagonizing him. Why?

"You three-legged, dickless dog. Your fucking eyes use two sets of cells, rods for dark and cones for the daylight. Why are pretending you don't know this?"

"Fine," Lowell said and flashed his lights at the oncoming vehicle, which was indeed gray and hard to see in the gloaming. As the car passed us, Lowell let down the window and gave them the finger and yelled, "Rods and cones, you cross-eyed redneck sons-of-a-bitches!" Not that they could hear him, mind you. That was for Lucas.

"Oh, fuck you, smart-ass rich boy," Lucas said.

"Check this out," Lowell said, looking in the rearview mirror. "Those bastards are turning around."

I kneeled in the seat and looked out the back. The gray car had indeed turned around and was now hauling ass toward us.

Lowell said, "Sit down and buckle up, Darlin'." And then he hit the gas, as my daddy used to say.

The Escalade could really fly, but in a quick minute that gray car pulled up alongside of us. The speedometer suggested we were doing eighty in a fifty-five-mile-an-hour zone. The road was straight and flat, but my heart was beating out of my chest. A man was halfway out the passenger window of the gray car, shaking his fist and screaming. He looked like a country meth head: skinny, wispy beard, sketchy tats, several important teeth AWOL. "Run these sons of bitches off the road," Lucas said.

"The hell you say," Lowell said. "I'm not even about to scratch my car over these dumbfucks."

"Then pull the fuck over."

"Why? Do you want to talk to them?"

Lowell slowed the car and stopped right in the middle of the road. The other car pulled ahead of us and stopped. Silently, I hoped no other car came up from behind and crashed into us. After all, it was dusk and we would be hard to see. Rods and cones.

The boys scrambled out of the car and stood in front of the Escalade. Two men emerged from the gray car.

They were redneck meth-head warriors. Home-cooked chemical knights-errant. Skinny as beanpoles, ripped-up jeans, one in a dirty wife-beater, the other bare-chested.

Lucas and Lowell had six inches and twenty pounds apiece on them. But the meth boys were not cowed. Wife-beater pulled a set of brass knuckles out of his pocket.

The shirtless one pointed past the boys into the Escalade at me. "That yo woman? 'Cause when we're done killing you, we're gonna fuck her. And gut her," and with this he snapped open a big-ass buck knife. Not too proud to say I got a real pit in my stomach.

I'm not sure what it was that set Lowell off. I like to think it was the overt and obscene threat to me. But he said, "You vile piece of shit," and strode toward them, pulling a pistol out of the back of his jeans and firing, shot after shot. I don't think he was trying to hit them though. The bullets all smashed into the gray car, popping holes in the back windshield and the trunk. The meth boys ducked and rolled on the ground and ran off into the woods. Lowell started after them, reloading as he walked, but Lucas grabbed him by the arm and pulled him back to the car. He put Lowell in the passenger side. Lowell cradled the gun in his hand like a baby bird. Lucas gunned the Escalade around the gray car and off down the highway.

We rode in silence for a while. Gritty smell of gunpowder. I was wondering when we were going to talk about all this. My heart was still pounding. Nobody said anything though. It was full-on dark when we pulled into the convenience store, mom and pop version. We were in the deep-ass country, so there was at least the possibility of some real cooked food up under some heat lamps. While I could get by on a supper of Slim Jims and pink Hostess Snowballs, it wasn't what I was truly craving. The boys got out and started rummaging around in the back-ety-back of the Escalade, pulling out the cooler, pouring off the water and rearranging the leftover warm beer and Cokes. I went ahead into the store. Still nobody had said a word about our confrontation with backwoods evil.

A little bell tinkled as the door swung shut behind me, and I got a feeling. It started as a prickling on the back of my neck that sizzled into a feverish burn that ran down my spine. No one behind the counter. Place deadly quiet. I only got about three steps in when the feeling overpowered me and stopped me dead in my tracks. Something was bad wrong. Feelings aren't always right, I know, but what are the consequences of ignoring your instincts? I mean, what are instincts for, if not to warn you off ruinous situations?

Looked around. Soul-sucking fluorescent lights, too bright, it seemed to me. Or maybe some biological response had blown my pupils wide open. Typical convenience store, except for the food display, which had everything a southerner might think up to deep-fry spread out under heat lamps: chicken and potatoes, of course, but also catfish, okra, pickles, Twinkies, gizzards,

Snickers bars—basically, the bumpy and potholed road to heart disease that I'd been hoping for when we stopped here. Music playing, cheap speakers nailed up next to the cigarette racks, some country singer, a woman, I didn't recognize the song. I stepped up to the counter and saw a lady lying on the floor on the other side. Blood everywhere. I had to grab my mouth to keep from crying out. Her throat cut. I turned around to look through the glass of the door, but I couldn't see the boys anywhere. I thought they were probably behind the car, still messing with the cooler and whatnot. I was about to back out of there when I heard something. A rustling. Then a man stepped out from behind a display of potato chips with three or four bags under his arm.

And a knife in his hand. A bloody knife. Literally dripping blood. Our eyes met. For a second, he looked scared. Then his face changed and he dropped the chips.

Tell me why I didn't run. How I turned into a cliché from a horror movie.

"So, little lady. You've come to join the revel. Because revelry is what we have here tonight. A revelry to raise the devil forever."

Opened my mouth but nothing came out; I wanted to leave but my legs felt like concrete. I smelled him from across the store: dirty, yeasty, sour.

"You know, my daddy said I'd never make it as a preacher. He was right, of course. He was always right. That's what *he* was, you know. A preacher. Beloved by his God, blessed of his God. Loved by congregations large and small all across this great Confederate land of ours. And the ladies of the choirs. Oh, they loved him too, don't you know it?"

He stomped one of the chip bags and it exploded.

"That didn't stop him, mind you, from dragging his wife and young'uns from pillar to post, forty years and forty nights in God's own desert, 'cause he just couldn't stay in one place so long. And thus it is, I've lived ever where, done most ever thing. But the calling. The calling."

Where were Lucas and Lowell? Surely they would walk through that door now. Bile churned in my stomach. Dizzy. My face burning.

"I wanted to follow in them footsteps, you know, as I'd followed him all my life. But as it turned out, it wasn't to be. So you know, Daddy said I lacked a certain johnny-knows-why. And I guess he was right."

"'Johnny knows why,'" I repeated dumbly.

"Right you are, little lady. Did you ever wonder? How Jesus can be the shepherd and the lamb? Oh, He saveth the little lamb, all right. Yes, He does. But for what? *For what!*"

"I don't know."

"For the sacrifice. For the knife, for the table, for our boundless hunger for blood and meat. Is that what Jesus is saving all us for? He was the Lamb. But he died blood and meat."

I threw up on the dirty linoleum.

"Ugh. That's a mess." He wrinkled his nose. "Don't you worry, sweetheart. You are forgiven, as you well know and the Book says. But your sins are trifling and hardly in need of divine pardon. Believe me, He didn't die for you. I'm sorry to have to tell you that, missy miss. This is a true saying: He died for sinners. Real sinners. Murderers, rapists, evildoers of all stripe. Child fuckers, mama killers, don't you know?"

I wiped my mouth and took a step back.

"Daddy said, 'It's some that have it and will hear the call and it's some that don't, and this boy is one of the latters.' So instead of sweet-talking 'em into Heaven, I'm sending 'em into Hell."

He raised his arm, the knife flashed in the fluorescents and he stepped toward me. I put my hands out and, yes, closed my eyes. Useless girl.

Thunk. That's a sound I can describe, like a baseball slapping into a catcher's mitt.

Then a sound I can't describe, which turned out to be Knife Boy hitting the floor in front of me. Maybe a load of laundry hitting the floor? Well, something hitting the floor.

For when I opened my eyes, he was, in fact, on the floor,

facedown, blood seeping out of the back of his head and Lowell looking down at him, holding—what? A stick of some kind. Lowell's face twisted into a shape I didn't recognize. Beyond anger or fear, maybe rage. I don't know. I really don't.

He looked up at me, and the face fell off him, and he was the Lowell I recognized, the one I know now, the one who cares for me, worries about me, protects me.

Lowell was still holding his arm in the air as if to swing it again. He came to himself, I guess, and dropped his arm.

He smiled and said, "Rebar. That's funny. You know, I was just telling Lucas what rebar is. Last week. He thought it was a good word but had never seen it or heard of it. He thought it was something I'd made up."

Then I felt Lucas's hands on my shoulders and he turned me away and led me to the door.

"Goddamn that son of a bitch," I said shakily.

"Easy, Darling. I think you might be in shock." He took me outside and put me in the back seat of the Escalade. "Why don't you lie down. I'll be right back."

I did that. I don't know how long it was before the two of them climbed into the front seat. I could smell fried food. They didn't say anything, and we drove away fast.

Some time passed, then Lowell said, "Hungry, sweetheart?"

I didn't say anything. I had lost my appetite.

"Sleeping?" Lowell asked.

Lucas said, "Probably. Pretty intense. I'd say you got there just in time."

"Punk-ass bitch."

"Really? 'Punk-ass bitch'? My, my, the diction on you. I can't hear Miss Eudora nor the Oxford bard anywhere in that phraseology."

"My mask is slipping."

"You can't blame the guy, you know."

"I hope to God I can," Lowell said. "I just sank a piece of rebar in his head. And—"

"Why?"

"What do you mean why?"

"Why did you bust him in the head with an iron rod? I mean, for instance, did you stand back, take a moment, think it though? Make a judgment as to that guy's deserving or not deserving of an iron rod upside his head? Did you find him 'blameworthy'?"

Lowell said nothing.

"I'm thinking, no. No, you didn't make a judgment. You didn't ask if he deserved it. Or in what degree. You hit him for, what I'm going to call, a spectrum of reasons. A smear of causality. You were scared, you were worried about Darling, adrenaline lit you up like a burning Christmas tree. Maybe somewhere deep inside you is an old-timey Southren gentleman (and here he put on an exaggerated Foghorn Leghorn accent) who quite naturally and as a matter of course brings down the whip onto the backs of the uppity."

"Fuck you," Lowell said.

Lucas softened his voice, modulated it down to what might be called a lover's tone, if you know what I mean. "Sorry. I'm only trying to say that we do what we do for a number of reasons, some of which we know, some of which we rationalize, but some of which we are only dimly aware of. And some we are aware of in no way at all."

"Please don't equate me with the southern aristocracy. My parents—"

"I know. I only said that to suggest that you—we, everybody—may have motivations of which we are unaware. And my point wasn't about you in any case. It was about the unfortunate young man back there in the store."

"Unfortunate?" I cried, almost yelling. No, I was yelling.

"Ah, so she is awake," Lucas said. "Fried Oreo, Darling?"

"He was going to kill me!"

"Yes. Yes, I'm sure you're right. Given the state of that poor lady working the cash register and her poor husband lying in the cooler, I have to concur. He was certainly going to kill you."

"And he's 'unfortunate'?"

"Look. We can reduce Lowell's infinite existential cosmic reaches to a map. We can shrink the map. The world is a pliable thing that can contract or expand. Consider your world, Darling, reaching from here back to your parents, to your relatives, out to your friends and acquaintances, and even reaching out to celebrities and politicians and musicians, in your world, and now consider how when you're in pain or you have the flu, the world contracts until it is no larger than the bed you lie in or, in fever, the extent of your body."

"I'm tired of this music," Lowell said.

Click, click, and a sweet-voiced guitar player began to sing soft borderline country music.

"What I'm saying is that, yes, we are determined, in every choice we make. Do you hear the contradiction at the very core of our lives? Do you hear: determined in every choice. We are in chains, biological, sociological, psychological chains, everywhere in chains and yet we must dance. Don't you see? Dancing in chains. We can at least be bright points against the background smear."

"I don't understand a damn word you're saying." I was probably yelling. "What are you saying?"

"Just that that crazy boy, and you hear that, right? Crazy? Just that he was probably in that store for a lot of reasons, some he knew, some he only vaguely knew, and some he didn't know at all. I'm just saying that it's not as simple as saying he chose to do something evil. I'm saying that biology and psychology and social forces come into play in every choice we make. No choice is entirely free. And thus, we are not entirely to blame for our actions. Anymore, I guess, than we are praiseworthy for our good deeds."

"And so—what? He's not to blame? We just let the bastard kill me and walk away?"

"Oh no. No, no, no. That's not what I'm saying. That crazy bastard had to be stopped. Just not for a bunch of simplified moral reasons. I mean, well, think of it this way. We shoot a rabid dog, not because he's evil, not because he's made poor moral choices, but because he's a danger."

"I don't care. Fuck that guy."

"Yes," Lucas said. "Fuck him, indeed."

The car came to a stop. I thought we might be home, but we were on a little bridge over a river or creek or something. Lowell stepped out of the car and flung something as hard as he could. A distant splash.

Rebar on water, I assumed.

That close call, that brush with death, at least I thought of it as my close call, it shook me up. To be that close to death, to being murdered, that was part of what haunted me, but what really got to me was the reason: killed not for being me, not for some crime or sin, not for some passion or for love or for hate, but for no reason. Just for being there. At that time. That's a terrible reason to die, for being in a time and place. I don't guess there are any good reasons to die. *Dulce et decorum est*, my sweet Arkansas ass. However hard I was falling for the boys, and I was falling for them, the act of saving my life sealed the deal. I owed them. I loved them.

And what did I think happened after Lucas put me in the car and went back into the store?

Well, in my child's imagination, I envisioned them putting a call in to 911 and reporting a murder. So why didn't we stay to talk to the cops? To explain what had happened?

I don't know. I didn't think about it at the time. I couldn't get past almost dying. I couldn't get past that they had saved me.

After the detective came to see me, I tried to google the event.

I didn't know the name of the store. I wasn't sure exactly where we were. Search terms: "Store clerk murdered. Arkansas."

"Three found dead in local convenience store." The story was from September.

"Sheriff's deputies were called to the Y'all Come Shop convenience store around eight o'clock last night after a customer reported finding two dead bodies in the store when she stopped in for milk. The sheriff's office says that Mary Lister, 58, of Springdale was found dead inside the store. She had been stabbed. Her husband, Marvin Lister, 63, was found dead in the cooler. He had been stabbed as well. Also found dead at the scene was Simon Simpson, 28, no known address. He died of injuries to his head. No suspects have been arrested."

The boys hadn't called 911. So what did they do in the store? Besides carrying out fried vittles? My worst fear was that they had finished the job on crazy Simon by beating his brains out with that piece of rebar. Which they took with them. And chucked into some river.

But why?

Not for me. Please not for me.

What did the police think had happened? They surely found the knife with those folks' blood and Simon's fingerprints. They must know he killed those people. But who do they think killed him?

What are the possibilities?

One of the Listers got in a few shots with a piece of rebar before succumbing to their wounds? And then what? Crawled back into the cooler to die? Dragged herself back behind the counter?

Can you google police reports?

I looked at the Springdale police department website. They had an incident report list. Then I remembered that it was sheriff's deputies that investigated, so I went to the Benton County sheriff's website, but it showed nothing in the way of crimes that were or had been investigated. I supposed I could call and ask about the progress of the investigation, but I'd seen way too many cop shows to do something so foolish as to draw attention to myself in regard to the incident.

What the hell happened to my life?

It was possible that ole Simon had expired from just the one hit that Lowell gave him. That can happen. Hit somebody just right with an iron bar in the head and they could die. Right?

So the boys just looked around in the store to make sure nothing could tie us to the crime. And grabbed some fried pickles. But why? Why not call the cops? Explain that it was self-defense?

Well, it would have been a lot of hassle. Cops, newspaper, who knows what else. Better to just walk away. That had to be it.

Better to walk away.

Not that ole Simon was flopping around on the floor and the boys finished him off.

Surely not.

I'm packing for the Thanksgiving break. I had originally hoped that the boys would ask me to go with them to Lowell's folks' house for the holiday. But of course, they didn't.

There is a soft knock on the door. Then another. I hear Lowell's voice, quiet: "Darlin'."

I fall backward onto the bed and then fling myself at the door. I stop. Slow down, slow down. I open the door. Lowell is alone. I don't throw myself at him. I don't hug him with all my might or kiss his neck and ask him to love me.

I say hey.

He says hey and comes into the room and looks around and finally sits on Delores's bed. I turn a chair around to face him and sit.

He's quiet. He is going to say something. My heart is pounding. I sit up straight, close my eyes, and take a deep breath. This is where he cuts me loose. This is the end, the little death, the distinguished thing. The dying fall.

"Darlin'."

"Don't. Please don't." I don't mean to say this. It comes out on its own. Like a yelp of pain. I can't control it. Who can control that?

He won't look at me. He's looking at his hands. He's wringing his hands. Wringing them. Like in a movie, in a book.

I cry.

This is what he doesn't want to see. He had such high hopes for me. I imagine. Liked to see me do well, succeed. Always a little surprised but pleased when I held my own. Pleased that I never got knocked down, that I always hit back, that I could lie without a hitch, that I had no tell. Little sister. Doing well, little sister.

"This last thing won't be for you."

"Last thing?"

"It's too hard. The risk is outsized. We have to leave you home."

"Last thing?"

"What lasts in the material world? Everything is a-passing away, Darlin'. You know that. Just like I do. There is no Ozymandias in Dixie because the irony would be lost on us. You're the arsonist's granddaughter. The ashes in your grate just the cold cinders of the Confederacy. You're Cinderella who knows there is not going to be any ball, nor carriage, nor prince. Those monuments all got burned down a long time ago. You ask me, I blame Descartes. Mind-body, my ass. We're bodies, Darlin'. The South was a body. Bodies fall, and they decay, and they return to simpler matter. And for all our love of the mind, of ideas, of philosophy, of theory, we love our bodies best. Our own, each other's. I love my body," and right here he finally looks up at me, "but it's just a weed, albeit a pretty weed." He shrugs. "An outlier with a duration somewhere between a mayfly and a star."

I could say:

You need me.

I can help.

I'm the best driver.

What I say is, "I thought you loved me. I thought y'all loved me. It's Lucas, isn't it. He sent you over here. What did I do? What did I do? Why doesn't he love me anymore? Lowell, don't you love me?"

"Love is such a blunt tool in trying to describe such a wide range of feelings and behaviors."

What I say is, "I need you. Help me. I'm lost."

Now he looks me hard right in the eyes. I can see it. I can see that he still loves me. He loves me. Just not enough. "I wasn't here tonight. For the official record. You haven't seen either of us since before we went to Mississippi. Which we didn't. You've never been to my house, my barn, et cetera. Okay?"

He kisses my wet cheek (first kiss from him). I imagine him tasting my tears. I wish they were a magic potion, a philter, that would enchant him, make him love me the way I want him to love me. But they're not magic, they're just tears, and he rises and leaves me without another word.

For one long night, I hate myself. I hate that I have given over to feelings, that I'm a child and a girl, not a woman. Not on my own feet, but dragging behind them, defining myself in their perceptions of me.

What the hell did I think I was doing?

❧

Wednesday afternoon, my parents pick me up and we drive to Jean and Ed's for Thanksgiving. Sleeping arrangements are a little tight: Ed's brother, Tom, and his wife, Bridgette, are here, sleeping in my room (well, cousin Janie's room), and I end up on the couch. The next day everyone is up early: my mother and Jean and Bridgette in the kitchen; Ed, my father, Tom outside, looking under the hood of Ed's car, talking politics, staying out of the way.

The house smells like cornbread and turkey and cinnamon. I go into the kitchen, but after I stick my fingers in everything and taste all the food, the women shoo me out.

"You're useless, Darlin'," Jean says. My mother turns and makes actual shooing motions with her hands and runs me out. I walk down the hall. The middle of the house is dark. I go out the front. The men are now down at the chicken houses, pointing and talking, looking like they're actually doing something.

Down to the road, and I head west, toward the river. Past the blasted fields, dead in winter, and across the bridge. I think about walking along the bank of the creek until I find the old swimming hole. That's what I should do. Instead, I keep walking, not admitting to myself that I'm headed for Zach's house.

It's cold and the wind is—I don't know—bracing? My eyes are watering and my nose running. At the top of the ridge I can see Zach's mama's house down in the holler, as Jean would say. Six cars are parked in the yard, shiny new cars that clearly belong to city folks out visiting for the holidays. I'm thinking that the rusty Oldsmobile probably belongs to the mama. Smoke rising up out of the chimney is ripped away by the wind. I'm standing in the worst possible place, on this ridge, in the wind, but I can't make myself go down to the house. I don't even know if Zach's there. I could pretend to be looking for Cody and Zach both, but I can't face their mama.

I walk down the hill and past the house and on for about a half mile. My toes are numb. I call myself an idiot and a coward and some other insults in the second person. Then I turn back for Jean's. When I get abreast of Zach's house again, three men come out of the house and get into a big red pickup truck. It roars to life and throws gravel backing up, then shoots down the driveway toward me. I step off the road in case I'm not clearly seen by the driver. The truck skids to a stop next to me and the window comes down.

The driver is Zach.

He's in his uniform, hair buzzed short, grinning from ear to ear.

He comes down out of the truck and stands before me.

"Darling."

He makes no move toward me, so I hurl myself against him and hug him as hard as I know how. It's a long hug. With me still clinging to him, he turns toward the truck and says, "Cody, look. It's Darling."

"Not blind, soldier boy. Darling, get up in here before you freeze to death."

I climb in and sit between the brothers.

Cody says, "Sorry, D. My brother lost all his manners over to

Iraq, not to mention a couple of toes off'n his foot. That's our cousin, Dupree, in the back seat there."

"Pleased to meet you," Dupree says. "Happy Thanksgiving."

"Where y'all going?" I say.

Zach says, "We're headed into town to try to find somebody open who'll sell us some beer."

Cody says, "'Course, we'll have to leave it in the truck. Mama won't tolerate no spirits in the house."

"It'll stay cold, that's for sure," I say.

We don't ever get all the way to town but find an open convenience store at a crossroads. We all go in. I get a Slim Jim and Coke. Cody says, "You're gonna spoil your appetite, Darling."

They throw a case of Miller Lite and a case of 7UPs on the counter and Zach says, "Ring up her goods too."

The girl behind the counter looks tired and crooks her finger at me to give her my stuff. Zach grabs the beer and Cody the 7UPs. Dupree lingers at the counter. I hear him say, "Sorry you're having to work on Thanksgiving," and he slides a ten-dollar bill across the counter to her. She picks it up and pushes it into her bra. Dupree smiles, but her expression doesn't change.

When we get back to Zach's house, Cody and Dupree grab the drinks and say goodbye and go into the house.

"You wanna come in for a minute?"

"I better not. Gotta get back for Jean's dinner."

"Lemme drive you."

"Why don't you walk me instead?"

We trudge down the long driveway to the road and turn toward Jean's house. He asks me about school, but I don't know what to say. Classes, studying, tests. It's all bullshit. I tell him some things but don't tell him anything, really. I ask him about the army, and he says some things, but I get the feeling he's leaving out stuff too, things he doesn't want me to know or just plain doesn't want to talk about. It's kind of awkward as we realize that we're just talking around things. So I tell him about trying to sing with Tommy Steele at Lucille's. I keep the story focused on the drummer and the crowd's reaction and the total chaos that came from it all. I make it a funny story. Zach is laughing. It's a good sound.

When we get to Jean's, we stand around in the front yard, stamping our feet, jamming our hands into our pockets. It's cold, and he needs to get on back home. I need to go inside. Jean peeks out from the front window. There's something between us that needs saying, but for the life of me I don't know what it is or how to say it.

Finally, he steps in and gives me a hug. I hug back pretty hard. I'm trembling. It's mostly cold but something else too. He waves at the house. I guess he's seen Jean too, then he turns and heads for home. I watch him going down the road until I can't see him anymore. I'm thinking that if this were a movie, I'd run down the road after him, I'd catch him and we'd look into each other's eyes. And I'd say something.

I just don't have any idea what that would be.

Thanksgiving dinner is perfect. Country cooking at its finest and we sit around the big table with the leaf put in and everybody is happy. Almost everybody. Everybody is eating, everybody is talking, Ed is sitting by my mama with his yellow pad between them, writing her notes between forkfuls of turkey and dressing. Once in a while someone turns to ask me about school or how I'm liking the beans or the dressing or some such, and I try to smile and respond, but I don't have much to say. I'm a little choked up, really. I think I've got Zach caught in my throat. Or maybe Lowell. Or Lucas. Dessert is pecan pie and store-bought ice cream. After dinner I go and lie down on Jean's bed.

It's deep afternoon when I come back out. Daddy and Mama and Ed are nodding in front of the television. Tom and Bridgette are nowhere to be seen. Probably catching a nap. Out the kitchen door it's a perfect Thanksgiving Day in Arkansas: cold, wind died down, thin gray clouds shading the woods and fields. Gold band belting the horizon.

Grandma Jean is standing down by the barbwire fence, pulling her coat tight around her.

"That was a mighty good feast," I say.

She turns and fixes me with a meaningful look.

"What's going on with you?"

"How so?"

"Your mama doesn't want you to go back to school."

"What are you talking about?"

"Something's going on over there at that college. What are you up into?"

"I'm not 'up into' anything. I'm studying and going to classes. You know?"

"So why doesn't your mama want you to go back?"

"Honestly, Jean, this is the first I'm hearing of it."

"Maybe something to do with your 'falling down' incident?"

"I can actually hear the quotation marks around 'falling down.'"

"I would hope you can."

"Jean, what are we talking about?"

She's quiet. Does she think I'm lying? What has she heard?

"Your mama knows things."

"That's cryptic."

"She's deaf."

"Duh."

"Stop being a smart ass and listen for a minute. Your mama"—and she actually lowers her voice as if we might be overheard, *as if my mother might hear*—"your mama knows things that nobody else knows. Until it's too late."

"I have no idea what you're talking about."

"For true? Honestly, Darling, I don't know what to believe with you."

"Since when? Mama hasn't said one word about me going back to school. Has she said something to you?"

"Not in so many words. She wrote me a note, just this morning, asking if you could stay out here with us till Christmas."

"You've got to be kidding. Let me see the note."

"She kept it. Folded it up and put it in her back pocket."

"And from that you inferred she doesn't want me to go back to school?"

"I don't know how you'd be here and at school at the same time."

"What in the world?"

"Just tell me the truth. Is something going on over to the school your mama and I ourta be worried about?"

I hesitate. I look at the sky.

"Okay," she says. "A wink's as good as a nod."

"Look. Everybody's got stuff. I've got some, but nothing I can't handle."

"If'n you say so."

"In any case, Mama's intuition isn't a yardstick I necessarily want to be measuring by."

"Fine."

"I mean, if you think there's something to it—"

"Hush. Let me tell you a story. One time, one awful time back when you were a baby, I foolishly consented to go on a car trip after Tommy died, with your parents and your other grandparents, Ruth and Richard. Five of us and you, screaming your head off, piled into that big old Buick Horace used to have, driving to Rock City in Tennessee."

"That's wild. How did all that come about?"

"Never mind that. I don't remember where it was exactly, but we stopped on the way there, and everybody got out to go in a Stuckey's or some such, everybody except for your grandma Ruth and me. We were in the back seat and I didn't want to climb out of that behemoth, so me and her just stayed put."

"Behemoth."

"Shut up. So we're sitting in the back seat of that car and, well, we didn't have a lot to say, I don't guess. Anywho, she was watching your mama who had gotten out and was standing off a ways, looking out into some trees in back of the store. I asked her if something was the matter. 'She sees something,' she said to me. I couldn't but think, to myself, mind you, that she sure didn't *hear* nothing, so I says, 'What does she see?'

"'Just how in the almighty Hell would I know?' is what she says back to me. Well, I musta looked a little startled because she closed her eyes and took a deep breath and said, 'She sees things.' 'And so do we all,' I says, in a kindly sharp way, dontcha know, being more than just a little ticked off in spite of my good Christian upbringing."

I cough, and she says, "First Peter, chapter three, verses eight and nine—"

"Jean."

"'Love as brethren. Be pitiful and be courteous, not rendering evil for evil or railing for railing.'"

"Or 'ticking for ticking'?"

"You are not as cute as you think you are, Darling Jean Bramlett."

"No, ma'am. I 'spect not."

"Anywho, she says that her girl sees spirits or ghosts or something."

"My mama."

"Uh-huh."

"So what kind of spirits or ghosts are we talking about here?"

"I don't mean 'ghosts' exactly. That's my word. Your grandma Ruth didn't say that. She was trying to say that your mama saw—and sees to this day, I reckon—*something*. And that whatever it is is like unto spirits and whatnot, but I don't think that she rightly knew exactly what it was that Lavinia truly saw."

"Get outta here."

"O ye of little. You know, Miss Smartypants, it's said that when a person loses his sight, he's just liable to find himself an increase in one of the other senses," Jean says, with a knowledgeable, or maybe, know-it-all tone in her voice.

"I've heard that," I say sarcastically.

"Well?"

"Well what, Jean? Surely you are not trying to tell me that

while maybe—and that's *maybe*—some deaf guy's eyesight might be, I don't know, stronger than other folks, or some blind guy's hearing gets better after he goes blind, that now somehow my own deaf mama's vision is so, what? Keen? So keen that she can see into the very etheric itself? That she can perceive such bodiless spirits and ghosts and apparitions, and—what? Manifestations and specters and phantasms, the very wraiths and ghouls and banshees that stand invisibly around us, for God's sake?"

"Without the smart-mouthy sarcasm, yes. That's what I'm saying."

"For pity sake, Jean."

She gives me a long look. A hard look. Then she says, "So you're saying that you've never seen your mama's—intuition or whatever at work, is that it? You've never noticed anything in her that seems beyond the ordinary and workaday?"

Something is there, right on the edge of my awareness.

"Your mama's different, Darling. I think you know it. I know it. I've seen it. I can't recall any particular something right now, but I have seen it, girl. What I can tell you is the story your grandma Ruth told me in the back of that car that long and miserable day. She told me that many years ago, when your mama was little, she was in the kitchen one morning, getting ready to make breakfast and that your mama was playing on the floor. And what Ruth said was that when she struck the match to light the pilot, your mama's head snapped up just exactly like she'd heard the scratching of that blessed match and that there was a look of complete and abject terror in the child's eyes."

"She couldn't have heard it."

"Ruth said that Lavinia jumped up and ran out the back door like a flash and that she herself was quick on the child's heels. Lavinia rounded the corner of the house and lit out across the back field. Ruth said she could see smoke coming up over the ridge and that when they topped the hill she could see that the back barn was afire. Ruth started hollering for Dick. Lavinia was on a dead run for the barn and would have run inside if Ruth hadn't overtaken the child and pushed her down. Then she turned and saw Dick coming over the far hill at the same time she heard her other kids screaming inside the barn. Dick wasn't going to make it in time so she motioned for Lavinia to stay put and she went into the barn herself."

"Jeez Louise. I never heard this story. What happened?"

"Well, she got the kids down from the loft somehow and got them out. She said that for all that her hair got burnt off and her dress was nigh on to ruined."

"It's a miracle."

"That she got them kids out and didn't die in that barn right alongside them, yes. A miracle. Thank God in His heaven for it. But what Lavinia did? What are you gonna call that, Darling?"

"Ordinarily I might be tempted to say that Grandma Ruth's mouth ain't no prayer book, but that wouldn't be rightly so."

"No kidding. The woman's a living saint. You should be so good."

"Look who's talking."

"I cannot but agree. All have sinned and so on, but your grandma Ruth's an exceptional woman. And while there's a great deal to be skeptical about in this world, if your grandma Ruth says it, I reckon I'm gonna have to take it at face value."

At that instant, the sun drops into the break between cloud and horizon and floods golden light all over us.

And in that golden moment, that thing, that memory/feeling thing finally breaches the event horizon of my consciousness: when I first came home with my materials about Chandler and spread them out on the dining-room table, Mama came in and looked over my shoulder. I gave her the brochure about the school, and I swear she blanched and dropped the thing like I'd handed her a copperhead. She composed herself pretty quick, but she did not pick the brochure up off the floor, and she left the room in a hurry. I didn't think much about it at the time. Or I misinterpreted it. In any case, the whole thing looks different to me now.

❧

The two weeks between the end of the Thanksgiving holiday and the winter break is a dead time at Chandler. The holidays are too close together. Nobody wants to be here or to study or do any work or go to classes. Even the professors are lethargic, dreamy, their lectures wandering, digressive, full of Christmas and solstice imagery. Everyone seems to be going through the motions, staring emptily at the walls of classrooms, in their heads already home, hall decked, chestnuts roasted, eggnog supped.

There's no "seems" for me. I am without question just going through the motions. Classes, dining hall, library. And now it's full Arkansas cold. Which is to say it's in the low, low 40s during the day. Winter-coat weather. Dry air, wood smoke, girls in knit hats. Boys blowing into their hands. I sit alone in the dining hall. I stare into my plate as if it were a tool of divination: what configurations are hidden among the slices of ham and kernels of corn? I try to see my future there. I cannot.

I haven't seen Lucas and Lowell since I got back. They aren't coming to Whitman's philosophy class anymore. I don't have any other friends. I came to college and made two friends and now they're gone. Did I make two friends or did I join a cult of personality? Is that what I am? A cult of one?

I've been warned (is *warned* the word? Is that what Lowell did, warn me?) to stay away. I have resisted the constant urge in my heart to go to their room and beat on the door, crying to be let in, to be taken in again. I have sat on the bench in front of the Christian Center, looking off into the western sky at sunset. *Go to the western gate, Darling Bramlett.* From there, one can see the front entrance to the men's dorm. *One.* What a deflection. Shoot, Darling. Can you not speak the truth? *I* can see it. I sit there, and I can see the entrance. I don't stare at it. I glance. When Whitman took attendance yesterday, and since my name is right after Lowell's on the roll, he gave me a pointed look when Lowell didn't answer. Again. I shrugged. *I have no answers for me, Dr. Whitman. What answers would I have for you?* I haven't seen the Escalade in the parking lot. Even now I peek around the dining hall, but they haven't been here and aren't here again.

Where are they?

Possibilities: they are avoiding me. Why? Don't they think I can take a hint? Not that telling me to fuck off was the subtlest of hints. Though they would be right. I can't take this hint.

They're dead. They've concocted some suicide pact and moved on beyond this plane to—

Horseshit.

They're gone. They fell into my life like some genius teenage French poet, seduced me into not having sex with them, and then vanished.

I walk in the falling dusk back toward the dorm from the dining hall. The sky is plunging toward indigo. I turn around and walk toward the Hill. I don't have on enough jacket for the approaching cold of dark, but I trudge on. Up the Hill. The sky is cloudless and the stars are rushing out of the blackness as fast as they can, hard, crystal points of bluish white light. Can I just say I feel super sorry for myself, abandoned, alone? Foolish?

The proverbial Fool on the proverbial Hill.

I approach the observatory. Is it a symbol? A symbol in the story of my own life? And what would it be a symbol of exactly? Is God a symbolist poet? Mocking me? Professor Blackwell says that the best way to recognize a symbol is that it is an object in a story that is absolutely out of place, that does not belong in the story: the monkey in "A Good Man Is Hard to Find" was the example she used. What would a monkey be doing at a run-down gas-station restaurant in the Deep South? Good question. And what did the monkey symbolize?

I forget now what she said. I should have asked the boys.

The observatory might make perfect sense on a college campus. But what it is doing in the arcing and quickly plunging narrative of my life?

The death of love? Love of death. The pull of sky, of light? The convergence of sex and downfall and ruination?

It's not really tall enough to be a phallic symbol. Though size is not supposed to be important, huh? It's a dauber of a phallus.

I approach the burned wall. And again, for the thousand and first time, wonder how much of the legend is true. The lovers. The light. The fire of photons magnified into a conflagration of joining. The hot room. The white room. The breaking of atomic bonds and their reunion in carbon and ash—

"Hello, Miss Bramlett."

I step back and trip over my own feet and go down onto my butt and slide a little ways down the Hill. Detective Somerset.

"Shoot!" I take his outstretched hand and pull myself up. "You may as well call me Darling since we're up here on the Hill together."

"Sorry. I didn't mean to scare you."

"You didn't scare me. You're not a monster or a vampire or something. What you did was startle me."

"What's the difference?"

"Think about it, Detective."

"Okay. I'll do some googling when I get home."

"Please tell me you're not up here looking for me."

"No, sorry. I'm not going to be able to tell you that."

"How did you know where to find me?"

"Actually, I followed you."

"That's not a little creepy."

"My job, you know."

It is full dark now. The lights from the college and the town throw some illumination up here. I can see his face but I cannot read his expression.

Is he going to put his hands on me? Is that what I want now?

"Do you know what this place is, Detective?"

"An observatory?"

"Not that place. This place. The Hill."

"Highest point in the county, I believe."

"It's a make-out place."

"Is it?"

Did he just soften his voice?

"Yes."

"I guess it's a falling down place too. I believe this is the second time you've fallen here." He pauses, but I don't say anything. Pebbles. "At least," he adds.

"So I'm guessing you didn't follow me up here to make out with me."

Why am I saying this?

"No," he says and his voice is hard now.

"I swear," I say, "I don't know anything about the fire. I didn't set it, and I don't know who did."

"What do you know about Laura Huddle?" he says.

That question is designed to catch me off guard, but I am ready for him. After the Muskogee remark, I understand that he knows a great deal about me. And about the boys. "I don't know that name."

He doesn't say anything, but I can see him nodding in the dark. "What do you know about Muskogee?"

Ah. There it is.

"It's a town in Oklahoma. Made famous by a country song. Willie Nelson or somebody."

"Merle Haggard."

"If you say so."

"Have you been there?"

Darling's first aphorism: a lie should be dangerously close to the truth. "Why do you ask? What's Muskogee got to do with the fire?"

"Asking questions is my job."

"Fine. Yes, I've been there. I took a road trip earlier this year."

"With Lucas Susskind and Lowell Alford."

"Yes."

A pause. Is he waiting for me to say something more? It's pretty clear now that he suspects something about the Y'all Come Shop.

"Do you have anything to add?" he says.

"Like what?"

"What happened?"

I dissemble. I lie by speaking truth. "We went to an old theater. We had lunch. We walked around the tourist areas."

"How about the trip?"

"How about it?"

"Anything unusual happen?"

"No. I slept most of the way."

"Both ways?"

"On the way home."

He hesitates, then says, "You're not a very good liar, Miss Bramlett."

"Well, if you're going to call me a liar right to my face, you should definitely call me Darling."

He says nothing.

"Most people won't call you a liar right to your face."

"The police will."

"Yup. I can see that they sure will."

"I don't think you fell down here the night I met you at the hospital."

"No? What do you think happened?"

"I think Patrick Mitchell, for some reason, beat you up."

"You don't think that."

"I do indeed."

"Well, wouldn't you have arrested him if you believed that?"

"One word from you and I would have."

"So it's my fault."

"That's not what I'm saying. You're conflating two different issues."

"'Conflating.' Good one, Detective."

"But if you mean he's not in jail because of you, then yes. You're to blame."

Everybody constructs a narrative. I'm trying to put together a story that explains the evidence he has on me.

"Do you remember that exact day that you and Mr. Alford and Mr. Susskind took that road trip to Muskogee?"

"Not off the top of my head. It was near the beginning of the semester."

"So—first or second week of September or thereabouts?"

"Sounds right."

"On the seventeenth of September of this year, there was an incident at the Y'all Come Shop convenience store on Highway 62. Some people were murdered. Now Highway 62 is the road you'd most likely have taken going from here to Muskogee. Is that right."

"Murdered? Is that what you said?"

"Yes, Miss Bramlett. Murdered."

I let that hang in the air between us. I'm hoping that the pause will make me seem confused.

Or concerned.

"What has that got to do with the fire? Are you thinking that I'm somehow connected to a murder now?"

"Did y'all take Highway 62 to Muskogee?"

"You've got to be kidding me. First, I'm a liar because I won't admit to a beating I didn't take. Then, I'm an arsonist, burning up the truck of a boy who didn't beat me up. And now I'm a murderer. Or an accomplice to murder. Shoot. No wonder you don't want to make out with me."

He finally does put his hands on me. He grabs me hard by the shoulders and shakes me.

"This is not a joke. We're talking about murder here. Three murders. This is not some college prank that gets out of control and burns down a frat house."

I pull loose from his grasp and say, "I didn't murder anybody."

"No. I don't think you did. I don't think you're capable of that."

"So what do you want from me?"

"Let me tell you what I think happened, Miss Bramlett. I think your friends, probably through an incredible coincidence of timing and place walked into that convenience store and found this worthless piece of shit who had just killed the store owner and his wife and that they then killed him for some reason, I don't know, maybe self-defense, but they beat his brains out with a piece of iron and just walked away. They didn't call the police or an ambulance or see if they could help those poor people, but just walked away."

"Bullshit. You don't know any of that. You don't know who was in that store. You don't even know if it's the same day we went to Muskogee. Or if we took the same road. Why do you imagine it was us? What have you got against us? Is it because I won't say Patrick beat me up? Is that it?"

"I don't know? If you mean that I can't prove it, well, you just hold tight. Because we found some vomit at the scene. Somebody was sickened by all that death and blood and horror and puked her guts out. We took samples of that vomit. We have DNA from that vomit. And I've been wondering if that DNA might match the DNA from a strand of hair from your hairbrush that was on your dresser when I came to see you."

I feel sick to my stomach.

"You took hair from my brush?"

He lets that hang for a moment. "No. But there may come a time when I show up with a warrant for your DNA. What are you going to do then?"

"Give it to you, I guess."

We stand there a minute or so. I can literally feel how pissed he is. Finally, he asks if I want him to walk me back to the dorm.

"You worried somebody's gonna beat me up, Detective? Again?"

Wrong thing to say. He turns and strides off down the Hill.

What's the matter with me? Why am I antagonizing a policeman? One who has my DNA at a crime scene?

❧

There's only one week left in the semester. Exam week. Still no sign of Lucas and Lowell. Maybe they're smarter than me and have lit out for the territories ahead of Detective Somerset finally coming to arrest us all. What am I saying? Of course they're smarter than me. On the other hand, where would I run to? My daddy can't fix this. Grandma Jean can't hide me. At least not forever.

Monday night, I'm sitting in front of the CC thinking about my algebra exam tomorrow when I see an old truck pull up behind the men's dorm. Something tickles my brain. It's the truck. It's *the* truck. Lowell's grandfather's truck. I creep through the shadows toward the parking lot and see the boys when they jump out of the truck and run into the dorm. They don't see me.

I walk over to where the truck is parked. I lean against it. I am not sure what to do. I guess I'm just going to wait for them to come back out and confront them. And tell them what? Ask them why they've abandoned me? Beg to be taken back into the fold, the blessed fold? Even as the little sister, not the role I wanted, but I'll take it now. I just want back in, back between them in the front seat, them looking at each other over my head at every foolish thing I say. I just want back in. I shift my position against the side of the truck, cock my hip, flip my hair back. I'm cool. I'm ready. They love me. At least Lowell does.

So maybe I just focus on Lowell. Maybe I can be the wedge that finally comes between them. The wedge that Sarah Jackson wanted to be but couldn't. Or at least the wedge that lets in just enough light so that I can be with them again. I know Lowell was reluctant to cut me loose that night in my room. All of that (or at least most of it) was coming from Lucas, I just know it. Lowell still loves me. On some level. Surely. I'll look him in the eyes. I'll see that love. I'll make him want me. I'll make him take me back.

How?

Whatever else I know, I know he loves Lucas more than he loves me.

Maybe I could say—

There is noise from the bed of the truck. I step around and

see something, someone writhing around, struggling. Then his face turns toward the light.

Detective Somerset.

One of his eyes is swollen shut. Duct tape over his mouth. Blood on his face.

Holy fuck all.

The world, which only a minute ago had seemed no larger than the distance between me and the door to the men's dorm, now expands, like the first moments of the big bang, to the farthest reaches of the universe. The stars stand out against the dark, spinning like in a Van Gogh.

And I'm telling the truth now: I do not know why I do this.

I climb into the back of the truck with him.

He grunts and jerks. He's on his side, and I get around behind him, thinking I can untie his hands. More duct tape. I claw at the tape, but there's no way to get him loose. I need a knife. I'm about to jump out and run to my room to get one when I hear the boys come banging out of the dorm. I lie down next to Somerset. He is knocking around, making a lot of noise. I shush him and he quiets.

The boys get in and start the truck and peel out, flinging Somerset and me around in the hard bed. We leave the college grounds and are soon speeding away. Going where?

Thirty minutes later I know. They're headed to the river.

The wind is ripping through me. I'm shivering, and so is Somerset, though I think for different reasons.

I lie back and hold the detective's arm and watch the shimmering, spinning stars above. I think I'm hallucinating. The air is cold and my lungs hurt. This is it. They are going to kill Somerset. Why? He must have tried to question them as aggressively as he questioned me on the Hill.

And they weren't having it.

After about an hour, the truck stops, and one of the boys gets out to jimmy the gate into the park. It's pitch dark, there are no streetlights here, so they have to drive slowly now, and as they navigate a curve in the narrow road, I jump out and roll off into the bushes. I assume they don't see me. They don't stop. They don't come back and look for me.

I have landed in stickery shrubs of some kind. Thorns claw at my clothes and yank me down when I try to get up. I'm dragging myself but it's as if a thousand hands are holding me back, some scratching my arms, my face. Some stabbing me. I tear myself loose and find the road.

By the time I get to Hippie John's canoe place, they are already on the water and headed downstream.

To that hole.

I look into the back of the truck. The detective is gone.

I can't figure out how they got a canoe loose. From what I can tell, they're all chained together. I shake the chains. I look for one that's not secured. No luck. So I step into the water. It is beyond freezing. I can see the flashlight from the boys' canoe flickering downstream. I'm up to my waist, then I back out and take off my coat. It's an army jacket. Belongs to Lowell. I can picture it, feel it really, soaking up gallons of river water and pulling me under, cold Ophelia sucking down death.

Turns out the river isn't super deep here. I'm still on my feet and the water is only chest high. I really only have to pull my feet up and try to tread water while the current carries me. I'm completely numb now. I grab at a vine to slow myself but my hand won't close on it good.

I can't see the flashlight anymore. I think there's a good chance I may die tonight.

I'm going to float away down this cold river until hypothermia paralyzes me and the water gets deep and I sink and I drown and I walk along the river bottom all the way to Hell.

On tiptoes now. Should have taken off my shoes. Heavy as bricks. Try to kick them off but can't.

A light, off to the left. I push that way, catch a limb in the crook of my elbow, hold on. Grab my way from slender tree to tree toward the light. I can see the canoe now, the boys standing waist deep in the water. They are trying to pull the detective out of the canoe. They are having some trouble.

"Just turn the fucking canoe over," Lucas says.

I can't feel my feet or the bottom of the river, but I am walking toward them. The canoe has a lot of primary stability and the boys are having trouble flipping it.

They're going to drown the detective.

Finally, they jump up and put all their weight on it and it flips. The other side of the canoe flies up and strikes them both in the face and the flashlight falls into the water.

So does Somerset.

There is much cursing and flailing and fumbling for the flashlight. I am there now. I feel around on the bottom for the detective, find him, my hands so numb I can barely get hold of him, but panic is a power, a potency I didn't know I had. I pull him up and rip the tape off his mouth and he gasps loudly for air.

"What the fuck?" Lucas has found the flashlight and is shining it on us. I'm holding the detective up out of the water. His hands are still taped behind his back and his feet are taped together too so he can't get his footing.

"Darlin'?" Lowell says. "How—what are you—?"

Lucas slogs angrily through the water and hits me in the side of the head with the flashlight. The detective slips through my hands and sinks. The blow warms me up a little. Lucas grabs me and turns me toward the cave/hole, illuminating it with the flashlight.

Lucas is shouting. "Is this what you want, Darling? Is this it? Sex and death? 'Cause here it is. Here's the lesson you've been waiting for: they're the same thing. We won't fuck you, but we will kill you. Is that what you've been wanting this whole time?"

I throw my elbow back into his throat and he staggers, dropping the flashlight again.

I grope for the detective, but I can't find him. I put my face in the water to try to reach the bottom of the river. My feet are so numb I could be standing on him and not know it. Hands grab me from behind. Lowell.

"Darlin'. You need to get out of here."

"How?"

Now Lucas shoves Lowell away and pushes my head under the water. I can hear Lowell saying, *Let her up!* This is it, I think.

I don't know if Lowell hit him or what, but Lucas lets go and I come sputtering up. I've swallowed a lot of water. I puke. I'm dizzy. The detective is floating face down between Lucas and Lowell. The clouds have broken above us and the moon, near on to full, is shining through the trees onto the water, white on black, rippling bars of vanilla light.

The boys stare at each other until Lucas snorts and says, "You stupid redneck bastard," and he drags the detective's body toward the cave. For a long moment, Lucas is gone inside the cave. He's cursing and splashing around. Finally, he emerges.

"Leave the hard work to me, you little shit."

Everyone is trembling. Cold water, cold air. I'm not sure how I'm standing. I don't seem to have any feet. Maybe they won't kill me after all.

Lucas says, "You're not keeping her," and he shakes his head. "No. You're not. She's gone. We lose her, right here, right now."

"No," Lowell says.

"This is all her fault." Lucas is yelling now. He's right in Lowell's face. "The fire, the rebar, all of this because of her."

Lowell pushes him away. "Get outta my face. You wanna blame her? Her? Bullshit. We made choices, old son. Ain't that what it's all about?"

"Don't fucking 'old son' me. What is she, your girlfriend now? You self-centered son of a bitch. You just need a witness. Shit, all you want is a fucking witness. The eye of the camera for your cornbread Confederate narcissism." To me, "You're a thing, Darling. A toy, a mirror, a looking glass he can see himself reflected in. That's all. That is all you ever were to him."

Lowell doesn't say anything. Is Lucas right?

"The frat house. Tell me that isn't on her," Lucas demands.

"Hey, Patrick Mitchell was your idea. You wanted to burn his truck. I was good with that. I did not agree to burn the whole goddamn house."

"But you should have. YOU FUCKING SHOULD HAVE. That bastard and his frat fuck friend beat the shit out of me, and you don't give a damn about that. But he slaps sweet Darling around a little, you're suddenly all, 'Oh, we gotta get him. He pushed Darling down and blacked her eye and hurt her. Oh, my poor Darlin'. We gotta get him.'"

"You're wrong."

"Am I? So what did we do about that other shitbird? Huh? Did we find him, did we fuck him up? He stomped me in the face and we let him walk away. The only reason we fucked over Mitchell was because of her! You didn't give a shit about what happened to me."

"No." Lowell's voice is softer now. "You're wrong. You're wrong."

"Can't tell it from where I'm standing."

There's a quiet moment. Then Lowell says, "She didn't finish off that ole boy in the store. That was you. That was all you."

"That was us. Us. And you goddamn well know it. And the only reason we were in that god-forsaken place to begin with was her! 'Oh, I'm hungry. Feed me.' You've just got to have a little pet, don't you? And your little pet needs feeding. No matter how she drags us down, slows us down, gearfucks everything we're trying to do. Oh, you've just got to have a mirror to see yourself in."

"Fuck you," Lowell says, but without anger.

"And ask yourself this. Would we be here right now? Would we be hiding a fucking POLICE DETECTIVE'S BODY right now, if not for her? Hasn't protecting her, avenging her, dragging her around behind us all this time brought a whole shitstorm down on us? You stupid shortsighted redneck. She's the problem. And, by god, I'm gonna fix this problem once and for all."

And with that, Lucas snaps open a buck knife and grabs me. I lose my balance and would go under but for Lucas holding me up by my hair. Moonlight fuzzes every surface, tree, water, boy. I notice that. Why do I notice that? Why is my life not flashing before my eyes? Why do I see the graceful image as if for a poem in the last moment of my life?

The sound of the gun is incredibly loud. Lucas lets go my hair and I sink but find my footing and rise up. There is a look on Lucas's face. The moonlight, the darkness, the conflict of emotions that must be roiling inside him. Black-looking blood spreading across his chest and he falls into Lowell's arms.

It's like a painting I've seen somewhere. The bleeding, dying lover, face upturned, the expression different parts pain, fear, loss, disappointment. Their faces are so close I think Lowell is going to kiss him. But Lucas's eyes close, his body sags, and Lowell lets him slip away into the water.

Will he kill me now?

But he turns and slogs through the water toward the cave, then past it and out into the swampy edge of the river. The last I see of him, he's trudging away, struggling against the weeds and bushes and pulling off his jacket and then his shirt. And he disappears into the darkness. He'll be naked in a minute, I know. Freezing, beautiful, a god in ruins.

No one's going to kill me, but I think I might die anyway. I can't feel my fingers or my face. The canoe has floated away. I try to swim, but I can't get enough forward motion to stay above the water and end up dragging myself from tree to tree until I finally get to the shallower part of the river and trudge against the current. I am not thinking about how far it is or even where I'm trying to go. Once or twice I stop and fall into the water, giving up, thinking I'll give up, just lie down, let it all go. Then I get up and walk. I drop my head and put one foot ahead of the other. When I see Hippie John's canoes, I fall to my hands and knees and crawl in the shallows the last few yards until I can pull myself out of the river.

The moon is setting. I'm beyond cold. The sand feels warm after the water, though I know it's not really. After an eternity, dawn. It's ruby fingers. Rosy? And finally John comes out of his shack, stretching, scratching, and he notices me. After finding that I am indeed alive, he calls 911.

I fall asleep in the back of the warm ambulance.

❧

The rest is, I suppose, history.

In the ambulance, I told the EMTs to call the cops, and when I wake in the hospital the next day, there are detectives from the state police in my room, drinking coffee and giving me the stink eye. Detective Somerset is missing, they say, and I'm guessing they have read his notes or files or something and have a pretty good idea that I am up to my neck in some bad shit.

They aren't wrong.

I tell them the whole story. Yes, the whole story.

They don't want to wait until I am feeling better, even though my father, who has come over from home, tells them I need some time, to rest, to recuperate. They tell him that there is a dead policeman stuffed into some bushes in a river somewhere and that they are, by god, going to bring his body home today. And that's what they do.

Dozens of policemen, highway patrolmen, and plainclothes cops are standing around Hippie John's shack when we get there. John is smiling and pointing at the canoes and down the river and I'm guessing he's hid his stash somewhere because there are cops in his shack, searching it for, I don't know, evidence? John, though, is unworried, smiling, high as the proverbial.

I'm not in handcuffs. Not yet, anyway.

The cops have much bigger boats and they load me into one. I show them the way to the cave. Men in diving suits, though the water is only waist deep, go in and pull out Somerset's body. I turn away. While it's true that I cannot make myself look at him, what I really don't want to see is Laura Huddle's body, if they should happen to find that in there too. They don't. Thank God. And even though I have told them the truth about trying to save him, I can feel their hatred for me radiating off them like fiery photons and burning me. About half the cops take Somerset's body in one of the boats back upriver toward the canoe shack. I'm in the other boat and we drift downstream about a mile until we find Lucas's body snagged in the bare limbs of a fallen tree. Now I don't turn away. He is so white. His eyes are closed but his mouth wide open as if still hectoring the world for his fate.

"And where's the other one?" This is the lead detective from the state. He's in his sixties, in full suit and overcoat, brush cut hair, cold blue eyes. When he looks at me, I think he sees me in jail.

"I told you. He walked off back there where they left Detective Somerset."

"He walked off. Uh-huh. And did you say he took off his clothes?"

"He took off his jacket and shirt. Then he was gone in the dark."

"Why didn't you go with him?"

I don't expect this question. I'm caught off guard, so I answer truthfully: "He didn't ask me." My answer surprises me.

"But you would have gone with him?"

"Don't know."

When Lucas's body has been pulled on board, the driver turns the boat around and pushes it back upstream. The old detective gets on his walkie-talkie and orders a search east of the river, in the direction Lowell headed. As he gives his orders, he takes one last look at me. I can't read it. Disgust? Disbelief? Certainly those. But something else? Hate? And why do I care and what difference does it make?

I'm taken to the second floor of the Parker Federal Building in Fort Smith. It's a fine old red-brick structure, like so many southern buildings. Two detectives from the state police interrogate me for some hours. One is older than the other, but they seem to be wearing exactly the same suit. Dark gray, with white shirts and blue ties. They question me for thirty, forty-five minutes, then leave me alone in the room for about the same amount of time, before they come back and ask me questions again. I've seen this on *Law and Order*. They don't believe me about Lowell. Or anything, probably. They keep asking me the same questions over and over in different ways. They're trying to trip me up, but since I'm telling them the unmitigated truth, nothing changes in my story, and they're frustrated. Finally, a lawyer shows up. Don Melnick. Donald. He comes into the room and looks at me first. "Not another word, Darling." He tells me that my father has sent him. He pats me on the shoulder, settles into a hard chair next to me. Then he looks at the detectives and tells them that he is going to take me home now.

The two policemen stink of coffee. They stare at Donald across the scarred table. They have offered me coffee ten times, but I don't trust them. Or their coffee. They offer the Donald nothing. They are shaking their heads no.

"No? So, how long have you been questioning her? Without a lawyer, I mean?"

"She didn't ask for a lawyer."

"Did you Mirandize her?"

The detectives look at each other.

Donald smiles. It's not a nice smile. "So—no. Okay. I think that's fine. Yes, that's fine. Now, as far as I can tell then, I mean, since you haven't Mirandized her nor have you arrested her, I'm thinking that she's clearly not a suspect in any crime. Right? So, I think—yes, I think that we're going to leave now," Donald says and starts to stand up.

"We may charge her," the older one says.

Donald slowly sits back down. He stares at the men for a long minute. He's completely calm. I'm shaking—it feels like a real turning point now that Donald is here—but he seems to be enjoying the back and forth with these men. It's like he knows he's already won but can't help running up the score.

"So. I see. All right. That's fine. Let me ask you then, with what do you imagine you might charge her exactly? For instance, oh, I don't know. I'm having trouble thinking of a charge. I mean, you know as well as I do she didn't kill your detective."

"We don't know that," the older one says.

Donald smiles. I guess he knows they do know that.

The younger one says, "Anyway, we can charge her with accessory."

Donald is shaking his head, almost sadly. "Fine. Well, and this is for the record now, nothing, and I do mean nothing, that she has said to you here today is going to be used in support of such a charge. You didn't Mirandize her? Really? In any case, if you make the charge, it will never stick. So. Let's look at the facts: she tried to help the detective, she came straight to the police after he was killed and told you everything. She has been completely forthcoming. Face it. You would never have found the detective's body without her help, nor would you have solved the Y'all Come Shop case. I mean, she's a cooperative witness, not a criminal. She's an innocent here."

The older detective turns his face to me and says, "She may not be guilty, but she's no innocent."

I know he's right. This feels like a charge that will stick. Stick to me for the rest of my life.

"Very poetic," Donald says. "Here's some prose you might enjoy. You have one minute to charge her. Otherwise, I am taking her home."

The detectives stare at Donald hard, as hard as they can, I think, but they're bluffing, even I can see that, and after a few long, long seconds, he stands up and pulls me to my feet and we walk out of the room and down the hall past the elevators to the stairs. He doesn't want to wait for the elevator. He's in a hurry, like maybe those cops will change their minds and come after us.

We push through the door into the stairwell. "I'm so tired," I say.

"I'm sure. My car is right outside. I'm taking you to Helena. Your parents are very anxious to have you home."

"Thank you for helping me."

"My job, Darling."

After only a couple of miles, Donald pulls the car over and moves me to the back seat where I lie down and sleep all the way home. My parents are standing in the doorway of our house like a picture postcard and my mother hugs me and hugs Donald and my father shakes his hand. The car nap refreshed me, no doubt, but I don't want to get into it with my parents, the whole thing I mean, right away, so I say I am tired and just want to go to bed, though I am hungry and smell my mother's cooking, her cornbread foremost.

I lie in my old bed and listen to the drone of voices. I can't make out the words, but Donald's voice is calm and calming and I know my parents will be relieved.

What will I be?

The day is darkening. I switch on the lamp. Then get under the covers. I can't shake the cold from the river. I look at the bookshelf. My favorite books are back at the dorm. There's nothing here I want to read. Thinking about the dorm worries me. All my stuff there. I can't go back. I've ruined the semester, my college career, my life. All my work down the drain. Down the river. I let myself cry a little, feel sorry for myself a little.

Then I picture Lowell. Walking off into those swampy woods.

You got off easy, I tell myself.

I miss all my exams and fail all my courses. My parents drive over to Chandler and gather my things from the dorm. They met with the dean while they were there, but so far, they haven't told me what transpired, and I have not yet dared to ask.

My mother loves Christmas. Not so much outside on the house or in the yard, but inside she decks the very halls. Every window is traced with lights, alternating white and blue. She pulls the pictures and prints down off the walls and wraps them like gifts and hangs them back up. Over the years, she has assembled her own little crèche that sits on a table in the front hall. No store-bought nativity for her, she has searched out and found the figurines and constructed a stable of sticks she picked up out from under our oak tree. Delicate white lights inside and out. Never satisfied, she regularly swaps out the statuettes. The

Wise Men are a fairly stable group, the donkey, the sheep, the oxen and the camels too. Mary has gone through a few incarnations, Joseph fewer, I think. On the other hand, the baby Jesus is in constant flux. She has a new one this year. She has a new one every year. One year she replaced the child mid-season. There's something weird about the whole deal. Out shopping, in little secondhand stores and the like, she selects the figures with her hands really, more so than with her eyes. Sometimes she keeps her eyes shut. She rubs them between the pads of her fingers. I have seen her do it. Once she picked up a Wise Man at the Wal-Mart in Jonesboro. She made this face like she smelled something bad and put the figure down and turned away without ever looking at it good. Year before last, I found a brace of goats in the trash out back. I don't know what they did wrong. The sheep, on the other hand, were still standing right outside the stable. Like I say, weird.

And she puts up two Christmas trees. Yes. Two of them. A big one in the living room in front of the picture window, so thickly decorated you can only infer that there's a tree under all the tinsel and strung popcorn and lights and beads and ornaments collected over my mother's entire life. It blazes like a symbol of something bright and holy and prescient. It dominates the front rooms of the house. It's a presence. A living presence.

And a smaller one, in my parents' bedroom. Oh, it's a live tree, all right. It's one you pass right by on the lot without even looking at on your way to the normal-size trees. Or it's the fallen leftover top of some too-tall tree cut to fit. Mama decorates it with one strand of small blue lights and an old star for the top. It's the star off her own mama's tree, Grandma Ruth's. This tree stands in the corner of the room, between the edge of the dresser and the mirrored closet door. She spends almost no time on it, but she clearly loves it more than anything else among all the trappings of the season. Sometimes she just sits on the corner of the bed and stares at it. And its reflection.

This year, since it looks like I'm home for good, she goes all out. The Tuesday before Christmas I get up and pour myself a cup of coffee and plop down on the couch in the living room. It's a bright day. The room is full of white light and I hear my father cursing out in the front yard. I'm thinking it's about thirty-five degrees out there and the wind is clearly blowing. Mr. Brumfield's pines across the street are swaying like hula dancers. I get up and peek around the tree out the window and there's my father wrapping a string of lights around the arborvitae bush. My mother is watching him, stamping her feet and clapping her hands to get his attention and correct his work. I am so not going out there.

The rest of the week is a lot of sitting around, reading, staring out the window. I'm a total veg. In fact, Jean gets me on the phone one day, calls me a slugabed, and tells me to get up off my lazy butt. But my parents don't pressure me. I finally do go shopping with my mother the Friday before Christmas, just so they'll have something under the tree from me. Pathetic. At the Penny's in Batesville, my mother hands me some cash and leaves me to wander around on my own. I'm a zombie shopper. There is no joy in me. I see a boy that looks like Lowell in men's wear. Okay, not that much like him, but I stare at the boy anyway.

On Christmas morning, the three of us sit in the living room, looking at the tree and drinking cinnamon-flavored coffee and opening presents. My parents have happy smiles. I assume they're just glad to have me home. But I'm wrong. *I suppose that should be my mantra now: wrong, wrong, wrong.* After we eat a breakfast of omelets and bacon and grits on TV trays in the living room, they take me outside. It's cold, dry, windy still. The sky is burning blue. There is a little red Toyota truck, five or six years old, sitting in the driveway and my father is dangling keys in front of my face.

It's my first car. Truck.

Cold blurry tears brim, fall, burn on my cheeks. I hug my father. "Go on," he says, and I get in the truck and crank it up. It's quiet and still in the little cab. It's no Escalade, but it's mine. The radio is tuned to a station playing Christmas music. My parents wave at me and then step back into the house and close the door. I back out of the driveway and drive the streets of our neighborhood. Folks wave at me, smiling. My father has told everyone, I suppose.

I get it. I'm welcome home. I can live here, go to the junior college, get back on track. They still haven't asked for any explanation of what happened. At least they haven't asked me. I don't know what all they asked Donald and what he might have told them. At a stop sign I put the truck in park and cry. Pathetic.

In the week between Christmas and New Year, I drive out to Grandma Jean's. Ed walks around my truck, nodding and giving it the once over.

"You're a lucky girl, Darling," he says.

"I suppose."

"No supposin'. You're lucky, all right." He hesitates. He wants to say something else. He's probably wondering if he's got the standing to give advice or comment on me and my life, given that he's just the step-grandfather. He sighs and says, "Things can go badly wrong when you're young, things that won't allow you to live the life you're aimed at. Not so with you. I see good things in your future. You're a good child, you'll find your way."

I'm turning into a crybaby. I have to look away and wipe my cold tears. Ed pats me on the shoulder and walks back into the house. Grandma Jean is standing at the front window, waving at me to come in.

I wave back at her but turn and walk down toward the road. What I'm thinking is that Ed is probably wrong. I don't think I'm the good child at all. At the road I turn back to look at the house and Jean is still there, at the front window, waving me into the warm house, with sweets and goodies for the good girl. Maybe what I am is Our Lady of Perpetual Questions. And here's one more: why do I think, why do I in fact know, as surely as I know my own name, that I would fare better, be happier, love life more, under Lucas's mocking of my feelings more so than Ed's countenancing of them? Why do I think I would be more at home, more comfortable and comforted, squeezed in between Lucas and Lowell in the front seat of the Escalade than in my own grandma's wolf-proof house?

I spend two nights with them. During the day, when I'm not underfoot, following Ed around the property or helping Jean clean the house, I drive around the countryside some. Drive past Zach's mama's house in particular. I don't know what I'm looking for. He's off in the army somewhere. I mean, he could come home for Christmas, I suppose. He came home for Thanksgiving, didn't he? There are cars out front, but that doesn't mean Zach's there. And I don't reckon his mama would cotton to me showing up out of the Christmas blue. *Cotton to.* The longer I'm away from Chandler, from the boys, the longer I'm here in the unreconstituted South, the more country I talk.

It's the second night. In the morning I'm driving back to Helena. Ed, having finished his supper, has gone down to the chicken house to check something or other, leaving Jean and me at the kitchen table. I'm under the impression that we're just stalling on getting the dishes done. But no.

She's let me alone long enough and now she fixes me with a long look over our plates. I see it coming and duck my head and push some black-eyed peas around, finally mashing them to mush between the tines of my fork.

"So. Are you gonna tell me about it or not?"

"I'm thinking not."

"Well, little missy, you couldn't be more wrong. Your parents can baby you and pussyfoot around you all they want, but I'm fixin' to hear it, you understand me?"

I sigh. "It's a long story, Jean."

"So, in the short eighteen years you been around, you've managed to put together a long story. Now don't that just take the rag off?" This is said sarcastically.

"I just mean that it's complicated."

"What in this green world of God's ain't?"

"And I'm not sure I really understand the whole deal myself."

"Hm, yeah. Eighteen. I'm shocked to my core."

"And—"

To her credit she doesn't prompt me. She leans back in the chair with her head cocked in an attitude that says, *Bring it on.*

"I'm not proud of some of it."

Nothing. Not even a change of expression.

"A lot of it."

She lifts her chin and says, "Ashamed of."

"Yes."

"Yes."

"So, there were these boys—"

"Boys? How many boys?"

"Two. Two boys. Lucas and Lowell."

"And which one did you like?"

"I don't know. Both, I guess."

"You guess!"

"Like I said, I'm confused. I was confused then, and I suppose I still am."

"All right. Did you go with both of them?"

"Go? Like go steady?"

"Did you bed down with them?"

"Oh. No, I didn't."

"Neither of them?"

"Nope."

"Which one did you want?"

Lowell.

"I don't know."

"Hm."

"What does that mean?"

"Nothing."

"Really."

"No. Not really. It means I think you do know but don't want to say one way or another and so you're hotfooting around the truth. I'm sure there's a fancy college word for such."

"Equivocation."

"Uh-huh. Came quick to your tongue, didn't it?"

"Easy as lying."

"Is that what it's come to, Darlin'? You're just a common liar now?"

"You have to lie sometimes, don't you?"

"Yes. Yes, you do. But that don't make it right. And, more to the point, you don't have to lie to me. Not now. Not never."

I take a deep breath. "Things got out of control."

"Whose control? Yours?"

"Maybe. I'm not sure. I don't think I ever was in control."

"Sounds like an excuse."

"It feels like I was just along for the ride."

"A ride you chose to climb on, I'm guessing."

I don't want to tell the story. Telling it will change it. The words I pick, if not perfect, or maybe even if they are perfect, will subvert the story, reduce it to anecdote, repeatable, simplified, lessened, diminished. Just then the lights flicker. Coincidence?

"Nobody's heard the story."

"I bet the state police has."

Ouch. "Not all of it."

"Ah."

"I don't think I want to tell all of it."

The back door bangs open and Ed staggers into the kitchen. He's wearing just his underpants which are torn and scorched looking. He's got a sheepish grin on his face, which I guess only makes sense inasmuch as he's standing there next to naked.

"Hell's bells, Ed! What in tarnation you been up to?"

"Got tangled up with the wiring down to the chicken house. Tore my clothes right off."

"My stars and garters. Darling, go get his bathrobe. Ed. Sit down right here," and she pushes him into a chair.

I run to their bedroom. Ed's bathrobe is hanging on the back of the door. When I get back to the kitchen, Jean is standing over him, eyeballing him for burns and cuts and whatnot.

"Don't this just beat all you ever stepped in. Darling, there's some salve behind the bathroom mirror. Get it for me, would you?"

She spends a good twenty minutes searching all over him, daubing ointment on burns and clucking her tongue. "You beat all, Ed Moore."

"I'm gonna need some new overhauls, I reckon," he says. "Them old ones is mostly confetti from what I can tell."

"Hush. I think maybe we ourta run you over to the 'mergency room."

"Nope. I'm just banged up a little. Still got all my faculties about me."

"How many fingers am I holding up?" Jean says and lifts her middle finger.

"Not in front of the young'uns, Jean."

And with that he gets up and pulls on his robe and leaves the kitchen without looking back and without another word.

"He's all right, I think," I say.

"He'll do in a pinch," Jean says and starts picking up gauze and tape and other implements of repair.

I say, "I might call the country nurse anyway, if I was you."

"First thing tomorrow. I don't know if she'll be working this week though." She steps into the hall and is gone a minute or two, looking in on Ed, I suppose. Then she comes back into the kitchen and sits at the table and puts her chin in her hand and says, "Don't think I forgot what we were talking about."

"Nobody's accusing you of the old-timer's disease."

"So, these boys. Tell me about 'em."

And in the end, words won't matter/ In the end, nothing stays the same. Some song. Where'd I hear it? The Escalade?

"They acted like I was their little sister."

"Really? I reckon that chawed you some."

"Am I gonna get running commentary on the whole story the whole time I'm telling it?"

"Probly."

"Yeah. Well, they were, what? Odd ducks? Is that what you'd call them? One was from Mississippi, the other California."

"Were they gay boyfriends? Is that what it was?"

"Maybe. I don't know. Yeah, in a way. There was something between them that wasn't just being friends and wasn't just love, though I suppose whatever it was had some of both of those things in it."

I think she'll interrupt here, but doesn't so I say, "I don't think they were, like, sex boyfriends. Though, now that I say that, I guess they probably did have sex sometimes. One time, at least. I truly don't know. If they had a sex life going on last semester, they did one hell of a job hiding it from me."

"And you didn't sleep with neither of them?"

"No."

She says nothing. But she's looking at me hard.

"I wanted to though."

"Uh-huh. Which 'un?"

"Both, I guess."

"Now don't that take the broom outta the closet?"

"One was prettier than the other. I liked him the best, but I'd have gone with either of them. Or both. Preferably both, I guess. I know how that sounds."

"Do you?"

"Bad."

"Yeah. But not as bad as all that, I don't reckon. You ain't the first woman to be in love with two men."

"I figured."

"Now, as a rule, we generally get shed of one before we take up with the next."

"Gotcha."

"So, you didn't sleep with 'em. What did you do?"

"This and that."

"Right. Well, 'this and that' don't generally draw the speculation of the state police."

"That's true. Um, what have you heard? Maybe I can just fill in the blanks."

"Nuh-uh. Don't fool with me, Darlin'. Start at the beginning."

"It's a long story."

"I can put on some coffee, if'n you like."

"Shoot. So, I get over to the school and right away these boys take notice of me and bring me to lunch out at this old barbecue place."

And I tell her the whole thing. At least more than I told the state police. There's a fair amount of *You don't say* and *No, you didn't*, but not much in the way of direct commentary from her. Until I get to Patrick Mitchell on the Hill.

"That's when you shoulda started to pray," she says. "God woulda helped you."

"I don't see how. These aren't Biblical times, Jean. God doesn't send no angels down for wrestling matches anymore."

"Shut up, you little fool. I mean God would have guided you. And particularly guided you to tell that detective, whatever his name was—"

"Somerset." It hurts some to say his name. Okay, not some. It hurts bad.

"—to tell him what that boy did and get his behind locked up. Then your friends wouldn't have set fire to his car."

"That's just what I was trying to prevent. I didn't want them to know who did it."

"But you couldn't. You didn't."

"You're saying it's my fault?"

"Yeah. And you know very well it is. At least that much of it is."

And by and by, I get to the part about the Y'all Come Shop. She cries a little, thinking how close I came to getting murdered along with those poor folks that ran the place, but she draws me up short with her analysis.

"You don't know for sure that your friends killed that crazy boy on purpose."

"Well, I'm pretty sure."

"Pretty sure is a long way from a conviction."

"We're not a court of law here, Jean. I know what I know."

"You maybe ourta give them the benefit of the doubt."

I don't know what to say to that, so I go on with the story. How Detective Somerset started putting the pieces together. How I looked into the whole Laura Huddle thing, the result of which she dismisses as nothing but gossip and hard feelings. Jean's a tough audience.

I tell her about the end of it. The river. Somerset in the water. Lucas wanting to kill me. Lowell.

"He's dead, I reckon," she says and shakes her head.

"I don't know what else he'd be," I say. "He'd would have turned up by now."

"Your story makes him come off as the good brother."

"They're not brothers."

"Maybe. Maybe they're just two sides of a coin."

I like the metaphor, but I can't see the full range of implications in it. I'll think about it later, maybe fix it up, find a way to make it my own. I tell her about dragging myself back up the river to Hippie John's place. I lay it on thick about how cold it was and all. She clucks her tongue and pats my hand. I tell her about the police coming and about me taking them down the river to where we found Detective Somerset's and Lucas's bodies. I give a full accounting of my interrogations by the police and of the lawyer Donald showing up and getting me out of there.

"And that's about it. Donald says it's over as far as I'm concerned. That I should forget about it, consider myself lucky I'm not dead."

"Smart lawyer."

"He's a nice guy."

"Yeah, I think maybe you should take a little break from the boys for a while, sweetheart."

The boys.

"I didn't mean it that way. I'm not interested in him."

"If'n you say so. I'm gonna go check on Ed."

The next morning I call the country nurse myself. Turns out

she is working this week. She says for us to haul Ed to the ER posthaste. I offer to go with them, but Jean says she's got it in hand and I should just head on back to Helena.

I lean into the car and give Ed a kiss. "Make her take you to Wal-Mart for some new overhauls."

He chuckles and takes my hand and tells me to drive safe and to say hey to my mama.

Jean is standing by the driver's-side door, looking at me over the roof of the car.

"When your school gets out, and if'n you can stay outta jail that long, come on back and spend some of your summer with us."

"I'll do that very thing," I say.

Arkansas winter is mostly gray, a little rainy, cold, but then uncomfortably warm right out of nowhere. In the weeks before and after New Year, I put a lot of miles on my truck. I'm driving like the boys would, like Lowell would, anyway: two-lane country roads, the longest way to anywhere, listening to music, their music mostly, The Electric Prunes, Madonna, Josh Pearson. I spent a lot of my Christmas-gift money on boy music. I stop on bridges, stare off into the trees, down into the water of whatever little creek is passing by. Can't get enough of moving water. My navigation consists of simply turning and turning onto smaller and smaller roads. The air is gray, the trees black, occasionally a field in beige or pale yellow, now and then houses out in the woods, up on hills, decorated with seasonal lights, blurry jewels up in among the dark trees. I haven't taken a dirt road yet. Staying on county pavement for now. Today I've found one, a bridge, if you can call it that. Really, it's just a little creek passing under a road. I pull off and park, then walk back onto the bridge where I can see the water. It's cold today. I can't see my breath, but the mist constantly falling is cold on my face.

The face of the water looking back at me is a gray and black Brutalist facade, if such a thing could find itself in constant flux. I stare at the water so long, I'm right on the edge of hallucination. It's quiet here. There's nothing on this road. I feel like the ascetic, the carmelite, marabout, and where is my scourge? What am I doing? Penance? Will I ask myself this question forever? Lady of Questions. When do I take the wheel? How long can I put off growing up?

Really?

When will I ask the right questions?

Just shut up, Darling. Where are my pebbles?

On New Year's Eve, my parents toast me. I've agreed to come home, live here, go to the junior college. I managed to make it sound like it was my choice. Like I had other options. Like I had free will.

There's still another week until my advent at Barnett, the junior college. I'm starting over: Freshman Comp, Intro to Sociology, algebra. Should be an easy semester, since I've all but passed the same courses at a real college. Now that I have my books back, I've been reading "Little Gidding," in fact all of the *Four Quartets*. I don't know why. Somebody said that when you don't know where you're going, any road will get you there. I can't say I'm making any progress. Despite my desperate-feeling drives in the country, I feel stuck.

On my last free Monday, I make up my mind to drive over to Kings River. My father has already left for work, and when I tell my mother that I'm just going to drive around, and even though I've done the same thing almost every day since they gave me the truck, she gives me a look. *Your mama knows things, Darling.* Does she know where I'm going? Or does she know something less specific than that, though of a similar nature? Maybe I'll stop by Jean and Ed's on my way back, spend the night. I don't know. I piddle around on the way, turning off on interesting-looking roads, sitting on bridges watching the ripply water, stopping for gas, for Slim Jims, Coke. It's late afternoon when I get there. I see Hippie John. He smiles and waves. When after a minute he recognizes me, he looks around, as if cops are going to start pouring out of the woods. I tell him I'm by myself.

"Nice truck," he says.

"Christmas gif', doc," I say.

He nods, then turns and looks out into the woods on the other side of the river. "That ole boy of yourn ever come back?" he says. "You know, the nekkid one?"

"Not that I know of," I say.

He shakes his head and sits on an overturned paint bucket and lights up a joint.

I ask him if I can get a canoe. I want to go down to the cave. I can't tell you why. I don't know why.

He looks doubtful.

"I have money," I say.

He carefully stubs out the joint and puts it into his shirt pocket.

"Let me carry you then," he says. "Dangerous to go by yourself, Darl. You cain't never know for certain what's out there."

He drags a blue and white canoe down to the water and gestures for me to get in. I sit in the front and he pushes off and we just float. It's colder out on the water so I pull my hoodie close. By and by, I think I recognize where we are and point over to the east bank, so John drops his paddle into the water, turning us. We float up into the trees and bump around among them. Then I see it. The cave is not recognizable as such anymore. The bent-over bushes and weeds that constituted the thing have been pulled apart, searched thoroughly, I imagine. Still I recognize it, maybe as much by the feeling of this place as anything else. The boys laughed at me when I suggested that there are evil places in the world. They were wrong. They were wrong about a lot of things, and this was one of them. *Was I one of them?*

"Yeah, this is the place," I say, so John ties the canoe to one of the skinny trees growing up out of the water. He's good company, ole Hippie John. *Wait. Did he call me Darl?* He's quiet, holding his peace, he doesn't hit on me. He leans back and fishes around in his pocket until he comes up with the joint. That smell, that sweet, acrid smell. My heart is full and bursting. That smell is my madeleine now, I guess, always evoking Lowell. *You little drama queen, Darl. Darl?*

We float there, I don't know, a half hour, forty-five minutes, tied against the slipstream which would bear us south if we were free. Through a clearing in the trees westward, the sun approaches the horizon, the burning color of cinnamon. The bottom of the globe seems to drip off and fall on the edge of the world, and then they fuse. The colors of the world are drawn up into the sky and the sharp edge of every shape darkens. In the crack between the worlds.

And still: what did I think I was doing?

The boys, the boys. They shape the creature that is I, invisible, still pulling on me, somewhere out there, out of sight, but strong, persistent, like dark matter.

ACKNOWLEDGMENTS

Portions of this book appeared in *Good Works Review* and *Shift: A Journal of Literary Oddities*.